THE WEREWOLF
MEETS HIS MATCH
NOCTURNE FALLS, BOOK TWO

Kristen Painter

THE WEREWOLF MEETS HIS MATCH:
Nocturne Falls, Book Two

ISBN: 978-1-941695-09-8

Published in the United States of America

Welcome to Nocturne Falls, the town that celebrates Halloween 365 days a year. The tourists think it's all a show: the vampires, the werewolves, the witches, the occasional gargoyle flying through the sky. But the supernaturals populating the town know better.

Living in Nocturne Falls means being yourself. Fangs, fur, and all.

Getting arrested wasn't on werewolf Ivy Kincaid's agenda when she arrived in Nocturne Falls, but her life rarely goes according to plan. The upside of spending the night in the local lock-up is finding a hotel room is no longer a worry...but the downside is the man she's come to marry will get his first impression of her behind bars. Not exactly the way Ivy was hoping to meet her pack's sworn enemy...aka her fiancé.

Sheriff (and werewolf) Hank Merrow is the alpha's heir. Everything he's ever done, from becoming an Army Ranger to serving in law enforcement, has been in preparation for the day he'll take over. Getting married to cement a shaky truce is no different. Hank will do his duty, even if it means shackling himself to a woman he has no intention of liking, let alone loving.

But Ivy is nothing like Hank expected. As feisty as she is beautiful, she's as determined as he is to make a go of marriage for the sake of peace between their packs. The trouble is, Ivy has secrets that could destroy everything Hank holds dear...including his newfound love for her.

Dedicated to my amazing readers:
Thanks for digging what I do!

Ivy Kincaid parked her inherited Harley Softail alongside a few other motorcycles in the back lot of a place called Howler's. The bike's metallic black paint looked great next to the other bikes. Sharp and on point. Small victories, right?

She swung off the bike and stood next to it. The other motorcycles seemed a good sign that this place had cheap beer and decent food, which sounded exactly like the kind of place she needed right now. Partially because of the long ride from Tennessee to Nocturne Falls. Mostly because of the reason she'd taken that ride. It was a doozy. The sort of reason that made a woman want a nice cold beer. Or three.

She'd come to this crazy tourist town to get married.

To a man she'd never met.

She knew his name. That was it. Not where he lived, not where he worked, not what he looked like.

She had two driving reasons for agreeing to such a crazy scheme. One of them was her father. No one said no to Clemens Kincaid. Not more than once anyway. The other...she glanced at the number five tattooed on the inside of her left wrist. The other reason was her heart and soul and the slim chance that this new life might also mean a new future.

She pulled off her helmet, stuck it on the back of her bike, then pulled the elastic off her braid and ran her hands through her hair, giving her scalp a little massage in the process. She kept her hair in a braid to minimize wind damage. Too bad minimizing the hits to the rest of her life wasn't that easy.

If it was, she wouldn't be here.

As it stood, this might be her last night without a man telling her what to do. Scratch that. Without a *husband* telling her what to do. Her father had been ordering her around her entire life, but she'd learned how to survive that. Mostly. The man who was about to be her husband was an unknown quantity. He could be worse than her father. She wasn't sure how, but the possibility existed.

She was supposed to text her father with proof of her arrival, but that could wait. Right now, she needed a break from everything that was about to happen to her. A little time to sit and unwind and not think.

But that was easier said than done.

With a resigned sigh and the weight of her future resting squarely on her strong shoulders, she headed inside Howler's. The large back room held pool tables, some dart boards and other bar games.

Booths lined the walls, and a few pub tables filled the vacant spots. She kept going, into the next room, and found her intended target, the bar. The place was busy but not crazy swamped. She grabbed a seat and ordered a beer and a grilled cheese, the cheapest thing on the list of sandwiches.

A quick assessment of the female bartender confirmed that this *was* Ivy's kind of place. The woman was definitely a shifter. Probably wolf, just like Ivy. Hard to get a clean scent with this many bodies in a place.

The bartender returned and dropped Ivy's beer off with a cold, frosted glass. "Your food will be right up. You want to run a tab?"

Ivy dropped a twenty on the bar. "I'll pay as I go." She didn't have a credit card to run a tab with anyway.

"Okay. Name's Bridget when you're ready for round two." She left to get Ivy's change.

Ivy ignored the glass and took a long, slow pull off the bottle, enjoying the icy cold liquid as it hit the back of her throat.

She sighed in pleasure. There wasn't much a cold beer or a good shag couldn't temporarily fix. Not that she'd had the latter in a long time. She took another sip of beer. Even with her sucky situation, she was feeling better. Not that she was one to feel sorry for herself. That was a fool's road, and her path was bumpy enough already.

The vibrations of the ride had left her a little antsy, making it hard to keep her butt on the stool. She scraped at the bottle's label with one zebra-striped nail.

"Hey, there," said a male voice. "Buy you a drink?"

She turned to see who was chatting her up.

Tourist. Probably. But then, technically so was she. She inhaled. Human definitely. She surveyed the man in all his casual, I'm on vacay glory. Cargo shorts, Key West T-shirt, sandals, bottle of Corona. She smiled. A Parrot Head was hitting on her? Wildly ballsy. She lifted her bottle. "I have one, thanks."

With a pleasant smile, she went back to watching the crowd. She got it, she really did. The Parrot Head probably imagined her as the bad girl, the forbidden fruit. He saw her leathers, the blue-black hair, the smoky makeup, and painted nails and made his assumption based on those externals. Not to mention the added pull of her werewolf pheromones. Shifter or human, they attracted all men.

Maybe he'd even seen the five on the inside of her wrist or the tattooed curl of her namesake plant peeking out over the collar of her vest. That particular spot of ink wound from her shoulder to just above her elbow. Delicate, feminine but undeniably a major piece of work.

"I could get the second round."

She turned back around and gave him points for not being a quitter. "I appreciate it, I really do, but despite your preconceived notions about me based on the way I look, I'm not the good time you're probably after."

He frowned. "You think a lot of yourself, don't you?"

Bridget the bartender dropped off a paper-lined red plastic basket with Ivy's sandwich and a mound of fries. She shot Ivy a look as if to ask if she needed to intervene.

Ivy gave a little shake of her head, then picked up her bottle and the food basket and stood. She was an inch taller than the Parrot Head thanks to her height and her lug-soled boots, but she wasn't looking to intimidate him, just be left alone. This conversation wasn't worth her time or energy, not when she had very little of the first and needed to conserve the second for whatever lay ahead. "Have a good night."

She left him with a scowl on his face and walked back to the pool room, the need to exert some energy rippling over her skin. She found a spot at the bar rail along the wall and settled in to eat her grilled cheese. It was good. Better than she'd expected for something so simple. She watched the tables. Playing a few rounds of pool might help shed some of her excess energy.

Taking to the woods for a run, her first choice, wasn't an option. Going full wolf in unfamiliar woods wasn't the most advisable decision, even if it was the one thing that would give her the most relief.

The full moon was four nights away. Close enough that the wildness inherent in her kind was already itching to be free, and if *she* was feeling it, so were the other shifters in the area. That meant there was too much of a chance she might cross into another shifter's territory and maybe have to brawl her way out.

Wouldn't do to meet her fiancé wearing the scrapes and bruises of a turf scuffle. Of course, she wouldn't know him unless she texted her father and got the rest of her intended's info. She prayed that he was kind and decent. Those things mattered far more than what he looked like, although it wouldn't hurt if he was all right looking.

She glanced over her shoulder. Parrot Head had made a smart decision and hadn't followed her into the game room.

From her spot near the back wall, she got the lay of the land while she ate. All three pool tables were in use and all had players waiting. She picked the shortest line and set a stack of quarters on the rail as a signal of her intention to play, then went back to eating and people watching. A few feet away, a couple stood face to face, the woman's voice quiet but strained, the man's louder. Possibly bolstered by alcohol.

Ivy watched them out of curiosity and a small sense of familiar dread. Her shifter hearing picked up their conversation easily.

He wore a sweat-stained Red Man chewing tobacco hat and a flannel shirt with the sleeves rolled up. He stared down at the woman, who cowered beside him like a whipped dog. "What did you say to that guy?"

The woman looked up, the corners of her mouth pulled taut. She shoved her hands into the pockets of her jean jacket and tugged it tight over her flowered sundress. "I didn't say anything to him."

"Well, he certainly thought he had a reason to talk to you. Did you smile at him? Make him think he had a chance?"

Ivy frowned, her dread realized. She knew guys like this. Controlling. Jealous. Always thinking the world was out to take away whatever crumbs they had. With a shake of her head, she went back to watching the tables and the players to see when her turn would come up.

But the woman's soft cry of pain pulled Ivy's

attention back. The man had a hold of the woman's wrist. She tugged but was unable to free herself. "Please, Jimmy. Let's just go home and—"

"And let that idiot ruin my vacation?" Jimmy's voice got louder, drawing a few stares, but he didn't seem to notice. "I don't think so. I'm going to stay here and have another beer, and you're going to shut your mouth and stop flirting with other men, or I'm going to teach you a lesson, you understand me?"

Ivy's hackles went up.

The woman nodded, her eyes filled with the kind of old fear that told Ivy this wasn't new behavior on the man's part.

She didn't wonder why women stayed with men like this. She knew. Even smart women sometimes found themselves in bad situations they couldn't see their way out of. And smart didn't always equal brave. Her mother was still with Ivy's father after nearly thirty years.

Patsy had stood up to Clemens once that Ivy could remember. Ivy had been eight or nine and she'd wanted a new bike of her own, not one of her brother's hand me downs. She wanted a girl's bike with pink streamers on the handles and a pink seat. Her mother had forced the issue with her father and ended up with a split lip and a loose front tooth. She'd never disagreed with Clemens again after that. Not for her own sake or her daughter's. Didn't help that Clemens Kincaid was an exceedingly powerful man. The alpha of the Tennessee pack.

This guy in the Red Man cap definitely wasn't an alpha anything and he definitely didn't look like a mover and a shaker, but then neither did Clemens. Her father's typical uniform was a dirty t-shirt and trucker jeans. But this guy in front of her gave off a real wannabe vibe. He just seemed like a lowlife who made himself feel like a big man by shoving his girl-friend around.

The woman chewed her lip and looked around the room from under the fringe of her bangs, and for a split second, she made eye contact with Ivy.

Ivy held the woman's gaze, but the woman bent her head and broke the contact after a long second.

Jimmy caught her movement and whipped around to see what she'd been looking at. He stared at Ivy. She stared back, unable to keep the challenge from her gaze. She wasn't about to be intimidated by a human.

He grinned and winked.

Apparently, he'd mistaken her dead-eye stare for flirting. She rolled her eyes and washed her last bit of grilled cheese down with her beer. How typical. Another guy looked at his girlfriend and it was a criminal offense, but if a woman looked at him, it was open season to flirt right back.

A cheer went up at the pool table closest to her

as the eight ball sank into a pocket, ending the game. She stepped forward to claim her spot, happy for the distraction.

Another beer and two wins later, she was ready to call it a night. Pool hadn't taken the place of a good, hard run, but it had filed the edges off the need. She returned her stick to the rack and was about to head out when a commotion erupted behind her.

She whipped around to see that Jimmy had apparently shoved his girlfriend into one of the pub tables, spilling the drinks and knocking over a chair. His girlfriend was still on the ground.

The edges of Ivy's vision went dark, tunneling down to a narrow point that focused on the man who'd just put his hands on a woman. She glared at him, then walked over and helped his girlfriend up. "You okay?"

The girlfriend nodded, but was holding her arm like it hurt.

"What's your name?"

"Sandra."

"Sandra, you know you need to leave him." Ivy couldn't stop herself from saying it even though she doubted it would make any difference.

"I can't," Sandra whispered. "We have a kid."

Ivy's anger notched up. "Even more reason."

Jimmy grabbed Sandra's other arm, but his gaze was on Ivy. "You stay out of this, you hear me?"

Ivy stood at eye level to Jimmy. She laughed in his face. "Unfortunately for you, chump, I'm not the kind of woman you can boss around." She leaned in. "You hear me?"

Jimmy muttered a curse and yanked on Sandra's arm, tugging her away from Ivy. Ivy let her go. Not her circus, not her monkeys.

Sandra said something to him about Ivy only trying to help.

Jimmy responded by slapping Sandra, causing her to cry out and a few other patrons to gasp, but no one made a move to help.

Ivy frowned as the circus became impossible to ignore. She stepped into Jimmy's personal space, anger funneling through her. "Touch her again and I'll lay you out."

He snorted. "You're cute until you open your mouth, and mouthy women need to learn their place. Why don't you find your way to the kitchen and make me a sandwich?"

"I already have one for you. Tastes like knuckles. Try it." Ivy hauled back and punched him in the eye. "Whoops. Missed your mouth."

The combination of her shifter strength and his clear inability to believe she'd actually hit him resulted in Jimmy going down hard.

He shook his head and struggled back to his feet a few seconds later. His eye was already starting to swell. His mouth twisted into an ugly sneer as he charged after Ivy, curses flying. She dodged him. A table went over. Glasses broke, beer spilled. He grabbed a pool stick and swung it. Ivy caught it and snapped it in half. A woman shrieked. Jimmy charged again and the next few minutes were a blur that ended in both of them getting handcuffed and hauled out of the bar by a pair of deputies.

Outside, Ivy and Jimmy were separated to opposite sides of the parking lot. Ivy got the female deputy. Her name plate said Blythe. Supernatural, but what kind, Ivy had no clue.

Blythe seemed a mix of perturbed and bored. "You have an ID on you?"

"Nope," Ivy lied. It was tucked deep in her boot. Any shifter in this area who knew anything knew the name Kincaid. The last thing Ivy wanted was her father getting involved in this. He'd no doubt find out soon enough, she just preferred that happened after it was all said and done.

Deputy Blythe sighed as she walked Ivy toward a nearby squad car. "Shifter, right?"

Ivy nodded. "Mm-hmm. What are you?"

Blythe ignored the question. "What happened?"

Ivy told her how things had gone down in the bar.

Blythe nodded while taking notes in a tablet. Finally, she closed the notebook. "All right." She opened the back door to the squad car and pointed. "In."

"Am I under arrest?"

"Not yet."

Ivy got into the car and the deputy walked away, probably to check on Jimmy. Ivy tipped her head back and stared at the car's headliner. Wouldn't be the first time she'd been arrested. Spending the night in county wouldn't be that big of a deal either. It would save her the trouble of spending what little money she had on a cheap motel. But they'd fingerprint her and, soon enough, figure out who she was.

Clemens Kincaid did not need to know his daughter, the child he already considered a huge disappointment, had gotten herself into trouble again. But if she didn't text him soon that she'd arrived, he'd get worried. Not about her, just that his big plan wouldn't come to fruition. That wasn't enough to make Ivy dig her phone out, though. Not yet anyway.

Maybe she could use her one phone call to reach out to Sam. Her younger brother had always had a soft spot for her. He might help. And be willing to keep it a secret from their father. Although lately, Clem's influence had started turning Sam cold toward her.

Maybe she wouldn't call anyone. She took a deep breath, trying to exhale the constant ache created by her messed-up life.

The car door opened. Deputy Blythe stood there. "Bad news. According to both your accounts, you struck first and Jimmy's pressing charges."

"Of course he is, even though he came after me with a pool stick. What's the good news?"

"He's drunk, so we're charging him, too. And because we don't like a long blotter in this town, you're both going into holding and then we'll reassess in the morning."

"Thanks." Ivy knew she was being thrown a bone. She'd happily gnaw on it.

The sheriff station was small, but had three holding cells. The deputies were smart enough to leave the empty one between her and Jimmy.

As they were booking her, she saw the sheriff's photo on the wall and read his name on the placard beneath it. That's when she realized just how deeply she'd stepped into it. Her heart sank. Any sense of hope, of a chance for a new start and a better future vanished.

The sheriff's name was Hank Merrow.

The same name as the man she'd come to marry.

After a long day of providing escort for the US Marshals Service, Hank pulled his duty car into the driveway to find another vehicle already there.

The Mercedes belonged to his parents, but they hadn't said anything about coming to visit. A sense of foreboding settled deep in his gut as he parked. His time with the Army Rangers had honed his already sharp shifter senses, so he knew when something bad was about to go down. He steeled himself for whatever that might be and went inside.

His parents had used the key he'd given them and were sitting in his kitchen, having coffee.

His dad sat on one of the bar stools at the kitchen counter. He gave Hank a nod and lifted his cup in greeting. "Son."

Hank nodded back. His father looked well. "Dad."

"Hank!" His mom smiled and gave him a big hug. "How are you, honey?"

"Good." His mother wasn't giving off any stressed vibes either. Maybe his gut had been wrong. That would be a first. "I didn't know you were coming. Have you been here long?"

"No, just a little bit," his mother answered. "Are you hungry? Did you just get off work? You don't have a thing to eat in this house. Did you have dinner at Howler's?"

"Belinda, leave the man be. He just got home." Griffin Merrow shook his head. "You're as bad as your sister, woman."

Hank kissed his mother's cheek. "Yes, I just got off work, and yes, I ate at Howler's. That's why I'm home so late." He glanced at his father. "Since you mentioned Aunt Birdie, are you staying with her?"

His mother raised her brows. "Is that your way of saying you don't want us?"

"It's my way of asking if you need the guest room."

"We do," his father answered. "But we'll be out of your hair first thing."

Hank retrieved a beer from the fridge, popped the top and leaned against the counter. "Quick trip. What's going on? Has to be important if you drove down."

"It is." Griff twisted the bar stool away from the counter to face his son. "You want to talk in the living room?"

Hank shook his head. His gut *hadn't* been wrong.

It was reassuring. To a degree. Depended on what the news was. "I'm good here."

"All right." Griff sighed. "You know that our pack owes a debt to Tennessee."

"Yes." Hank already didn't like the direction this was going. A decade ago, through a strange twist of events, Hank's younger brother, Titus, had been in a car accident in the Smoky Mountains. Through another strange twist, the alpha of the Tennessee pack had been on the scene and saved Titus's life. And so the debt had been created.

Griff crossed his arms. "That debt has been called. With conditions."

"You've been in talks with Clemens Kincaid?" The man might have saved Titus's life, but he was a criminal. Hell, his whole family was nothing but thugs. Moonshiners, gun runners, gamblers, they made their money skirting the law. They gave decent shifters a bad name.

"Yes. Talks he initiated. He wants a truce."

"I'm sure that's not all he wants."

"It's not. He wants me to allow their bourbon to be sold in Georgia."

"It already is."

"Technically. He wants me to lift the ban."

"That's not such a big deal." Bourbon and auto parts stores were the Kincaids' two legit businesses. Griffin Merrow had declared Kincaid bourbon off limits to all weres were in the state of Georgia, which meant not only did shifter-owned stores and bars like Bridget's not carry it, but with Griffin's influence neither did a lot of human-owned places. "Bridget won't like it. You want me to talk to her?"

Griff nodded. "Sure. But that's not why we're here."

Hank sipped his beer. "What do you need me to do?"

Griff hesitated, an uncharacteristic move for the man who had been alpha of the Georgia Pack for the last thirty-two years. Hank braced himself for the thing his gut had been warning him about. "Clemens is insisting on a marriage to seal the deal. His daughter. My son."

From the concern in his mother's eyes and the reluctant tone of his father's voice, Hank got the picture. A pack leader's sons often had to marry for the sake of power or place. Being firstborn meant Hank would be the likely choice but Griff had said "My son" not "You" so Hank assumed Titus was the sacrificial lamb. "You know I'd do anything for you and the pack, but there's no way I can talk Titus into this. He's in love with Zoe. He wants to marry that girl. It doesn't matter who talks to him, he's not going to give her up."

Griff cleared his throat. "This isn't about Titus."

Hank set his beer down and crossed his arms.

There it was. "Clemens wants *me* to marry his daughter."

Griff's slow nod answered Hank.

Belinda clucked her tongue and looked skyward. "A Kincaid married to the next-in-line alpha. It's a power play."

"Clearly." Hank shook his head but kept his eyes on his father. "We're the bigger, more powerful pack. It's ours to refuse. You could still lift the ban on Kincaid bourbon."

"Clemens has promised a war if we refuse and he'd have some grounds, since we'd essentially be refusing to repay a debt we owe."

It hadn't been that long since Kincaids and Merrows had been ripping each other's throats out. Returning to that kind of bloodshed would destroy all of them. "It won't come to that. I won't let it."

Griff took a breath, unhappiness adding lines to his aging face. "I wouldn't wish this on you, son."

Hank put his hands on the counter behind him and leaned back. "I've known all my life that an arranged marriage was a possibility."

"Yes, but to a Kincaid?" His mother shuddered like the idea was about to give her the vapors.

"Granted, that wasn't an alliance that ever crossed my mind." Hank stared at the hardwood floor. If the Kincaid women were anything like the

Kincaid men, marriage to one would be a hard, miserable road. Especially for an officer of the law.

"Hank, you're a good son. You've gone above and beyond to turn yourself into the kind of man any pack would be proud to call alpha. If you want to refuse this, I will understand. And so will the pack. No one will hold it against you."

Hank looked up. "And be the reason war comes to our pack? No. I've seen enough of that. I won't be responsible for bringing that nightmare to the pack I love."

Belinda blinked hard. "Are you saying you'll marry her?"

"I'm saying I'll meet her and make a decision."

"You don't have much time. As of tomorrow, we're three days from the next full moon."

Hank narrowed his eyes. "I know marriages usually take place on the day of the full moon, but why this coming one? Why not next month?"

"Another one of Clemens' stipulations."

"Something wrong with his daughter?"

Griff shook his head. "He says not. I think he's afraid if you spend too much time with her, you'll back out."

Hank swore softly and stared out the kitchen window for a moment. Married. "Three days from tomorrow."

"And if you do decide to back out..."

"I won't." He took another sip of his beer as memories filtered through his mind. "I've done a tour in Afghanistan and one in Iraq. Being married to a Kincaid can't be that bad."

"Don't say that until you meet her," Belinda said.

Griff got up, walked over to Belinda and put his arm around her. "You know your mother and I had an arranged marriage. Maybe this girl won't be so bad. Maybe you'll grow to like each other."

Hank nodded. "Maybe. Maybe not. But if this Kincaid woman expects a love match, she's going to be sorely disappointed."

"I'm sure she knows the same as you do that it's strictly to seal the treaty."

"Good." Hank finished his beer. "I'm going to turn in. Lot to think about and I have to be at work tomorrow."

His father exhaled a long breath. Like he was relieved, but still unhappy. "I'll call Clemens in the morning, give him the word. He said he'd send me some info on the daughter as soon as he knew you were in."

"All right. You need anything before I head up?"

Griff hugged Belinda a little closer. "We're good. We know where everything is."

She smiled sadly. "Night, honey."

"Night, Mom." Hank stuck the empty bottle in the recycling and went upstairs. He stared at himself in the bathroom mirror, trying to see himself as a husband.

To a Kincaid.

It wasn't an image he could reconcile. Soldier, yes. Sheriff, yes. Spouse, no.

That night he dreamed about being arrested and sent to prison as the judge announced that was what happened to men who married criminals.

After a night like that, he was ready to get up. He went for a run as dawn was breaking. The morning air usually helped clear his head. Not today. He turned back for home and a long hot shower, the unsettled feeling in his belly impossible to shake.

He saw his parents off before going into the station, but their visit made him late because his mother insisted on making him breakfast and then he had to stop by Howler's to check in on his sister, Bridget, like he did every morning. Howler's didn't open until eleven for lunch, but Bridget was there early every morning, doing the paperwork and making sure things were exactly the way she wanted. He kept the visit quick and the news about the marriage to himself. She'd find out soon enough.

When he walked into the station, Birdie Caruthers, his aunt and, unfortunately, receptionist, was already there.

Her carefully drawn-on brows arched. "Look at you strolling in at noon."

"It's nine thirty." He picked up his messages. "Anything happen yesterday?"

"Two in the holding cells. Reports are on your desk." She got up to refill her coffee. As usual, she didn't ask if he wanted any.

He went into his office and picked up the reports from his desk. One Jane Doe and one Jimmy Philips. Patted down, but not searched. Arrests pending. He looked around the door to see Birdie. "A Jane Doe? That's odd." Who didn't have ID in this age? "They're still in holding?"

She nodded. "I got them breakfast from Mummy's."

He went back to reading the reports. The two had been involved in a drunken brawl at Howler's, of all places. Bridget, who was also the bar's owner, hadn't said a word about it when he'd seen her. Like her silence was going to make a difference. Did she think he wouldn't find out? "This is exactly why I never take days off."

Birdie frowned at him and came to stand in his open door. "Going on a field trip with the Marshals isn't really a day off."

"It wasn't a field—" The phone rang, saving him from debating that point with her. He gave Birdie a sharp look. "Answer that."

She wrinkled her nose and headed back to her desk. He was about to close the door when she crooked the phone between her head and shoulder and punched the hold button. "It's for you."

Birdie might be his aunt, but she was a horrible receptionist. If not for the glue of nepotism holding her in her job, he would have fired her a long time ago. "Who is it?"

She shrugged. "You want me to ask?"

"Yes. When you answer. That's what a receptionist does."

"Don't sass me, sassmouth."

"I'm not—never mind." It was easier just to take the call. He closed the door, sat down at his desk and picked up the phone. "Sheriff Merrow."

"Hank, it's Dad." Hank relaxed at the deep timbre of his father's voice. "Thanks for putting us up last night. Listen, I'm serious when I say if you want to back out of this, you can. If Kincaid brings a war, we'll deal with it."

Hank would never let that happen. "I'm sure it will all work out." Sacrifice was nothing new to a soldier. "How did Birdie not recognize your voice?"

His father snorted. "I've been practicing a British accent."

Hank shook his head. "Whatever works."

Griffin's laughter was followed by a sobering sigh. "I love you, son. You're going to make a great alpha someday."

"That'll be a long time from now." Hank didn't

want to think about the day he'd replace his father as alpha of the Georgia pack, even though it was a role Hank had been preparing for all his life. First by going into the military, then by accepting the Ellinghams' backing to run for sheriff when he got out—an election he'd won handily—but being prepared for the job didn't mean he was anticipating it. Some alphas stepped down. A rare few were overthrown. Most kept the role until their death.

"Let's hope. Anyway, I just wanted to let you know I spoke to Clemens this morning and he'll be emailing you his daughter's details soon. What that entails, I have no idea."

"Once I get her name, I can do my own background check."

"Which is probably why he didn't send them to us sooner. I'm surprised you couldn't find her info yourself."

"I just got into the office, haven't had a chance to check. And it's not like it's going to make a difference."

"True. Anyway, Clemens said to expect her soon, so keep an eye out."

Hank sighed. "I have a feeling she won't be hard to find."

"Let me know how things go."

"Will do. Talk to you later." Hank hung up, then checked his email. Nothing yet. Back to work. Actual work. Searching for his bride-to-be wasn't how he wanted to spend his time. He'd deal with that soon enough. Right now, he had two full holding cells that needed his attention.

He reached for the intercom to talk to Birdie, then realized the pointlessness of that action. He got up and went out to her desk. "Anything come back on Jane Doe's prints yet?"

"Nothing. You going to let her go?"

"Not if Mr. Philips wants to press charges. Did you run the prints wide?"

Birdie shook her head. "Just through the state database."

"Run them through IAFIS. Has to be a reason she wouldn't give us her name or ID. Philips awake yet?"

Birdie started typing. "He was snoring last time I was in there. Probably hung over. Didn't even touch his breakfast." She shook her head. "Terrible waste of Mummy's pancakes if you ask me."

"Blueberry?"

"Mm-hmm."

"Terrible waste is right." He headed back to the cells. Number one held Mr. Philips. He was sitting on the cot with his head between his hands, moaning.

"Good morning, Mr. Philips."

The man groaned and didn't raise his head. "What's good about it?"

"You're still alive. And you're not in county."

The man heaved, but managed to hold it down.

"Since we'd both like you out of here as soon as possible, I need to know if you plan on pressing charges against the woman who hit you."

"Hell, yes, I'm pressing charges." He raised his head. His face was black and blue, and his right eye was almost swollen shut.

Hank hadn't expected the damage to be that extensive. The report said Jane Doe had hit him with her fist. Mr. Philips looked like he'd spent time in a batting cage with no helmet and an inability to duck. "You puke in my cell, you're cleaning it up."

He walked down to cell number three.

The woman inside lay on the narrow cot, one long, shapely leather-clad leg crossed over the other, arms folded behind her head like she hadn't a care in the world. She looked up at him as he stopped in front of the bars, batted her dark lashes and smiled. "Morning, Sheriff. I take it you're not here to send me on my way seeing as how Short Bus has decided to press charges against me."

He stared at her, unable to help himself. He'd always had a thing for bad girls. What red-blooded man didn't? And everything about her, from the silky mane of her black hair to the pout of her too-full lips to the generous curves of her body, said she was trouble. He cleared his throat and reminded himself that his love for bad girls did not include those currently housed in his holding cells. "You want to tell me your name?"

"Prints didn't come back yet, huh?" She studied her zebra-striped nails. Hank wondered what they'd feel like raking down his back.

The thought caught him so off guard, he shook his head.

"Not yet then." She nodded.

So she knew a little bit about the system. Repeat offender most likely. Really not anyone he needed to know outside of these walls. He'd keep the fact that they were checking her prints against the national database to himself for the moment. "You want to tell me what happened?"

"I'm sure you read the report. I hit him."

"Why?"

She flicked her gaze to him. Her big brown eyes held no remorse. "You really care?"

"Humor me."

She swung her long legs down, planted her feet on the floor and leaned back, her hands on the edge of the cot. "He got handsy with his girlfriend. Knocked her down. I told him not to do it again. He didn't listen." She shrugged. "I decided to teach him a lesson since no one else in his life had."

Hank frowned. He probably would have done the same thing. And left the same amount of bruising. She had to be shifter. Or some kind of supernatural. He inhaled, but the smell of shifter was everywhere in the station with himself, Deputy Cruz and Birdie being here all the time. "What did you say your name was?"

"I didn't." With a smirk, she lay down on the cot and returned to inspecting her nails.

Hank went back to his office to start the paperwork on her charges. His inbox chimed as he sat down. He pulled up the message from Clemens Kincaid with the subject line, *Your new wife*, and opened it, scrolling down to the attached picture. He stared in disbelief, a growl building in his throat. "Hell no. This is the woman I'm supposed to marry?"

"What was that, Hank?" Birdie called out.

"Nothing. And you can cancel the IAFIS search. I already know who she is." He ran a quick background search, printed out the info and tucked it into a file, then marched back to cell number three and glared at the woman inside it. Flirting with bad girls was one thing.

Marrying one was another.

Anger made his jaw tight. "You're Ivy Kincaid."

Her smile dropped and the slightest hint of fear played through her smoky eyes before she dropped her gaze and straightened upright on the cot. "And you're Hank Merrow."

Was she afraid of him? He hadn't expected that. But then, their packs had been enemies since well before either of them was born. Afraid was probably an understatement.

She must be terrified of him. Of what he might do to her. She was being offered to him like a piece of property, all to firm up a deal. Knowing her father, she'd probably had less say about this than he did.

That took the sizzle out of his shock. She had no more to do with this than the man in the moon. With a heavy sigh, he lifted the keys from his belt and unlocked the cell. "Let's go to my office."

Hank Merrow was gorgeous. Not average good-looking, not handsome at the right angle, not all right with dim lighting. *Gorgeous.* Which was both a blessing and a curse. He was the kind of hot that gave a woman wicked thoughts and sucked the sense out of her head. Ivy tried not to fidget in the wooden chair across from his desk, but parts of her were getting uncomfortably warm.

She tried to remind herself that Hank Merrow, while still the enemy and a complete question mark, might also turn out to be her salvation. It was a helluva shot, but once her father had told her she'd be marrying a Merrow to seal the new treaty, she'd decided to think positively. To make the most of this new situation. To believe that life really could get better.

Because the alternative was unthinkable. And this certainly couldn't be worse.

Hank's lips were moving.

She leaned forward. "What?"

"I said how long have you been in town?"

"Oh, uh, just since last night."

"First night in town and you get drunk, start a fight and end up arrested? What do you plan on doing for an encore?"

She crossed her arms. So he was a hard ass. She'd had a lot of practice dealing with those. "I wasn't drunk. I'd had two beers. And I didn't really start that fight—"

"You already told me you hit him." He opened a file and read. "And I quote, 'Then I punched him.'"

"Look, I know what I said, but the guy was a creep and he deserved it. I told you what happened. He was roughing up his girlfriend."

Hank stared at her, his blue eyes stupidly mesmerizing. He must really be something in full wolf form. Finally he blew out a breath. "I'll talk him into dropping the charges."

"You will? Thank you. I guess you don't want your fiancée to have an arrest record, huh?" She smiled hopefully.

"Did you think I wouldn't check up on you?" He flipped to a new page in the file. "You already have one. And don't use that word."

"What word?" She knew perfectly well what word he meant. She just wanted him to say it so he'd get used to the idea.

"Fiancée."

The way he grimaced when he said it almost

made her snort. "Don't worry. You only have to call me that for three more days."

He frowned. "Why's that?"

"Because after that I'll be your *wife*."

His frown deepened.

She settled into the chair a little more then pointed at the file. "That arrest was for protesting the use of a rather controversial pesticide in Smoky Mountains National Park."

He grunted. "You're a tree hugger?"

She narrowed her eyes. "Have you ever run through that park?"

"The Georgia Pack hasn't been allowed access to that park since—"

She held her hand up. "Right, sorry. I forgot about the edict." Her father had declared the park off limits to anyone who wasn't a registered member of the Tennessee Pack. "But I can tell you it's beautiful. The kind of place that makes you forget your troubles and makes you glad to be a shifter. Completely spectacular. And the Army Corp of Engineers was going to bombard the place with a pesticide that would kill off this little black beetle that sometimes infests the trees. I'm all for saving trees, but that pesticide had the potential to kill off some of the other native species...birds, fish, you name it."

He squinted. "You'd rather the beetle lived and the trees died?"

"No." She rolled her eyes. "But there was a safer solution."

"Such as?"

"Increasing the population of woodpeckers in the area. You know, set up a breeding program, that kind of thing."

"Uh huh." He flipped to another page. "And the grand theft auto?"

"I was eighteen and only along for the ride. My biggest crime was a bad choice in male companionship. Besides, that charge got pleaded down to unauthorized use of a motor vehicle. Which is a misdemeanor, in case you didn't know."

"I did know, thanks."

The slight sarcasm in his tone frustrated her. "Dude, I was eighteen. Didn't you ever do anything stupid when you were eighteen?"

A cloud of emotion flickered in his gaze for a hot second, then it was gone. "No." He closed the file. "Where are you staying?"

"The holding cell is pretty comfortable."

"I'm serious. Where are you staying?"

"Don't know yet. Got any recommendations?"

His eyes narrowed. "How much can you afford?"

"Something between bench in the park and youth hostel." It would be funny if it wasn't true.

He sighed. "I have a guest room. You can stay with me. We need to get to know each other anyway."

Since her father had sent her here with very little money and a threat hanging over her head, she'd take it. She had no choice. Not until the marriage was official. After that, she was getting Charlie back and the two of them were getting away from anyone who knew the name Kincaid. They'd have their fresh start and a chance to live their lives anyway they wanted to. "No monkey business. We may be getting married, but I don't know you from a hole in the ground. I'm not just going to jump into bed with you because—"

He held up his hand. "That's the last thing on my mind, I promise you."

She smiled, knowing it was in her best interests to be as charming and likable as possible. Starting now. "In that case, it's so gentlemanly of you to offer. You won't even know I'm there."

He snorted. "Somehow I doubt that."

BIRDIE STARED at Hank like he'd grown a horn. She gave Ivy a quick, judgmental glance, then returned to Hank. "You're leaving with *her*."

Hank grunted. "I'll explain later, Birdie. You know how to reach me."

She shook her head. "But I don't understand…"

Hank pointed Ivy toward the back door of the station. "Car's that way."

Ivy kept her mouth shut until he opened the door on the passenger's side for her and she got in. "That's a relief. For a second I thought I might have to ride in the back again."

He gave her a look as he shut the door and went around to the driver's side.

"Your receptionist isn't going to be happy when my prints come back and she finds out I'm a Kincaid."

He pulled out of the lot. "I'll deal with my aunt."

"She's your aunt?" Ivy laughed. "Wow. I would not have figured that."

"She's a good woman. Just nosy. And terrible at her job."

"I'm guessing it's the family connection that keeps her there?"

He nodded.

She started to lift her feet like she was going to put them on the dash, then apparently thought better of it. "That's how a lot of Kincaids keep their jobs, too."

He glanced at her. "Like who?"

"Like my older brothers."

"They pretty deep in your father's pocket?"

She twisted to face him. "You asking me as a law man or my intended?"

"Just trying to learn more about the family I'm marrying into."

She hesitated. "Yeah, they're in deep. If they'd been arrested, my father would have just flown in and paid off whoever it took to get them out. Because that's how Clemens Kincaid rolls when it comes to his boys. Speaking of, can we not let him know about this incident? Although I do need to tell him I've arrived."

"I won't bring it up if you don't." Hank glanced over at her. "And with you? How's ol' Clem roll with you?"

She stared forward, but that didn't hide the anger in her eyes. "He pretty much ignored me until he'd realized there was something to gain in marrying me off."

Hank couldn't imagine his father treating Bridget like a commodity. She'd always been his princess, his baby girl. And he'd always made sure her brothers treated her that way too. Hank pulled into Howler's back lot. A lone Softail sat in the parking lot. It was a sweet ride, made even sweeter by the thought of Ivy on it. "That your bike?"

"Yep." She opened the door, looking back at him like she expected him to say something else.

If he'd upset her with the questions, he hadn't meant to. But he also didn't know how to apologize for trying to find out more about her. All he could come up with was, "Follow me home. It's not far."

"Right behind you." She shut the door and climbed onto her bike, popping her helmet on before starting the engine. Why hadn't she taken off instead of coming here to begin with? There was still a chance she'd run but Hank figured she was more scared of Clem than she was of him. Clem had a reputation for punishing pack members who disobeyed him. Hank supposed that extended to family as well.

He turned out of the lot toward home. She stayed behind him and as she followed him through town, he tried to see things through her eyes. The place was packed with tourists, many kitted up in Nocturne Falls T-shirts, but some were in costumes or half-masks or face paint. The kids were decked out in their favorite Halloween get-ups. It probably seemed crazy to her, and it was in a way, but he admired the cleverness of it. Being a supernatural and not having to hide your real identity all the time made life so much easier.

They left the town behind and drove into the hills, and the countryside grew more rural. He pulled into the entrance of his community, tapped the clicker pinned to his sun visor and waited for the gate to open, then went in slowly so she could keep up with him.

He tried to see his neighborhood the same way he'd seen the town.

The houses in the secluded development were good sized, all stone and wood with neat front yards. She was the daughter of a wealthy alpha and, judging by the Harley she rode, probably lived in a pretty nice place. What would she think of his house? He'd never cared much what anyone had thought of his home before now, but this was a different situation.

He parked in the driveway and got out of his duty car, leaving it outside although he'd opened one of the three garage doors.

She pulled in beside his car, shut the bike down, took off her helmet and flicked her long hair free, still straddling the bike. Her hotness in that moment was not lost on Hank. She squinted at the house. Her smile grew incredulous as she looked at the forest behind it, then to his neighbors on either side. "Really? You live *here*."

"Problem?" He liked it. If she was used to something grander...tough.

"First of all, don't you think *Wolf Creek* is a little on the nose as your chosen place of residence?"

They'd passed the sign on their way in. He'd never given it much thought. Wolf Creek was one of the main tributaries that fed the falls. It was also a gated community especially for shifters, designed to keep human tourists out. For their own safety. Full moons tended to make things a little hairy.

Literally.

He grunted, having no real response.

She waved a finger at him. "That noise you make? That's not an answer, you know."

"Wolf Creek is where I live. If you don't like it—"

"No, I think it's beautiful."

"Then what's the matter?"

"Nothing, it's just...it's probably a little forward of me to ask this, but seeing as how we're about to be married and all, how in the hell do you afford a house like this in a gated community? How much does the sheriff of this burg make?"

He glanced at the house behind him. It was a good house. Craftsman. Solid timbers. Stonework. Well worth the money from his pack dividends. Although, part of it was gifted to him when he'd accepted the position of Nocturne Falls sheriff. The Ellinghams liked to offer deals that were hard to turn down.

Before he could answer, she walked past him into the garage and let out a soft whoop of surprise.

"Is this what I think it is?" She now stood beside his pride and joy. Touching it. Her fingers trailed over the only non-related female he'd ever let spend the night. His 1968 Pontiac GTO. "Sweet ride. *Sweet.* But again, how can you afford this incredible piece of machinery?"

"I—"

"Are you kidding?" She opened the car door and stuck her head inside. "Is this the Ram Air package?"

"Yes." His hands flexed, the urge to pull her out of the vehicle warring with what he knew was proper behavior. Which would be the exact opposite of what would happen if he touched her. And those curves.

Truth was, he'd lied to her in his office. Taking her to bed had definitely been in his thoughts.

She straightened and looked at him, but didn't shut the door. "Black on black."

He nodded, impressed. He'd never known a woman who knew much about cars, but it followed since the Kincaids ran auto shops.

Her brows lifted. "There were only ten of these produced."

"Five actually."

She laughed. "Very good. I already knew that, I just wanted to see if you did, too." She whistled and went back to admiring the car. "I'd have said yes based on this gorgeous hunk of metal alone. When do I get to drive it?"

"You don't. Bring your bike into the empty bay."

To her credit, there was no pouting in response. "So the neighbors don't see?"

"Something like that." He started toward the house, then paused. "Where are your things?"

"In the saddlebags."

He looked back at the bike. There was no way those saddlebags held more than a weekend's worth of clothes. That was good. Meant she didn't intend to stay long. Maybe they could get married and go their separate ways. A marriage in name only sort of thing.

Or maybe she was planning on refusing. Would Clem allow that? Hank thought not. But she might be working on a way around that.

Something inside him deflated a little at the thought. Why her refusing should bother him, he had no idea.

Either way, they had a lot to talk about. He waited at the entrance to the house until she'd wheeled her bike in, then he closed the garage door and opened the one to the house. She unhitched her saddlebags and carried them, one in each hand. He let her go in first.

She brushed past him. Slowly. It was the closest they'd been since being alone in his office. Even after a night in lockup, she smelled faintly floral with the pleasant earthy undertone of all shifters. She stopped, forcing him to share the doorway with her. "Thanks, by the way."

Up close, her eyes were the color of good, aged whiskey. The kind of burnt, liquid brown a man could drown in. Her lips had the color and ripe fullness of fresh berries. It wouldn't take much to taste them. Just lean across a few inches, put his mouth on hers. But he couldn't. Not after their conversation in his office. He forced his gaze to meet her eyes. "For what?"

"You could have sent me packing the minute you figured out who I was and what I was here for."

"I'm the son of the alpha. You're the daughter of one. You know as well as I do the obligations that come with those roles."

She nodded, her gaze skimming over his chest and shoulders like she was taking his measurements. Then the sad, fearful expression he'd seen in her once before returned for a moment. "I do."

She went inside, giving him a chance to breathe. There was something about her, something powerful that drew him to her like a dog to a bone. Or a red-blooded man to a hot biker chick. He closed his eyes and leaned against the door. The full moon was three days away.

That's all it was. Moon fever.

That rush of hormones and endorphins that charged every shifter's system until they had a chance to run it off. Or find another way to put it to use.

Which they would not be doing.

He closed the door behind him.

She stood in the kitchen, looking very feminine in his very masculine home. She swept a length of hair behind her shoulder. "Your house is amazing. Like something out of a magazine. A men's magazine, but still."

"Thank you." Had that actually been a compliment? He wasn't sure. "You...need anything?"

She laughed, a light, sweet sound that reminded him of clear water and sunshine. "I need everything. A room, a shower, a meal. Preferably in that order." She held her hands out. "Sorry, but that's my current status."

"Right. I'll show you your room."

It was upstairs, next to the room he used as a gym. On the other side of that was his bedroom. The only reason he even had a guest room was because Bridget and his mother had insisted he needed one.

He pushed the door open. "I need to wash the sheets. My parents just stayed and I didn't know you were going to be here so soon."

"I can do that." Ivy smiled as she looked around. "There's no way you decorated this yourself."

"My sister did it. Too much?" It was to him. All those extra pillows on the bed seemed pointless.

They basically existed to be taken off and put back on the bed. No other purpose.

"No, it's perfect."

He watched her walk in. Took note of how nicely shaped her backside was and how long her legs were. Reminded himself again to keep his gaze at eye level. "As for food, I don't cook much." Or at all, really.

She put her saddlebags on the bed. "Whatever you've got. I'm not picky." She was still looking around at the room. "And I'm so hungry even a PB&J would be manna right now. Those pancakes were good, but you know how it is when the full moon is near. Hungry all the time."

He nodded. "I can do better than that."

Or could he? He scratched his head. He couldn't remember the last time he'd gotten groceries that weren't six-packs of beer or PowerBars. He usually ate lunch and dinner at Howler's if he wasn't tied up with work, which in Nocturne Falls was rare. Eating there was his way of spending time with Bridget. Didn't hurt that the food was above and beyond anything he could make for himself. And free, despite the many times he'd tried to pay. "I better check the fridge first. Come down when you're ready."

"Okay, thanks." She nodded, eyes bright, but looking a little bit overwhelmed.

Was that because of him? He left her in the room and went downstairs. When he hit the kitchen, he paused to splay his hands on the granite counter. He leaned in, taking a deep breath of air that didn't hold her intoxicating perfume. Was he really about to marry this woman? He'd never thought of himself as husband material, even though he'd been born into a position that ensured marriage was in his future.

Problem was, the future he'd done his best to prepare for was not being a husband. It was all about becoming alpha. He'd gone into the Army Rangers, something he knew had made his father proud. After two tours, Hank had had enough and taken on the job of sheriff in this crazy town.

The things he knew about were strategy, leadership, discipline, rules, and teamwork. What he didn't know about were relationships with women.

Or marriage.

He knew what a loving relationship looked like from his parents, but their arranged match was nothing like this one.

There was no question whether he'd agree to it. He would. It was his duty as the firstborn of the alpha, and he wouldn't have a pack war on his hands.

He'd seen enough bloodshed in his days. No way was he going to be responsible for bringing even a piece of that to his family, his pack or the town that had become a sanctuary for him, his brother, and his sister.

Enough thinking. He'd made his decision. He'd do his duty. Ivy wasn't the worst the Kincaids could have offered him, that was for sure.

He went to the fridge. Bare. Unless ketchup, a jar of olives, or two-day-old pizza qualified as lunch. Or beer. He never drank when he was on duty. Never. And rarely before five, but today…today might be an exception.

No. There were no exceptions to hard and fast rules. That's how things went south.

He grabbed a bottle of Coke, twisted the top off and drank it while he checked the freezer. Bridget had stocked it with a few things—a lasagna and two tubs of chili, but both of those would take some defrosting.

That gave him only a few options. Run to the store for food, which meant leaving Ivy alone in his house. He wasn't comfortable with that. Not yet. That left him with calling in an order to Howler's. Technically, they didn't deliver, but Bridget would send one of the bus boys for him.

He picked up the phone and dialed.

"Howler's. Bridget speaking."

"Hey, Bridge. What's the special today?"

"Hey, bro! Bacon cheeseburgers with Cajun fries. You coming in for lunch?"

"Not today. Can you send two with the works to my house?"

"Working on a case from home?"

"Something like that." He'd break the news about Ivy to her and Titus later.

"You got it, brosef."

"Thanks." He hung up.

Footsteps padded down the steps. "I take it the fridge was bare?"

"Yes, I..." He turned around and immediately understood why Ivy's clothes had fit in her saddle-bags. There wasn't much to them. The denim cutoffs and purple tank top she wore would have fit in the glove box of his duty car. Or maybe his back pocket.

She was fresh from the shower, and her hair hung in long, damp strands around her face. She'd washed her makeup off and now wore none. Or very little. Hank didn't know enough about it to tell which. Either way, she was still gorgeous. Maybe a little less intimidating fresh-faced.

Lacy black bra straps peeked from under the skinny tank top, making him wonder what the rest of her underthings looked like. A delicate vine tattoo trailed from her shoulder to her elbow on her right arm.

And her legs...her legs were endless and tan and endless. Her toes were painted bright, glittery blue.

In need of a diversion, he straightened the towel

hanging over the sink cabinet door. "No, nothing in the fridge. I ordered bacon burgers and fries."

"Sounds good to me. Can I get one of those?"

He looked up. "What?"

She pointed to the Coke in his hand. "A soda."

"Sure. You can have anything. Help yourself to whatever you want."

She opened the fridge and laughed. "I see why you ordered out."

"I need to get to the grocery store."

She grabbed a Coke, twisted off the top and leaned against the counter. She held the bottle out to him. "Cheers. Here's to...getting to know each other."

He could drink to that. Especially if it meant finding out the truth behind her reason for being here and not running. Intuition told him it was more than just obligation but he wouldn't be surprised if a lot of her motivation was fear of her father. He tapped his bottle against hers and they both drank.

She wiped her mouth with the back of her hand when she was done. "I could do that for you, you know."

"Do what?" Damn, she was distracting with that much skin showing.

"Groceries." She shrugged. "It's not a big deal. Just like washing the sheets. I'd like to be useful while I'm here."

While she was here. Made it sound temporary.

Maybe his theory about them being married in name only was on target. "You don't mind?"

"Not at all."

"That would be good. You've got to eat."

"And you don't?"

"I don't eat at home much."

She nodded like she was processing what that meant. "I won't see much of you, is that what you're saying?"

"I..." He didn't want to leave her alone in the house but now that he thought about it, what choice did he have? He had to go back to work and he couldn't exactly have her hang out at the station all day. "I eat at Howler's most of the time."

"I think I'll avoid that place if it's all right with you."

"My sister owns it."

She set her soda on the counter. "Awesome."

He frowned. "What's wrong with that?"

"Nothing, I just didn't realize how many bad first impressions I'd made already."

"Bridget didn't say anything to me about what happened."

"Bridget? As in the woman behind the bar?"

He nodded.

"I was right about her being a shifter." Ivy sighed. "Any other Merrows in town I should know about?"

"My brother, Titus. He's the fire chief."

"The one my father saved?"

"Mm-hmm." He leaned on the counter. "And now that Clemens has called in that debt, neither of us has much say in the matter."

"Does that mean you're in?"

"Aren't you?"

She laughed bitterly. "Refuse an order from Clemens Kincaid? I'm a lot smarter than I look."

"You look plenty smart to me." She did. There was a bright, determined spark in her gaze. Like a woman with a plan. It was both encouraging and unsettling. "What do you do?"

"What's my trade, you mean?"

He nodded.

"I do hair. I guess I should look for a salon in town, see if I can rent a chair. Or maybe get my foot in as a receptionist."

"Are you planning on staying here?"

She gave him an odd look. "You must have a different definition of married than I do."

"I just thought...you didn't bring much with you." So much for his deductive powers.

She shrugged. "I figured we'd get to know each other, make sure we were compatible enough to make it work, then I'd get the rest of my stuff."

At the word stuff, she glanced at the tattoo on the inside of her left wrist and her mouth bent in an odd way. His gut told him that tattoo was significant. He wondered what it meant to her. When she was ready, he was sure she'd tell him. "If you want to get groceries, that would be good. I'll drop you off at the store, then head into the office. You can call me when you're ready to go and I'll come get you and bring you back."

"Okay. Happy to do it."

"I'll be right back." He jogged upstairs to the small safe installed in the wall of his walk-in closet. He punched in the code, took out three hundred dollars, locked it back up and returned to the kitchen.

He put the money on the counter. "That should cover it."

She nodded at the bills. "Yeah, definitely. Anything you don't like?"

"No. I'll eat whatever."

The radio attached to his shoulder squawked. "Hank?"

He pinched it to respond. "Birdie, you're supposed to call me Sheriff."

"Why? You forget what your job is?"

Ivy laughed, quickly covering her mouth with her hand.

He sighed and spoke into the radio. "What do you need?"

The doorbell rang. Ivy held up her hands and whispered, "I'll get it."

He nodded and listened as Birdie rambled on about a tourist with a parking ticket complaint, turning to watch Ivy.

Maybe he'd find a way to let Birdie go and make Ivy the new receptionist. He'd have to see if there was a rule about the sheriff's receptionist having a record. Ivy sauntered toward the front door, her hips swaying gently. Even if there was a rule, maybe an exception could be made. Having her at the station would be a great way to keep an eye on her.

Which, as it turned out, was quite a pleasurable activity.

Ivy opened the door and stared into the face of the woman who'd brought her a beer and a grilled cheese last night. The bartender from Howler's. Hank's sister. She had a large brown sack in one hand. The grease-stained bag gave off delicious aromas and Ivy realized in that instant Hank had ordered the food from Howler's.

Oh boy. This was gonna be fun. "Hi there."

Bridget stared back. "You look famil—aren't you the woman they arrested in my bar last night?"

"In the back parking lot and not an actual arrest because the charges were dropped, but yes."

Bridget frowned, which made her no less pretty. Bridget's deep auburn looked like it was bottle-enhanced, but so what? It worked really well on her. There was something reassuring about Hank's sister being well put together. "What are you doing in my brother's house? Are the holding cells full?"

"No! He brought me here. In fact..." Ivy took a breath, the truth on the tip of her tongue. "We're going to be—"

"Bridget." Hank hustled past Ivy to take the bag

from his sister's hand. "You should have sent one of the bar backs."

Bridget frowned. "Why? So I wouldn't see you shacked up with a perp?" She clucked her tongue and shook her head. "I know you haven't gotten any in a while, but this is sad."

Ivy put her hands on her hips. "I'm not a perp." Well, she sort of was. Still. Harsh. Interesting that Handsome Hank hadn't been scoring lately. What was up with that? She'd have thought the local talent would be all over Mr. Single-In-Uniform.

"Bridget, it's not what you think, and I'll explain later," Hank said. He started to close the door.

Bridget stuck her foot in the way. "Why not now?"

"Shouldn't you be watching your bar?"

"Don't change the subject." Bridget shot Ivy a look. "What *are* you doing here?"

Ivy answered, "Like I was about to say, we're supposed to be mar—"

"Later, Bridget." He glared at Ivy.

Ivy crossed her arms. "What's the matter? Don't want your sister to know you're about to get hitched to a Kincaid?"

Bridget swiveled toward Ivy like she was on a pivot. "What did you just say?"

Hank muttered a dirty word. "Living room. Both of you."

Bridget's face was screwed up six ways to Sunday, but she stepped inside. He shut the door, steam almost visible from his ears. Poor guy. Apparently, he'd wanted to keep his nuptials a secret. Too bad. Ivy had enough secrets to keep to be adding one more to the list. He pointed toward the interior of the house and both women headed in that direction. He followed after them.

Ivy let Bridget lead since she hadn't had a tour of the place yet. The living room was quite a space. Bridget sat on one end of a massive brown leather sofa, so Ivy took the opposite end. A huge stone fireplace and mammoth flat-screen fought for attention in the room. Definitely a guy's room. There wasn't much in the way of personal touches, but maybe that was because he worked a lot. Or because there was no woman in his life, outside of his sister, to do that sort of stuff.

Hank must have dropped the food off in the kitchen, because he no longer had the bag when he came in. "Bridget, just listen until I'm done. You can ask questions later."

"You're not the boss of me."

"Bridge, please."

She sighed. "Go on."

Hank spilled the details of the treaty and the marriage that would seal it. Ivy watched Bridget's face.

Her expressions ranged from anger to horror to sympathy. Clearly she and her brother were a lot closer than Ivy and her brothers. Hank took a deep breath and finished. "So that's it. Ivy and I are going to take the next few days to make sure we're compatible, but that's basically a formality at this point. The marriage will happen in three days. On the full moon."

Bridget frowned. "Dad said you had to do this?"

"No. He gave me an out. But if the marriage doesn't happen, Clemens has promised war. I'm not doing that to my family or my pack."

Ivy sucked in a breath, surprised her father had gone so far as to threaten war. He did whatever he thought necessary to get what he wanted, but going to war would be a new low even for him.

Hank and Bridget looked at her.

Ivy shook her head. "I'm sorry. I didn't know."

"Really?" Bridget's brows went up. "You had no idea?"

"*No*, I didn't." Ivy shot a look right back at her. "Believe me or don't, but I'm not exactly part of my father's inner circle. I didn't even know about this marriage deal until yesterday." And then her father had given her half an hour to pack and get moving, which was the real reason she'd brought only a few things with her.

And she still hadn't texted him. Well, screw him.

He had to know she was here. She'd call as soon as she damn well got around to it.

Bridget made a soft noise. "That sucks. It all sucks, actually."

"It's what happens to the children of pack leaders." Hank stared at his sister pointedly. "You know that. I know that. Ivy knows that. And we aren't always privy to the details."

Bridget looked at Ivy again, this time her gaze a little softer. "You're lucky you ended up with Hank. It could have been a lot worse."

Ivy held back a snort. Bridget really had no idea what worse was. "I don't really know your brother yet, but I'm sure that's true."

Bridget returned her attention to Hank. "You're definitely going to get married?"

"You see another option?"

"No." Bridget sighed and leaned back, her gaze shifting to Ivy once again. "You do anything to hurt him, and I swear I will—"

"Bridget," Hank interrupted. "Making threats in front of an officer of the law isn't advisable. Not to mention that's my soon-to-be wife you're threatening." Hank's face was as serious as could be.

"And?" Bridget challenged him.

Ivy snorted out a laugh.

Hank and Bridget looked at her again.

"Sorry, but the whole soon-to-be wife thing just

sounds so...weird." She composed herself, because there was no doubt by Bridget's stern expression that she was serious. "I promise I'm not here to cause trouble. Despite my start."

Bridget nodded. "Good." She stuck her hand out. "Kincaid or not, I guess you're about to be part of the family. We should get to know each other. I'll give you my cell number in case you need anything."

Ivy tried not to let her mouth hang open at Bridget's sudden acceptance. She couldn't imagine a Kincaid saying the same thing to a Merrow. Didn't mean she trusted the woman yet, but she shook Bridget's hand anyway. Of course, neither she nor her brother knew exactly what this marriage to Ivy meant, but they'd find out as soon as the deal was sealed per her father's orders. Remorse built in her belly. Neither Hank nor his sister deserved the trick Clemens was about to play on their pack. "Thank you. I really appreciate that."

Ivy's stomach growled.

Bridget grinned and hooked a thumb toward the kitchen. "Go appreciate the food I brought before it gets any colder." She nodded at Hank as she stood. "You, too. Come on, Ivy, I'll give you my number in the kitchen."

The three of them headed in that direction, and a few minutes later, Ivy had Bridget's cell number programmed into her phone, Bridget had left, and

Ivy was chowing down on the best lukewarm bacon cheeseburger she'd eaten in her life.

She swallowed the bite she'd just taken. "Your sister's nice."

"Did you expect her not to be?" Hank downed three fries at once. "Other than her threat to hurt you if you hurt me, of course."

"That's just sibling love." Ivy remembered that, but since her youngest brother, Sam, had fallen under their father's sway, he'd drifted away from her. She tucked a piece of lettuce back under the bun. "I'm a Kincaid. I expected to be treated like one."

"That's where you went wrong. Assuming we'd act the way your family would."

She nodded. "That's for sure."

Hank was gruff, but that was no big deal. Sure, Bridget had started out skeptical, but who wouldn't? And after Hank had told her how things were going to be, she'd become friendly. Yes, it could just be a front, but she'd seemed genuine.

The fact that Hank and his sister were so accepting of Ivy made it that much harder for her to keep quiet about the truth behind the marriage. But Ivy's father had sworn her to secrecy with the kind of threats that made Bridget's seem like compliments. Ivy glanced at the five on her wrist, struggling not to let her thoughts go to a very dark place.

"What does that mean?"

She looked up. "What?"

"The five on your wrist."

She turned her wrist against her thigh. "Nothing." Nothing she could tell him about.

He didn't seem like he believed her answer, but he didn't press her further. "You okay?"

She forced a smile. "Great."

He grunted. "We should go. I need to get back to the station."

"And I need to get groceries." She jumped to her feet and started cleaning up.

He grabbed her arm, the touch of his rough hand almost paralyzing her. "You don't have to do that."

She swallowed down the panic sparked by his touch, knowing he'd meant only to catch her attention. Not start her heart revving like a big block engine. *Breathe.* "I don't have to do what?"

"Clean up. You're a guest."

She focused on his words, on his voice—anything but his hand on her arm. "I'm going to be your wife."

He shook his head as his thumb made a lazy arc on her skin. The panic was gone, replaced by the kind of heat that built low in her body. His brows furrowed. "Still doesn't mean you have to wait on me hand and foot."

Something inside her melted a little, and her breath caught in her throat for a very different reason. "I don't mind," she said softly. Her instincts told her that this man was nothing like her father. Not someone to fear.

Not entirely. He was still an alpha. Maybe not in charge of his own pack yet, but that day would come. He could change her future. Or ruin it, but that seemed less likely the more she got to know him. She, on the other hand, might truly ruin his future. And she was regretting that with greater intensity every passing second.

"Fair enough."

But he didn't move his hand, and her pulse refused to drop down to a normal rate. Damn the full moon's pull.

He finally let her go, tipping his head slightly. "Do I scare you?"

She laughed nervously. "No." Yes. Because what if...she actually fell for him? That scared the hell out of her.

He stood, and the space between them disappeared. "I would never hurt you."

He towered over her. The instinct to back up kicked in hard. Crowding him in public was one thing, in private it was a whole different story. Bravado was easy to come by with an audience. Still, she refused to move. She didn't want to show him the fear that had been beaten into her. He was *not* her father. She opened her mouth and tried to find an answer that wasn't a lie, but she couldn't.

Gently, he lifted her chin and looked her in the eyes. "You don't know that, do you?"

She slanted her gaze away.

"I give you my word. Can you accept that?"

She nodded. "Yes."

He took his hand away. The loss of contact should have soothed her. It didn't. "I don't expect you to trust me overnight."

She hadn't imagined he'd be this understanding, this tender. "Okay."

"I'm sure your father told you differently all your life, but being a Merrow doesn't mean I'm a monster."

She smiled without effort and met his gaze. "I'm figuring that out."

The real monster was Clemens Kincaid.

Hank smiled, and a flash of the wildness within him danced in his eyes, turning them feral gold. A muscle in his jaw twitched. He bent his head and pressed his mouth to hers, hard and fast and possessive in its intent.

Her body responded with a sudden craving for more and the awakening of her own wildness. Just as she was about to reach for him, he pulled back.

He shook his head, breathing hard. "I shouldn't have done that. Sorry."

"No, it was...fine." It was *so* much better than fine. The fact that she could string words together into a coherent sentence was a miracle. "We're going to be married. Kissing is the least of our issues."

"I thought you were worried I might try to get you into bed."

She swallowed. "Kissing and sleeping together are two very different things." Although right now, she could see how one would lead to the other very quickly with a man who made her feel this deliciously light-headed after one kiss.

He grunted. The gold in his eyes was gone, and the sheriff was back in control. "Get whatever you need. I'll be in the car."

And with that, he went out the garage door. A few seconds later, the engine started.

She slumped against the counter and took a few breaths in an effort to calm her heart, which was now pounding all over again. This man was nothing like what she'd expected. He was So. Much. Better.

She hadn't prepared for this. For wanting to be in his arms, for enjoying the way he kissed, for even being kissed. For the slim possibility that she might...fall...in love.

Outside of her father, nothing in her life had ever scared her quite so much. She couldn't let her heart get involved, couldn't let herself care. She'd be the one who ended up getting hurt. Especially when Hank found out the truth.

She grabbed the money he'd laid out on the counter, tucked it safely into her bra and left the house. She slipped into the squad car, front seat this time. The dash was covered in police equipment, a laptop on a movable arm, a radio, a mounted camera and some other things she didn't recognize.

She clicked her seat belt into place and folded her hands in her lap while Hank drove. They were both wolves, both equipped with the same sense of smell. There was no way either of them could deny the pheromones they were each giving off. The kiss had started something. Or unleashed something. It was like a bad case of full moon fever. Maybe the worst case.

And yet they were both quiet on the way to the grocery store. As if that could stop whatever they'd just started. She kept replaying the kiss and he...she had no idea what went on in his head. Maybe he wasn't thinking about the kiss. Maybe he was thinking about the next person he was going to arrest.

He pulled up and idled out in front of the Shop & Save. "You have everything you need?"

She nodded and unclipped her seat belt.

"You don't have a purse."

"I don't need one." She opened the door and

climbed out, in desperate need for air untainted by
Hank Merrow's male scent.

"Where's the money I gave you?"

She leaned back into the car. "In my bra."

His gaze went right to her cleavage, then he
jerked his head away like he'd accidentally stared
into the sun and suddenly remembered it could
make him go blind. "Oh."

She grinned.

He swallowed, eyes straight ahead. "Call me
when you're done."

"Don't you want to know where my cell phone
is?" It was in her back pocket, along with her ID.

"No."

"See you later." She closed the door and gave
him a little wave.

A couple of people gave her curious looks as the
squad car pulled away. People talked in small towns.
She could only guess what stories they'd be sharing
over dinner tonight about the tattooed woman
getting out of the sheriff's car. Handsome Hank was
going to get a rep. With a smirk on her face, she
grabbed a cart and headed into the store.

She'd been given the nickname Poison in high
school. Tuning out gossips and bullies was nothing
new to her. It was how she'd survived her childhood
and her father's endless berating.

She took a second to suss out the unfamiliar

layout of the store, then pushed the cart toward produce. Hank said he'd eat anything, but she knew how to cook for men. Especially shifter men whose metabolisms meant they were always hungry. Meat, potatoes, sweets and beer.

Red skin potatoes were on sale, but russets were the best for baking. She weighed the choices until she remembered she had three hundred dollars to shop with. Hank didn't seem like the kind who cared if she used coupons or not, either, and what mattered most right now was making him happy.

She got a small bag of each.

Shopping without a list was tricky, but she mentally planned a week's worth of suppers, with leftovers that could be had for lunch and then some basics for breakfast. By the time she was done, her cart was full and she felt like nothing had been forgotten.

Including the dinner she planned to make him tonight. Steak, baked potatoes with all the fixings and chocolate cake made with her secret ingredient: coffee instead of water. Not that secret maybe, but still delicious.

She got in the checkout line and dialed his number.

"Merrow." His gravelly voice filled her ear and raised happy little goose bumps on her arms. Okay, her hormones really needed to chill out.

"Hi, it's Ivy. I'm in the checkout lane."

"Be there in five."

"See you then."

He grunted in acknowledgment and hung up.

She tucked her phone into her back pocket as the line moved forward. It took her a second to get her cart going, too long, apparently, for whoever was driving the cart behind her. It bumped her. She turned to see who the responsible party was.

"Sorry about that," the older woman clutching the cart's handle said. "It got away from me."

Not likely, but Ivy let it go. "It's all right."

"Say," the woman continued. "Didn't the sheriff drop you off?"

Small towns never disappointed. Ivy squinted at the woman. "Is that who that was?"

Confusion clouded the woman's face.

Ivy turned back around, pushing her cart up to the conveyer. She went to work unloading her groceries and humming *Going To The Chapel* while smiling to herself.

"Paper or plastic?" the cashier asked.

Crap. She didn't have any canvas bags. "Plastic. You have a recycling bin for those where I can bring them back?"

The woman nodded. "Up front."

"Okay, plastic is fine then."

"That's very conscientious of you," the woman

behind Ivy chimed in, her cart still following way too close. "Not many young folks these days care about the environment."

Ivy leaned toward the woman. "You know who else loves the environment?"

The woman grinned, apparently tickled to finally have gotten a conversation going. "Who?"

"The sheriff," Ivy whispered.

The woman's smile flattened and she hmphed out a little sigh.

Ivy went back to her groceries, doing nothing to hold back her smirk.

The cashier rang up the last item. "Two hundred and thirty-eight dollars and seventeen cents. Will that be cash or credit?"

"Cash." Ivy dug the three bills out of her bra, earning a soft, disapproving gasp from Cart Woman, and paid. She waited for her change, then stuffed that into the pocket of her cut offs. Transaction completed, she pushed her cart out of the air conditioned store and into the warm Georgia day.

Hank was already there on the curb, leaning against the squad car looking exceptionally handsome in his uniform and permanent scowl. He looked climbable. Wow, she needed to run some of this energy off and bad.

He peeled off the side of the car and helped her load the bags into the trunk. "I'd ask if you found everything but judging from the bags, you bought the whole store."

That familiar twinge of panic returned. Had she spent too much? She found her bravado. "If you don't like what I bought, you can do your own shopping next time."

He looked at her. "I was kidding."

"Oh. Right." She laughed, feeling a little sheepish. "Yeah, I bought a lot. Sorry."

"If anyone's going to apologize, it's me. I had nothing in the house. You fixed that. Thanks."

He opened the car door for her. She got in, then he went around to his side.

As soon as he was in and his door was shut, she dug the change from her pocket and held it out to him. "Here's what's left over."

"Keep it. You might need it for something else."

She hesitated, not quite sure what to make of that, then stuffed the bills and change back in her pocket. "Okay. I'll keep it for household stuff."

"Use it for whatever. I don't care."

She nodded. "Thanks."

She turned toward the window so he couldn't see her face. He was kind, generous, earnest...he was the polar opposite of most of the men she'd grown up with. Even if he'd been hideous, which he so wasn't, she'd be worried about falling for him.

Hell, she was already falling for him.

She closed her eyes and took a few breaths. This was bad. The kind of bad that wasn't going to be fixed by her splitting as soon as the deal was done. No, these were the sorts of feelings that settled into genuine heartache and a lifetime of regret.

She had to call home. Had to talk to Charlie. Had to remind herself why she was doing this.

Or she was going to turn tail and run.

5

Something was up with Ivy. Something was unsettling her. Hank didn't need his sheriff instincts or military training to figure that out. Maybe it was just because she was in a strange town, about to marry a strange man from the family who'd been feuding with her family since before either of them was born.

That was enough to upset anyone. Hell, it upset him for a second or two, but women attached emotion to everything. To him this marriage was a business transaction. One he hadn't given much thought to, although he'd known it was a possibility since he'd understood his place as the pack leader's firstborn. Clearly an oversight on his part. This marriage was going to last the rest of his life. He would have to find a way to make it work.

And he knew enough to know that making it work meant keeping Ivy happy. Happy wife, happy life was a saying for a reason.

But whatever was going on with her now was her business. She'd come to terms with the marriage in her own time. If she didn't, she'd be miserable for the rest of her life no matter what he did. With that in mind, he let her be. Suspects he could interrogate all day long. But a woman like Ivy was a complicated creature beyond his ken. Actually, most women were. His mother, aunt and sister included.

He pulled into the driveway and hit the button to raise the garage door. After parking, he got out and opened Ivy's door for her, then popped the trunk and grabbed two big handfuls of bags. No rat poison in any of them that he could see, so that was a good sign.

He went through the garage, leaving the house door open for her. As he set the bags on the kitchen counter, the knowledge that he'd have to leave her in the house alone became apparent.

What other choice did he have? Bring her to the station? And have her do what? Sit in his office for the rest of the day like she was a child to be watched? Make her fair game for one of Birdie's interrogations? Neither one of them wanted that.

He sighed. This would be their first experiment in trust.

He almost bumped into her on his way out for a second load of groceries.

"Sorry." She quickly got out of his way.

"No, you go." He moved to the side, watching her go past. For a woman with so much outward confidence, she had a wariness about her that was baffling. Was that Clemens' doing? Had he demanded a level of deferential treatment that had shaped her whole life? Hank set the bags on the counter and waited until she came back. "Why don't you start unpacking and I'll bring the rest in?"

"Okay." She tucked a strand of blue-black hair behind one ear adorned with a silver hoop, then went to work unloading the goods.

It only took him one more trip to bring the rest of the bags in. The counters were full. "You need anything else? I have to get back to the station."

She shut the fridge. "I think I'm good. I have plenty to keep me busy until you come home for dinner. You will be coming home for dinner, won't you?"

He didn't usually, but he also didn't usually have a woman waiting for him. Actually, he never had a woman waiting for him. "Do you want me to?"

Her brows bent. "Of course. It *is* your house. And how else are we going to get to know each other? Besides, I'm making dinner."

"Right. Seven then." That would give him time to swing by Howler's and check on Bridget. Make sure she wasn't freaking out over this marriage thing.

"Seven. Good."

"I'll call if something comes up."

Her mouth bunched to one side. "I was wondering..."

He waited.

"I could really use a run. This close to the full moon and all." She shrugged. "You know how it is."

He did know. The wildness had been scratching at his skin, especially with an available female in such close proximity, and there was no better way to release that wildness than a run. Well, there was a better way, but he wasn't going there with Ivy. Yet. "A run sounds great. After dinner."

She smiled, turning her already pretty face into something amazing. "Okay, good."

"See you later then." For a split second, he thought he should kiss her goodbye, but that's what couples did when they were comfortable with each other and that wasn't a word either one of them could apply to this relationship. If this could even be called a relationship. Arrangement might be all it ever was. He hoped that wasn't the case, but it was a possibility, especially in this kind of situation. With a small shake of his head, he went back to the car and got in. He sat for a minute, not going anywhere.

There was a woman in his kitchen unpacking groceries, who was clearly planning on cooking him a meal. A woman who was not his sister.

A woman who would be his wife in three days.

His life had done a one-eighty and he was essentially powerless to stop it.

The strangest part was, he wasn't sure he wanted

to. After all, this was what being next in line for alpha meant. Responsibility. Tradition. Sacrifice.

He went to put his keys in the ignition and realized he must have left them on the kitchen counter. He went back inside.

Ivy wasn't in the kitchen, but he heard her voice coming from the living room. She sounded stressed. He peered around the corner. She was on the phone, pacing in front of the fireplace.

"Yes, I'm here. In his house. I know I was supposed to text, but that's not how things went."

He shouldn't be eavesdropping. She was probably just checking in, letting someone know she had arrived. He started for the kitchen and his keys.

"Let me talk to Charlie."

He stopped walking, the sound of another man's name cutting through him. Of course there was another man. A woman like Ivy wouldn't be unattached.

Ivy sighed. "You have to let me talk to him at some point. He must miss me. At least tell him I love him."

Hank had never given it a thought, but it made so much sense. No wonder she'd tensed when he'd touched her. When he'd kissed her. And it explained why she seemed so torn about the whole thing.

Her father was forcing her to marry Hank for the

sake of the pack, Ivy's wants and needs and emotions be damned.

There was no way this would end well. Ivy would come to resent him, always seeing him as the man who'd cost her her happiness. It made Hank a little sad for both of them, and with that realization, he left.

He'd heard all he needed to hear.

IVY HUNG up and sat on the couch, letting her head hang down as she dealt with the emotions running through her. She wanted to cry and scream and break things, but none of that was going to change anything. Besides, she needed to focus her energy on making this situation work so that she and Charlie would never have to go through this again.

There were two options. Marry Hank, satisfy her father's demands, then take Charlie and run. And pray that her father didn't care enough about either one of them to bother looking.

Or *maybe* she could get Hank to fall for her, to really love her. Then, after he learned the truth, he might take pity on them and let them stay.

At the very least, he might not make them go back to Tennessee. Back to Clemens Kincaid.

That's all she really wanted for her and Charlie.

Freedom from the tyranny of her father. But getting that freedom was going to come at Hank's expense, no matter which route she chose.

She closed her eyes and inhaled, then blew out the breath slowly and opened her eyes again. She could at least give life with Hank a shot. He seemed like a decent man. Maybe he'd understand.

Maybe.

And if he didn't, running was still an option.

Her mind made up, she stood, tucked her phone in her pocket and went back to the kitchen to lose herself in the chores of putting the rest of the groceries away and baking a cake.

The oven had just come up to temperature when Hank charged through the front door, nearly scaring the daylights out of her. She jumped, jerking the mixer out of the bowl and splattering chocolate cake batter over herself and half the kitchen. He'd barely been gone an hour. "Are you trying to give me a heart attack?"

He looked stern. Not that that was so unusual. "We need to talk."

"Apparently." She put the mixer down, leaned against the counter and crossed her arms. She couldn't imagine what was wrong, but a small twitch of concern settled in her belly. "What's got you all worked up?"

"You. This...arrangement."

And there it was. She nodded. "Just hit you, did it? Blew your mind with a moment of, Oh crap, I'm marrying a Kincaid?" She sighed. "I feel ya. I really do."

"No." He huffed out a breath, big bad wolf style. "I know you're in love with another man. I can't marry a woman who's going to resent me and make my life miserable for something I can't help, so we need to work this out *now*."

She stared at him, wondering how he'd come to that conclusion. "Um...what?"

"Are you saying you're not in love with someone else?"

"I'm saying there's no other man, and I don't know what you're talking about."

He growled, his eyes sparking gold. "Do *not* lie to me. I hate lies. I heard you on the phone. Heard you asking for Charlie."

"Calm down, Merrow." She frowned, but her stomach rolled with a greater anxiety. The secret she'd been sworn to keep was on the verge of surfacing and it was very clearly too soon. Duty or not, Hank probably didn't like her enough at this point to forgive her for the whole thing. "For someone who hates lies, you sure have no problem eavesdropping, huh?"

That took the vinegar out of him. "Just tell me the truth. What am I getting into?"

She closed her eyes for a moment and took a breath. She could tell him the truth without revealing everything. It was the only way to hang on to her hope for a better life. The only way she might avoid her father's wrath and a lifetime of looking over her shoulder. She tensed in anticipation of his reaction. "Charlie is my son."

Hank's shoulders dropped and his face went slack, the frustration draining away. "You have a kid? Where is he?"

"At my parents." Anger had begun to simmer down deep. A little of it was because Hank was judging her for something he'd only overheard, but the bulk of her anger remained directed at her father for using Charlie as a pawn. And for being such a crappy human being.

A few beats passed before he spoke. "Why didn't you say something? That's an important detail, don't you think?"

Her anger hit a boiling point but Clemens wasn't there for her to lash out at, so Hank got the brunt of it. "My son is more than a *detail* and I didn't tell you yet because we've barely learned each other's first names. Maybe I was going to tell you at dinner." She wasn't. "Ever consider that?"

"No," he muttered.

He didn't deserve her ire, but she couldn't stop herself. There was too much built up emotion in her and it needed an outlet. "I get that you think your job makes you above the law but eavesdropping is a pretty crappy way to start out a new relationship."

So was withholding information, but what choice did she have? "Maybe it's stupid to think this can work. We don't know each other at all. I'm not sure we can even like each other. I need some air."

"Ivy."

She stormed out of the kitchen with no idea where she was going. Wasn't like the place belonged to her.

She ended up in the garage, next to her motorcycle. She wanted to leave even though she knew she couldn't. She had to stay here and see this thing through, but hearing Charlie referred to as a detail, like he was just one more box to be checked off, really riled her. Like the way Clemens had referred to her precious Charlie as a "weapon of mass humiliation".

She sighed and wrapped her arms around herself. She missed Charlie so much. She just wanted to pull him close and bury her nose in his hair and smell his sweet little boy smell.

Hank stomped down the garage steps. "Ivy—"

"What?" She whipped around, knowing her eyes must be gilded with the storm of emotions inside her.

He held his hands up. "I'm sorry. You're right. I

shouldn't have eavesdropped. And your son is definitely more than a detail. But you should have said something."

"Again, you were one meal away from finding out." She hated lying to Hank, but protecting Charlie and preserving the sliver of hope that she could make a better life for her son meant more. And what was she going to do? Tell Hank her father had sworn her to secrecy? That her father was trying to pawn off his unwanted grandchild onto another pack?

Hank raked a hand through his hair. "How old is...Charlie?"

"Just turned seven."

Hank nodded. "Just had his first moon, did he?"

"Last month. His birthday's May fifth." That wasn't adding to the lie, just answering in the vaguest way she knew how.

His eyes narrowed. "Does that date have anything to do with the five tattooed on your wrist?"

She smiled a little, feeling bad for dumping her anger on him. "You're pretty perceptive."

He shrugged, his broad shoulders pulling at his uniform in the most distracting way. Heaven help her, he was unfairly beautiful. "It's my job."

A moment of silence passed before he spoke again. "You understand why my knowing about your son is such a big deal, right?"

She understood. Too well. And there lay the crux

of the whole thing. "Because if we marry, you have to take him as your firstborn. Unless you have another kid I don't know about."

He shook his head.

She put into words what she knew he must be thinking about. "I can understand if finding out about Charlie makes you want to back out of the deal. A lot of men, especially those in line to be alpha, would demand their firstborn be a child of their own blood."

"I'm not most men. And I'm not backing out." He gave her a very serious look. "But you can't keep anything from me. If this is going to work, even on the most basic level, we have to be honest with each other."

She hesitated, then nodded. "I agree, but again, that comes down to trust and right now...I don't trust you yet. Just like I'm sure you don't trust me. And until we get to that point, you can't expect me to just go spilling my guts to you."

He rested one hand on his holstered duty weapon. "No. You're right. If this is going to work, then we—I—have to work at it. Anything worth having is worth working for."

Her brows rose. "You think this truce is that important?"

"I think you are."

She swallowed while her insides did a weird, fluttery thing. "Oh."

"Starting tonight, I'm going to work on showing you that."

"How?"

His eyes narrowed a little. Like he'd figured something out. "I'm going to woo you."

He was going to woo *her*. That was unexpected. She thought about how she could make him fall for her so hard that the truth about Charlie wouldn't change a thing. She'd just give his wooing right back to him. She lifted her chin and stared right back at him. "I like the sound of that."

"Good." His thick brows knit in seeming concern. "Just because you're a sure thing, you shouldn't be treated like one. I don't want you to feel like I'm taking this arranged marriage for granted. I'm not always so good with words but this way I can show you."

She put her hands on her hips and cocked one out to the side. "I like that you're willing to put in some effort to romance me. Do I get to make requests?"

"Sure." He made a face. "Like what exactly?"

"I don't know yet. But don't worry, I'm not going to ask you to carve my name on the hood of your GTO."

He cringed. "Is that a thing?"

"No, and I would never want you to do something that sacrilegious as proof of your affections."

"That's a relief." He smiled. A half-smile, but the corners of his mouth were going in the right direction so she wasn't going to nitpick. "So...romance. And wooing. And pursuing. Not exactly my area of expertise, but..." He shrugged and seemed deep in thought. "I was an Army Ranger, I'm sure I can figure this out."

She held out her hand. "Then it's a deal."

"What's a deal?"

"You woo me, I'll trust you. And together we'll figure this marriage thing out."

"And finally have peace between our families. Agreed." He took her hand, but instead of shaking it, he pulled her toward him, causing her to lean into him. "You have little spots of chocolate batter all over you, you know."

He was rock hard and smelled like the woods on a rainy evening. She sucked in a breath, inhaling more of his intoxicating scent. What had he said? Something about the cake batter. "I hope you like chocolate."

"I love it." His mouth found her jaw.

She closed her eyes and leaned into him a little more. He didn't budge. "I'm...so...*oh*...glad."

His mouth went lower, nibbling off the chocolate splatters as he went until he worked his way back to her lips and kissed her properly. The sweetness of the batter lingered on his tongue as it slid over hers. She moaned softly.

It had been a long, long time since she'd been this thoroughly kissed or had this much man to cling to. A long damn time.

Her body surged with need, fueled by the impending full moon. Judging by the grip of his hands and the possessiveness of his mouth on hers, he was feeling the same thing. When he broke the kiss, they were both panting.

"I should go back to the station." He pulled her along with him as he shuffled backward toward the steps, eyes golden and driving her mad.

She nodded and pointed toward the kitchen as she went along. "And I should get that cake in the oven."

"I'll, uh, see you at seven." He walked them up the stairs and back into the house.

"For dinner."

"For dinner," he repeated as he finally let go of her with one more quick kiss.

But even as he headed out to the squad car, she had a feeling dinner wasn't all that was on the menu.

"I said I'd woo her, which she seemed to like. But…" Hank propped himself on the edge of Bridget's desk in the tiny closet of a room she called Howler's office. "I don't have a clue where to start."

Bridget snickered. "You're such a man."

"Which is why I'm here. Can you help me or not?" He raised his brows to punctuate the questions.

"Of course I can help you. I'm a bartender. It's practically like being a relationship therapist. Also, in case you hadn't noticed, I'm a woman. I know what works and what doesn't. What's the plan for tonight?"

"She's making dinner and then I said we'd go out for a run."

Bridget's brows shot up. "*Hello.* A little romp in the woods three nights away from a full moon? You know where that's going to lead."

"We're *not* having sex." Hormones ran especially high close to a full moon, but they needed to burn off the building energy or it was only going to get worse. Granted, sometimes a good run was like foreplay, but this was strictly going to be about releasing excess energy. "Not tonight. Not tomorrow night. Maybe not even for a while after we're married. It has to be when she's ready."

"That's really sweet, Hank, but you know as well as I do what a run can do to you. Sure, it burns off energy. But it can also fill you with a whole 'nother kind."

"I know. But jumping into the physical side of things isn't the best way to start a relationship that's going to end up in marriage. Is it?"

Bridget shrugged. "Again, you are such a man."

Why were women so confusing? "Are you saying I should sleep with her?"

"Do you want to?"

"Yes, but that's not the point." The thought of Ivy beneath him, stripped bare, and his to pleasure filled him with such bone deep desire that he almost needed to sit down.

"If that's not the point, why did your eyes change color?" Bridget shook her head. "Dude, you've got it bad. I'm a little surprised. I didn't think you of all people would go in for the criminal element."

"She's not a criminal." Irritation edged his voice. "Stop calling her that."

Bridget's brows seemed permanently stuck in the air. "You're defending a Kincaid?"

"A Kincaid who's about to be my wife. You

befriended her. Why are you giving me such a hard time?"

"I'm not giving you a hard time, just curious why you're all into her. And I befriended her because you know what they say, keep your friends close and your enemies closer."

"I'm 'into her' because I'm about to be married to her and better to like her than not, don't you think? Why don't you trust her?"

"Do you?"

He exhaled. "She's alone in my house right now. I'm trying to think positively." He lifted his hand. "I do trust her. Until she gives me a reason not to. Cut her some slack. I get the sense she hasn't had an easy life with Clemens Kincaid as a father." He cleared his throat. "Or as a single mother."

Bridget almost fell off her chair. "What?"

"She's got a kid."

"Where is he?"

"With her parents." He could see the wheels in Bridget's mind turning. "It's not a big deal."

"Like hell it isn't. You have to accept that kid as your own."

"I know. And I'm okay with that." He shot her a look. "So you need to be too. Understand?"

Bridget held up her hands. "If you're okay with it, then I will be too." Her eyebrows bounced once in a 'how about that' expression. "Okay, back to you and your need for romance. Let's take it one day at a time, shall we? If she's making dinner, you should bring flowers. Not those awful limp things from the buckets in the produce section of the Shop & Save. Nice flowers. Go see Marigold over at the Enchanted Garden. She'll fix you up."

He hesitated. Marigold Williams was one of three sisters, who along with their mother, Corette, were the most well-known witches in town. Alice Bishop was probably the most powerful, but she worked exclusively for Elenora Ellingham and tended to keep to herself. "At what cost? I'm not giving her any of my hair or anything weird like that."

Bridget rolled her eyes. "Not every bunch of flowers she sells comes with a witchy price attached to it. Just tell her what you need. She's got a gift. With flowers. Now I have a bar to run and you have a woman to get home to."

She laughed. "Wow, that sounds even weirder out loud."

"It's not that weird." He opened the door.

"It's totally weird. You haven't had a girlfriend in how long? Since the Rangers? Bro, do your parts even work?"

"Don't worry about my parts." He frowned at her, but there was no denying he'd had a long dry spell. Deliberately. But Bridge didn't need to know that.

"Why *haven't* you had a girlfriend?"

"I've been busy." Truth, he'd never seen a reason to get involved, knowing that an arranged marriage would most likely be required of him as the pack leader's firstborn. And so, instead of entangling himself in a relationship that would only come to a forced end when his father dictated it, he'd opted to avoid relationships altogether.

It was also a way to spare Bridget and Titus from having to sacrifice their happiness for the sake of the pack. If he was available to be married off, they wouldn't have to be.

For a soldier, sacrifice was easy. Being sheriff felt very much the same. Long hours, hard work, sometimes unfavorable conditions, the willingness to be the first line of defense...it was what he did best. Who his father had raised him to be.

Bridget sighed. "Well, I guess you'll have to find a way to be less busy now, huh?"

"I guess. Thanks for the advice." He left and drove to the Enchanted Garden.

Not until he called out if anyone was there did Marigold come out from the back room. She had a leaf in her wild brunette hair and a piece of green tape stuck to the front of her work apron. "Hey, Sheriff, what can I do for you?"

"I need flowers."

Her eyes widened a little. "Good thing you came

here then. What's the occasion?"

"Dinner."

She nodded, leaning forward a bit. "With?"

He wasn't ready to make the marriage pact public. "A woman."

Marigold pursed her lips. "Is this a romantic thing?"

"Yes. Romantic."

She tapped her fingers on the counter. "You're not giving me a lot to go on."

"I want her to feel...wooed."

"Ah. All right." She held up a finger. "Give me a few minutes."

A few minutes passed and Marigold returned with what seemed like a bush in her hand. "What do you think?"

"That's a lot of flowers."

"It's a medium-size bouquet. It's not that many."

Looked like a lot to him. "And a woman will like that?"

Marigold gave him a withering glance. "Most women I know would love this."

"Good." He whipped out his credit card, but held it just off the counter. "You didn't put anything witchy in there, did you?"

"Did you want me to?"

"No."

"Then you're in luck. I charge extra for that

anyway."

"Good to know." He dropped his card on the counter. "Could you send a bouquet like this to my house every day for the next three days? Not the same bouquet. Different. But similar." Why was this so hard?

Marigold nodded. "Absolutely. You want me to send this one?"

"No, I'll take that one with me."

"You have a vase, right?"

He opened his mouth, then closed it again. He had no idea if he had a vase.

She waved her hand. "If you don't, call me and I'll send one with tomorrow's delivery. You want a card with them?"

"Is that what people do?"

"Normally, yes." Her eyes narrowed. "Haven't you ever sent flowers before?"

"No." He and his siblings often sent flowers to his mother for her birthday, but Bridget always took care of the details. "What do you put on the card?"

"Whatever you want to say." She pointed to a clear plastic stand in front of the register that held three rows of small, mostly white cards. "You can pick any one you like, but I'll need three of them for the rest of the deliveries."

He grunted. The cards all looked the same to him. He pulled out the first one.

She pushed a pen toward him. "You probably don't want that one."

"Why not?"

She pointed at the flowing script at the top. "This says In Sympathy. The woman in question might not feel too wooed if she thinks she's getting funeral flowers."

With a small noise, he stuck the card back into the holder.

Marigold lifted out another one. "How's this?"

The card had a zebra-striped border outlined in bright pink. Very girly. And Ivy's nails had been zebra-striped. "That one's good."

He grabbed the pen and jotted down the first thing that came to mind.

To Ivy, from Hank.

Not the most poetic thing he'd ever written, but the point was the flowers, not the card.

Marigold sighed. "Sorry, no."

He looked up. "What?"

She pointed at the card. "Is that really what you're going to say?"

He held back a growl. "You have a better suggestion?"

"Only like a thousand of them."

He waited. "Such as?"

"You need to write from your heart, not your head. To and from are not romantic."

Neither am I, thought Hank. He came up with something that didn't make Marigold wince, then wrote three more like that, paid, took the bouquet she had made up and headed home, his head reeling like he'd been trying to understand a foreign language.

He parked his duty car in front of the garage. It was odd to come home to his own house and find it lit up. It was even stranger to walk inside and feel the hum of activity. He glanced at the clock on the dash. He was fifteen minutes late, thanks to the stop for flowers. He hoped Ivy wasn't going to nag him about that.

His stomach rumbled as he approached the kitchen and the delicious smells of dinner reached him. He stopped just outside the kitchen, a little overwhelmed by the thought that it could always be this way.

Someone waiting for him.

That hadn't happened since he'd been a boy living at home, and that someone had been his mother. Now, that someone was a very sexy, very beautiful woman who would soon be his in every sense of the word.

The reality of that sent a tingle of sensation down his spine and a sharp jolt of possibility into his bloodstream.

He held the flowers behind his back as he

walked in. "Smells good in here."

Ivy was at the counter, icing the chocolate cake. A plate near the stove held two steaks waiting to be cooked. She turned as he came in and smiled. "Hey, welcome home. How was your day?"

"Busy." Not a word about him being late. He smiled. "I brought you these." He pulled the flowers from behind his back.

Her face lit up as she took them. She stuck her nose in them and inhaled. "They're gorgeous and they smell like spring." Her eyes suddenly went liquid. "I don't think anyone's ever brought me flowers before. Thank you."

"No one's ever brought you flowers?" That angered him for reasons he couldn't pinpoint, but also gave him a sense of happiness that he'd been the first.

She shrugged, a sad smile bending her mouth. "I'm not that kind of girl, I guess."

"You are now."

She blinked and her smile lost its sad edge. "This is a good start to the wooing. Do you have a vase I can put these in?"

Apparently, vases were more important than he'd realized. "I have no idea."

"You probably don't, but I'll find something." She licked her top lip, the tip of her pink tongue impossible to look away from.

The tingle that had gone down his spine zipped to a new location. His mind wasn't on the flowers anymore. Or dinner. Full moon or not, being around Ivy had a marked effect on him. He wanted her in a way that erased all rational thought.

She made shooing motions at him. "Go change, dinner's almost ready."

He stayed where he was. "Don't I get something for the flowers?"

She tipped her head. "Like what?"

"Like a kiss." He wanted more than that, but all in good time.

She bit her lip. "I think that's fair."

She put the flowers on the counter, her hands on his chest and went up on her tiptoes as she tilted toward him and pressed her lush mouth to his.

His hands settled on her hips of their own volition.

She kissed him tentatively, the pressure of her mouth soft, the movements sweetly hesitant. Then her hands rose to twine around his neck, and she leaned into him, a soft growl of pleasure rumbling from her throat.

He matched her growl with one of his own. His hands slid down to cup her backside, his palms filling with her firm flesh. He pulled her in closer until the line of their bodies meshed. Heat burned through him everywhere she touched him. The kind of fire only one thing would quench.

He broke the kiss and sucked in a deep gulp of air, but all he could taste was her. All he *wanted* to taste was her. "I'll go change."

THE SECOND HANK was out of the kitchen, Ivy pressed her forehead to the granite countertop in an effort to cool herself off. The man was like lava. Hot, delicious lava she wanted to ride like a brand new Harley.

And he was giving her dirty thoughts. No, the full moon fever was giving her dirty thoughts. At least it was partly full moon fever. It had to be, because there was no other reason for her to be so attracted to a man who not only came from the family that was her family's sworn enemy, but a cop.

A Kincaid, hot and bothered over a *cop*.

No wonder her father had had such a big laugh over this whole setup. Not only was he getting rid of his disappointing daughter and her dud of a kid— her father's words—but he was shifting their care and responsibility onto a man he couldn't stand for a multitude of reasons. Merrow, lawman, bringer of flowers, respecter of women.

Exactly the sort of man her father loved to hate.

Exactly the sort of man she dreamed about because she'd never thought he could be real. Handsome Hank, the dream come true.

She stood up. The granite hadn't cooled her off as much as she'd hoped, but they were going out for a run later, and that would do wonders. So long as they could keep it in their pants until the run. And after.

She grabbed the flowers, stuck them in an iced tea pitcher filled with water, then cranked up the burner beneath the grill pan. Hank might not do a lot of cooking, but his kitchen was well stocked with equipment. Maybe that was Bridget's doing.

Hank came back downstairs as she was flipping the steaks. He was barefooted, wearing jeans and a t-shirt and his hair was damp. He must have showered. It was the first time she'd seen him out of uniform. She wasn't sure which look she preferred. Both were unfairly nice. "Damn, those smell good."

She returned her attention to the steaks. "I hope they taste as good."

"I'm sure they will." He went to the fridge. "You want a beer?"

"No, thanks."

He gave her an odd look. "Wine? I have some of that too."

"No, I don't like to drink before a run." Not her first run with him anyway. The hormones were already weakening her inhibitions. She didn't need alcohol to help that along any further.

He nodded and put the beer back. "That's a good idea."

"Don't not drink on my account."

"I'm good."

He came to stand next to her by the stove. The clean scent of soap and his natural earthy maleness wafted off him. She glanced up at him. Damp hair was a good look on him.

Hell, everything was a good look on him.

"What?" he asked.

"Nothing." She smiled and poked at the steaks with the tongs just to give herself something to do. "You smell clean."

"And you still smell like chocolate."

She put the tongs down and turned, almost running into him as he bent toward her. Had he been about to sniff her hair? "Sorry. I tried to clean all the batter off."

Gold haloed his irises. "Nothing to be sorry for. I like chocolate, remember?"

For a second she thought he was going to kiss her again. She was okay with that, but the phone rang and brought the moment to an end.

He went to answer it. "Hello?" He asked a second time, then hung up. "No one there."

"Wrong number probably."

"Probably." He stayed on the other side of the kitchen. "You need help with anything?"

Getting her pants off. She took a breath. "Sure. You can get the salad and the dressing out of the fridge. I bought Italian and blue cheese. Whatever you want is fine with me."

She put the steaks on a platter and brought them to the table to rest while she took the baked potatoes out of the oven. She brought them over as well, then loaded the biggest steak onto Hank's plate. Lastly, she added the pitcher of flowers to the table. She wasn't about to let his effort go unappreciated.

By the time they were done eating, they'd talked about cars, their families (mostly his) and somehow completely avoided the topic of the wedding only being three days away.

Three freaking days. It was hard to imagine that in such a short time she was going to be a Merrow. She prayed that was enough to make things better for her and Charlie.

Hank helped her clear the dishes and clean up. Based on what she knew about him so far, she had a good feeling about the future. So long as Charlie's... disability was something Hank could accept. And Hank would forgive her for keeping it a secret until after they were married.

But what else could she do? Clemens had given her no other choice.

The woods behind Hank's house were thick with trees, their branches dressed with the rich green leaves of early summer. Insects buzzed and an owl hooted in the distance, their voices carrying easily on the warm evening air. Ivy clenched and unclenched her hands, practically vibrating with the need to run.

Hank stood at her side. "You ready?"

"You have no idea. Anything I need to know? Territory wise? Or whatever?"

"I'm the alpha's son. I can pretty much run where I want."

A remote howl disturbed the calm, punctuating her thoughts. She put them into words. "We're three nights from the full moon and clearly, this community is full of shifters. No matter who you are, we're bound to cross another were's path."

"True. But that's okay. The shifters in Nocturne Falls aren't hard-liners. Keep a respectful distance and you'll be fine. Plus, you're with me."

"I'll stick close." Not so close his pheromones

overwhelmed her and made her offer herself up like a tasty snack, but within reason.

"Then let's go." He leaped forward, his clothes becoming his fur as he shifted mid-air and landed several feet away as an enormous silver and gray wolf. He turned back to look at her. Even his markings were handsome. How was this guy not taken?

A thought for another time. She leaped like he had, giving herself over to the night. The change swept through her the moment she was airborne. She landed on all fours, the joy of being in her animal form intoxicating.

Caught up in the moment, she ran toward Hank and stuck her muzzle in his neck. She pulled away a second later, pawing at the ground like she hadn't just done that.

His lips curled in a wolfy grin and he lifted a paw, then trotted deeper into the forest. She joined him, staying a few paces back and to his right flank. Their communication was limited to body language and some vocalizations, but that's how most weres communicated anyway. *If* they bonded at some point, they might be able to share thoughts. It happened only to those with strong bloodlines and a true connection.

She didn't hold out hope for that. Not in an arranged marriage. But that didn't matter now. All that mattered was the ground beneath her feet, the wind in her fur and the loamy scent of the world surrounding her. The freedom of the moment. The exhilaration of the run.

Hank glanced back, saw she was at his flank and woofed.

She woofed back, ready to run.

He dipped his head and took off, his massive paws digging into the soft earth and flinging clumps of mossy dirt. She sped up to match him, pacing him as they tore through the woods. Here and there, more howls filled the night. Other shifters reveling in the release of the wildness that had been building with the waxing of the moon.

How long they ran she wasn't sure, but it was good and long and when they finally slowed, they were near a waterfall. They panted with the exercise and the thrill of the run. Her blood thrummed with the joy of it. Hank bent to drink and she joined him, staying a few feet downstream, even though the embarrassing urge to nuzzle him again was almost stronger than the urge not to.

An unfamiliar scent brought her head up from the water. Two large, black wolves stood deep in the trees on the other side of the bubbling stream that tapered off the waterfall. They made no move to come down and drink. She studied them, trying to see them better, but they were almost hidden by the undergrowth.

And they were staring at her.

She stared back, her hackles lifting out of instinct. She remembered what Hank had said about the shifters here not being hard-liners and forced herself to relax. The wolves made no moves, just watched. Were they waiting for her and Hank to be done drinking?

The wind shifted and Hank's head came up. She looked at him, then toward the two wolves, but they were gone.

Had she imagined them? No. Their scents had been real. Maybe they'd disappeared so quickly because they'd recognized Hank. She stared into the woods, trying to find them again, but all she saw were trees painted silver with moonlight.

Teeth nipped her left flank. She yipped and jumped away. Hank stood there, jaw open, tongue lolling out, laughing wolf-style.

She rammed her head into his shoulder and danced away, woofing. He followed after her. She took off, weaving through trees, leaping fallen logs, barreling through thickets of shrubs. He caught her quickly, and she realized that her ability to pace him earlier had only been because he'd allowed it.

He tackled her, knocking her to the ground and standing over her. He nuzzled her neck the way she'd done to him earlier, nipping playfully and snorting in clear amusement. In human form, Hank wasn't nearly this playful. Maybe he felt freer as his wolf. Whatever, she liked this side of him.

A lot.

Her nose was full of his scent, and her body came alive with the need to act on those pheromones. Instead, she put her paws on his chest and shoved him off, scampering away with a challenging bark. He came after her, catching her immediately and taking her to the ground again.

This time he touched his nose to hers and whined softly.

He was courting her, wolf-style.

And it was working.

If they'd been in human form, she would have jumped him. As it was, she was barely holding on to decent behavior. She got to her feet and shook her head. He bowed on his front legs and shook his head, too, flicking his ears back.

He understood.

He took off in a gentle trot, then stopped and looked back at her. She joined him, and he started up again.

They stayed side by side until they returned to his house, then he shook himself back into his human form.

She did the same, the excitement of the run electric in her blood. Like all shifters, their clothes and pelts exchanged places when they shifted unless they'd started out in nothing but skin. When she was alone in familiar woods that was her first option. But being naked with Hank? That wasn't a bridge she was ready to cross. Not when she'd started this run. Now, with the night air draping her like silk, being naked with Hank seemed like a grand idea.

She tipped her head back and inhaled deeply, trying to rid herself of the throbbing need pushing her closer and closer to action. Action that would take her down a path there would be no returning from. She sighed. "That was a great run."

He grunted affirmatively.

She glanced at him.

From the smoldering gold in his eyes, he needed something more.

Her.

HANK only barely kept himself from lunging at her. "Go inside."

"Aren't you coming with me?"

"Not yet." He shouldn't have played with her like that. Being so close to her in wolf form had only aroused an unquenchable need. He'd known that was a risk and yet, he'd done it anyway. Running with her, going wolf with her, had made denying that side of himself impossible. She was too large a temptation. And he'd given in. He just hadn't bargained on how strong his desire for her would be. "I need to run."

She shook her head, the slightest hint of gold dancing in her eyes. "We just ran."

"It wasn't enough." Actually, it had been too much. Too much inhaling her scent and sharing her space combined with the pull of the moon and the power of the night. He ached with wanting her. Ached to claim her as his mate, right then and there.

But that was too much, too soon. He didn't make rash decisions. About anything. There was a right way and a wrong way to do things, and he always chose the right way.

That was what any good alpha would do.

Her eyes flashed gold, and she took a step toward him, hips swaying with the kind of deliberate movement that told him she understood exactly what he was feeling. "And if you don't run?"

He swallowed, fists tight at his sides. "I won't sleep."

She swayed closer. "Maybe I won't sleep either."

He did the impossible and backed up. No matter what he was feeling, this decision was hers to make. "I want you, Ivy." Understatement of the year. "I think you can tell. But it's too soon. I think you know that, too."

She took another step toward him, head lowering as she took a breath. "What I know is the moon is making me crazy." Her eyes went full gold, and she massaged the back of her neck. "I feel like I'm in heat around you. Which isn't a bad thing, considering we're about to be married."

He stopped retreating, mesmerized by the play of moonlight on the curves of her body. Someday, when they were married, they were going to do the run the right way. Clothes-free. The thought caused his fists to press hard against his thighs. Breathing normally became a concentrated effort. Standing there without making a move became a timed event. Another minute and his reserve would be gone. She deserved to know that. "My control is almost shot."

She came closer still. "Control is overrated."

The muscles in his jaw twitched. Desire owned him. Somehow, he made rational words come out of his mouth. "We should get to know each other better."

An inch, maybe two separated them. She didn't touch him, maybe because she knew that if she did, that would be the end of this conversation. She tipped her head back and stared into his eyes. "What better way to get to know each other could there be than giving in to the moon's pull?"

His body tightened, every fiber taut with need. His voice came out a gruff scrape. "Are you saying yes?"

She nodded. Her lids were heavy with desire as her lips parted. "Take me to bed, Hank."

He was very good at following orders.

She'd lost her head to the full moon fever. Hard. Ivy stood at the living room windows, her gaze lost in the tangle of trees at the edge of Hank's property line. Dawn was still minutes away, but she'd been unable to sleep.

She plucked at the hem of his borrowed t-shirt with her free hand, her other wrapped around a cup of coffee that wasn't doing enough to perk her up. His scent surrounded her, not just on the t-shirt but on her skin. Every inhalation reminded her of the man she'd come here to marry. And deceive.

Steam curled up from her coffee cup. Her sigh pushed it away.

She hadn't wanted to sleep with him—well, she *had*, but not like this. Not while she was still holding back the truth about Charlie. It felt wrong to give herself to Hank that way when she wasn't being honest with him.

Couldn't be honest with him.

Damn her father and his cruel, manipulative ways.

Now, when Hank found out, he'd think she'd

slept with him in an attempt to snare him deeper in her web. And that might make him feel used. Might make him hate her.

He'd probably be right to.

She swallowed down a hard knot of pain and dropped her gaze to stare into her coffee. Hank was a good man. An amazing man. So much better than she could have ever hoped for. Better than she'd dreamed of. Funny how her father's scheming had brought her Hank and would inevitably take him away.

She was going to get her heart broken, and this time, it wasn't going to heal. Her life was so freaking unfair. She closed her eyes and took a breath. Enough wallowing.

Self-pity was pointless. It wasn't going to change anything. Better to focus on finding a way to fix things.

She could tell Hank the truth right now. Hank seemed like a trustworthy guy. But she'd trusted a man before, a man she'd had no reason to doubt, and been betrayed. What if she'd misjudged Hank? What if he used the information to get the Merrows out of their debt? Then there'd be no marriage at all. It would save the Merrows. But it would destroy her. Clemens would blame her for the whole thing falling apart.

Her *and* Charlie.

But Charlie would pay the price.

She bit back a sob. She couldn't risk her son's life for the sake of her own comfort.

"You okay?"

At the sound of Hank's voice, she turned. He was more gorgeous than ever with the look of sleepy satisfaction on his handsome mug. "Did I wake you? I was trying to be quiet."

He padded up to her, wearing nothing but pajama pants, and wrapped his arms around her waist. "I wish you had woken me up. But then you'd still be in bed."

She smiled, unable to help herself. Gruff, serious Hank was anything *but* in bed. The man was an artist with his hands. Generous, giving, and wicked in the best possible ways. She hadn't been so thoroughly shagged in...ever. "Sorry, I couldn't sleep." She lifted her cup. "I made coffee."

"Something wrong?"

Everything. "Nothing. Just restless with the full moon so close, I guess."

He lifted one hand to her chin and tipped her face toward him, then planted a soft, closed-mouth kiss on her lips. "Please don't regret last night."

She shook her head. "I don't. I promise. Last night was amazing."

He grinned. The smile lit his face so brightly it

was like staring into the sun. "Damn straight it was. You hungry? I'm starving."

"Sure, what do you want for breakfast?"

He made a face at her. "For you to sit down and enjoy your coffee while I fix it." He grabbed her hand and pulled her toward the kitchen.

She went along with him, balancing her cup to keep from spilling coffee on the hardwood floors. "You cook?"

He snorted. "No, but I can make breakfast."

"Uh-huh."

He looked at her. "Do you doubt me, woman?"

"I'm just saying it's pretty hard to believe judging by the state of your refrigerator yesterday." She liked this new playful side of him. It seemed he'd let his guard down. Like she was catching a glimpse of the man without the weight of sheriff and firstborn riding his shoulders.

No doubt that would change when he learned what her father had put her up to. She pushed that thought away and tried to focus on the present.

"You sit here." He pointed at one of the bar stools at the raised breakfast bar.

She climbed into the chair. She'd been a child the last time someone had made breakfast for her.

He opened the fridge. "What'll it be?"

She decided to go big, knowing she'd probably end up doing the cooking, but then she'd planned on that anyway. She thought about what she'd bought yesterday and based her choice on that. "Blueberry pancakes."

"Good choice."

"Really?"

He looked over his shoulder at her, his brows angled down in a victorious expression. "Thought you were going to trip me up with that, didn't you?"

She laughed. "Yeah, I kinda did. Good thing I bought blueberries. Are they better than Mummy's?"

He hesitated. "You won't have to eat them in a holding cell."

"Sold."

He pulled the ingredients together and got to work, refusing to let her help. Once the ingredients were mixed, he pulled out the griddle, greased it and set it to heat up. Then he refilled her coffee, fixed himself a cup, and leaned against the counter facing her. "Tell me about your son."

The lightness of the moment disappeared with those words. A wave of desperation went through her. She missed Charlie so much it hurt. She tried to cover by taking a sip of her coffee. She swallowed and chose her words carefully so she could stay truthful. "He's a good kid. Quiet. A little on the shy side. Kinda small for his age."

"So was I."

She raised her brows. "You were small for your

age."

"Almost dead last in the percentages." He turned, ran his fingers under the tap then flicked the water onto the griddle. It sizzled, so he poured thick circles of batter onto it. More sizzling followed, sending up the most delicious aroma. He dropped big handfuls of berries into each one. "Until I hit puberty. Put on seventeen inches and forty-three pounds in a year and a half."

"That's crazy."

"Hurt like a mother, too."

"I'll bet." For the first time, hope for Charlie bloomed within her. "Kincaid men get their size early."

Pancakes cooking and coffee in hand, he went back to leaning. He swallowed another sip of coffee. "Charlie's dad still in the picture?"

All the inevitable questions. "No. He was for a little bit, but then he just up and left. Haven't heard another word from him. Which I'm fine with. I don't need the reminder." Still, she'd thought Eric had been a different kind of man. But she'd been wrong. And might be again. She twisted her cup, turning it slowly until the handle was perpendicular to the edge of the granite.

"We don't have to—"

"You have a right to know." She blew out a small breath, feeling the old regrets tugging at her happiness as images of Eric filled her mind. "I met him the summer before my last year of college."

"You went to college?" He held a hand up. "Sorry, didn't mean that like it sounded."

"No, I get it. Kincaids aren't known for their academic prowess." She smiled grimly. "I was determined not to be a typical Kincaid. Anyway, I thought I was in love and, long story short, he wasn't. He disappeared before Charlie was born."

"You ever try to track him down? Get support out of him?"

She shook her head. "And risk having to fight him for custody? Or see him happily married with kids and have him reject Charlie all over again? No, thanks. Really, I'd be fine never seeing him again."

Hank nodded. "What about college?"

"I managed another semester, but it was a hard pregnancy." She stared into her cup. "I always figured I'd go back and finish that one last semester, but it never happened."

"Doesn't mean it still couldn't."

She laughed. "Yeah, I suppose so."

"What did you major in?"

"Business. I thought it would be a ticket out of Kincaid country. Instead, I ended up going to the local beauty school after Charlie was born and staying right where I was." The weight of her broken dreams weighed heavy on her.

"Maybe I can be that ticket."

He said it so quietly, she almost wasn't sure she'd heard it. She looked up. "I didn't mean to imply—"

"I know." He took a long, thoughtful pause. "I like you, Ivy. And you're going to be my wife. I want you to be happy. I want...us to be happy."

She stared at him, not quite able to process that idea.

He turned back to the griddle and flipped the pancakes. "Why didn't Charlie come with you?"

Because Clemens knew she would have run. "My father thought it would be easier for us to get to know each other without a kid underfoot."

"And Charlie's staying with his grandparents?"

"Mm-hmm." Staying and being held hostage were two sides of the same coin when you were a Kincaid.

"You want to go get him?"

She froze at the thought of that confrontation. Hank and her father, her son caught in between and the truth being used like a weapon to beat her precious boy down even further. "*No.*"

Hank slanted his eyes at her. "It was just a suggestion."

She made herself smile. And breathe normally. "It's a great one, but I want to make sure this whole thing is going to work out before I introduce him to you."

That sounded like a weak excuse even to her but she wasn't sure what else to say. School was out for the summer so she couldn't use that.

Hank shrugged and went back to plating breakfast. "Whatever you think is best."

Her shoulders dropped in relief. She slid out of her seat, done with the conversation. "I'll set the table."

"Good, because we're ready to eat."

She collected silverware, napkins and the syrup. "What time do you have to be at the station?"

"Half an hour." He brought the plates over. "What are you going to do today?"

She set two places, then grabbed her coffee and sat at one of them. "I hadn't thought about it."

"You know how to get back into town." He put a short stack of pancakes in front of her, then took his spot. "Why don't you go explore? See the town you're about to become a resident of. Nocturne Falls is anything but boring."

"So I've heard." The town was well known amongst supernaturals as the place to live if you wanted the most freedom to be yourself. Celebrating Halloween three hundred and sixty-five days a year made that possible.

"And if you stop by the station at noon, I might be able to break away for lunch."

She grinned. "Are you making a date with me?"

"You're the one who agreed to the wooing." He winked at her as he carved up a forkful of pancake and stuffed it in his mouth.

That she had. "I'm glad you don't think you're off the hook for that after last night."

He swallowed, his seriousness returning along with a hint of gold in his eyes. "If anything, last night showed me that making you happy is a very worthwhile endeavor. One I will be pursuing many, many more times."

She did her best not to show how light-headed and swoony those words made her, but a little sound of pleasure escaped anyway. She covered with a bite of pancakes. More sounds of pleasure ensued. "These are really good."

He preened. "I'm not without some skills."

"Yes, you proved that last night. I just didn't think you could manage breakfast, too."

He chuckled and leaned in to kiss her syrup-sticky mouth.

They finally came up for air, finished breakfast and a few minutes later, she sent him off to work with a promise to see him at lunch and another long kiss that almost ended up with them back in bed.

Life was remarkably good.

She hoped it stayed that way, but so far, that wasn't her track record.

For once in her less than illustrious career as the receptionist for the Nocturne Fall's sheriff's department, Birdie was at her desk before Hank arrived. He checked his watch. That explained it. He was six minutes late.

He grinned. The kiss had been worth it.

"Something's wrong," Birdie chirped.

He stopped in front of her desk to pick up his messages. "What's that?"

"I have no idea, but you're late and you're smiling. Are you feeling all right? Bend down so I can feel your forehead."

He frowned at her. "I'm fine." He turned one of the message slips so she could see it. "What does this say?"

She squinted at it. "Beats me."

"It's your handwriting."

Her brows lifted. "Can you always read *your* handwriting?"

"Yes. Because it's my handwriting." But he was in too good of a mood to let Birdie's nonsense get to him.

"You're just trying to change the subject. What's going on with you?"

"Nothing. I'm just happy. Or I was until I got in here. I'll be in my office."

"You want coffee?"

"That would be great." Now who wasn't acting like themselves?

"Then you should probably go buy some. We're all out."

And that explained it. At least he'd had coffee at home. Shaking his head, he took ten dollars out of petty cash and slapped it on her desk. "Go to the Shop & Save and buy some. Please."

"Who's going to answer the phones?"

"I will. Go."

"This doesn't mean you're off the hook. I'm going to figure out what's going on with you soon enough."

Everyone would. He just wanted another day of peacefulness before the town erupted with the news that he was getting married. To a Kincaid. "Now. *Please.*"

With a put-upon sigh and no small amount of muttering, she gathered up her purse and headed out.

He went into his office to check his email and work on the week's schedule. Besides himself and Deputies Cruz and Blythe, he had another four on the night-shift crew. Night shift in this town had been much easier to fill. In addition, he had five more reserve deputies he could call up in times of need. But those were few and far between in this town. He paused for a moment to enjoy the quiet. His mind went straight to Ivy. Hard to keep his mind on anything but her. Very hard.

He found himself staring at words on the screen, but not really seeing them. Random smiles found their way onto his face. No wonder Birdie thought he was acting strange, because he was.

He was falling for Ivy.

Or maybe he'd already fallen. Whatever the case, there were worse things than being infatuated with the woman you were going to marry.

He sent Bridget a text to reserve one of the back booths for him for lunch. It was a big step to go out in public with Ivy. The tourists wouldn't care, but the locals would be abuzz with the news.

He sighed. He ought to tell Birdie now. If she found out secondhand, she'd make his life miserable.

And he was going to need a ring. He frowned. That was another area he had no expertise in. Maybe he'd take Ivy down to Illusions after lunch and see if the jewelry store had a ring she liked.

His smile came back. Maybe it was the wolf in him, but there was something deeply satisfying about the idea of making Ivy officially his. He *knew* it was his wolf that fueled that kind of possessiveness and would cause him to protect her with his life if need be. Thankfully, having the treaty in place meant life should be fairly peaceful.

He leaned back in his chair and kicked his feet up onto the desk. Would they bond? Having the mental communication would be nice, but he knew it wasn't a guarantee. Bonding came most often with love matches, which this wasn't.

Although the more time they spent together, the less it felt like an arranged marriage. How was it possible that they were so well matched?

He tapped the end of his pencil on the desk as a sliver of suspicion shot through him. Was there a chance Ivy was just telling him what he wanted to hear? Acting the way she thought he'd want her to act?

There was always a chance, but if the military had honed his already keen instincts, working as sheriff had put a fine point on them. He sensed no guile in her feelings toward him. And thinking his intended was setting him up in some elaborate ruse was a dangerous path to follow. Being skeptical was one thing, being paranoid was another.

He pushed that from his mind and went back to work. Birdie returned from the store a few minutes later, erasing the quiet. She was humming some-thing to herself. Loudly.

"Birdie, come in here please."

"What?" She stuck her head in through his office door, a grocery sack swinging from her hand. There was a bag of coffee and a bakery box.

He inhaled and picked up the sugary scent of chocolate glazed donuts. The woman had a worse sweet tooth than he did. He should have brought her a slice of Ivy's chocolate cake. "Come in and shut the door."

She squinted at him. "I thought you wanted me to make coffee."

"I do. But that can wait. I need to talk to you."

"Hmph." The suspicion in her eyes grew. "If this is another attempt to fire me, I will call your mother faster than you can—"

"Aunt Birdie, I'm not firing you." *If only.* The *aunt* part got her attention. He rarely called her that. Didn't feel appropriate. Especially not in an official setting like the sheriff's department.

She came in, shut the door and sat, resting the bag at her feet. "What's all this about?"

"Everyone in town is going to know soon enough, but I figured you ought to hear it from me. I'm getting married."

Her whoop of joy nearly blew out his eardrums. "Hank, that is wonderful! I didn't even know you were dating anyone. Who is she? Do I know her?

When's the wedding? Oh, I'm so happy. What does my sister think?"

He held a hand up. "Take a breath, Birdie. It's an arranged marriage."

That settled her down. "Arranged? Why on earth is your father doing that to you? In this day and age—"

"It's the final seal on a truce between the Merrows and the Kincaids."

She recoiled in horror. "You're marrying a Kincaid? My poor boy, your father should be ashamed of himself putting you in that kind of position. Just wait until I talk to my sister. I mean, look at that awful Kincaid woman who was in here the other night. I can't imagine my sweet nephew having to spend the rest of his life with *that* kind of woman."

He narrowed his gaze, but she didn't seem to pick up on the consternation flowing through him. "What kind of woman would that be, Aunt Birdie?"

"You know." She waved her hand. "*Loose.*"

"And you can tell she's *loose* how?"

"The makeup and the motorcycle and the leathers and the tattoos. Especially the tattoos. She's probably covered with them. Probably has a list of her ex-boyfriends on her somewhere."

"She doesn't. And she's not covered with them." He knew, because he'd seen every inch of her. "She's got exactly three. The number five on the inside of her wrist, a piece of ivy on her arm and shoulder and a tiny heart on her left ankle."

Birdie's gaze narrowed suspiciously. "How do you know that?"

"Because Ivy Kincaid is the woman I'm marrying. Do I really need to explain how I know about her tattoos?"

Birdie's eyes rounded. "Hank!"

"Ivy's coming here today, and we're going to lunch. If you are anything *but* nice to her, I will fire you for real. Do you understand?"

She nodded, silent. But the silence only lasted a few seconds. "You...like her?"

"I do."

"Is she the reason you were smiling this morning?"

"She is."

Birdie took a moment to ponder that. "If she makes you smile, then I like that. But she'd better be a good wife to you or I'll have a few words of my own for her. You can't stop me from doing that."

"She made me a steak dinner last night. Baked a chocolate cake from scratch."

Birdie hmphed. "Lots of women bake. Doesn't mean she's the right one for my nephew."

He leaned forward. "Listen to me. Ivy's in the same spot I am, but as it so happens, we get on well."

His aunt's chin went a little higher in the air. "Apparently if you've seen *all* her tattoos."

"She's got enough to deal with without adding my crazy aunt to the mix. Be nice. Or you will have a *lot* of time off." He pointed toward the front office. "Coffee."

She stood and picked up her bag, marching away without another word. She came back a minute later with a manila envelope in her hand. "This was on my desk. Has your name on it. And I am *not* crazy."

"Where did it come from?"

She shrugged. "Someone must have dropped it off when we were talking."

He took it from her. "Coffee made yet?"

"I'm working on it, you ungrateful child."

He smirked as she left. Sheriff Merrow was scrawled on the front of the envelope in barely legible writing, the black ballpoint ink a little smudged, but not enough that he could make out a fingerprint.

He tapped the contents of the envelope down to the bottom, then slit the top open with his pocket knife. He pulled out three grainy cell phone pics that had been printed on regular printer paper. Each one showed the same thing.

Ivy with a little boy. Had to be Charlie. Hank studied the photos, the sense that he was viewing a private moment giving him a second of unease.

Obviously she hadn't known these pictures were being taken.

Looked like they were outside a school. Charlie was a reed. A short reed. Hank shook his head, sympathy for the kid already growing. The way Charlie smiled up at Ivy made it clear the kid thought the world of his mother.

Hank stared at the pictures. Someone had delivered these for a reason. Did they think Ivy wasn't going to tell him about Charlie? That by showing Hank these pictures, they'd create trouble? Why else would they be delivered without a word?

He held the photos up and inhaled. They reeked of shifter. Which didn't do much to narrow down the field of suspects.

He tucked them away, almost forgetting about them until hours later when Ivy came in. Her voice in the reception area got him up from his desk. He opened his office door and leaned against the jam, taking in the sleek glory that was his bride-to-be.

Gorgeous in jeans and a black tank top with silver studs along the neckline, she stood in front of Birdie's desk, biting her lip and looking like she was about to bolt.

Probably because Birdie was giving her the third degree. "So you're marrying my Hank, are you? How many times have you been married before? What kind of housekeeper are you? You know he likes a neat house—"

"Birdie." Hank barked his aunt's name out like a command.

The grilling came to a fast end as Birdie whipped around. Not even an ounce of guilt colored her face, the old battle ax. "I was just about to let you know your *fiancée's* here."

"I see that. Stop harassing her."

Birdie's mouth thinned to a hard line. He looked at Ivy and tipped his head toward the space behind him. "Come into the office for a second."

She did as he asked. He shut the door as soon as she was inside and pulled her into a kiss, unable to keep from groping her a little as he did. A soft, possessive growl slipped from his throat, and he nipped her bottom lip.

She sucked in a breath and pushed at his chest, her eyes half-gold with the same thing he was feeling. "Not that that wasn't the best greeting I've had in a long time, but what's gotten into you?"

He honestly didn't know. He'd never felt this out of control before in his life. "You have."

She stayed in his arms, eyes slitting down to half as she raked him with a languid glance. "I think it's moon fever."

"Maybe." He gave her a few inches of room but didn't release her entirely. "You want me to stop?"

She pursed her lips like she was trying not to laugh. "No. It's kinda nice to have a guy who looks like you all hot and bothered by little ol' me."

He snorted. "Little ol' you?"

She leaned back and frowned. "What's that supposed to mean?"

"You're not a little delicate flower. Which I like." He grabbed her hips. "You're tall and built, and I couldn't ask for more. It's nice to be with a woman I don't feel like I'm going to break."

Her eyes narrowed and she maintained her distance. "Are you saying you've been with a lot of women?"

"No." He let her go, wondering what she'd think of his long, self-imposed dry spell.

"Did I ruin the moment?"

He shook his head. "I haven't been with a woman in four, maybe five years."

She looked a little horrified. "Why? There's certainly nothing wrong with you physically to keep you from...indulging."

He shrugged and pulled out one of his office chairs for her before he sat on the edge of his desk. "I didn't want to get involved because I knew this day might come."

She took the chair and beamed up at him. "So basically, you were waiting for me?"

He laughed softly. "Yeah, I guess I was."

Looking very pleased with that answer, she blinked her big brown eyes at him. "Where are you taking me for lunch?"

"Howler's."

She rolled her gaze toward the ceiling. "Oh good, the scene of the crime."

"Do you want to go somewhere else? I was thinking you could get to know Bridget a little better if we—"

"It's fine. I'm a big girl, as you said." She grinned. "I can handle it."

"Good, because after lunch, I have a surprise for you."

She perked up. "More wooing?"

"You could say that. Speaking of surprises, I got a delivery today." He reached behind him and dug out the envelope. He shook the pictures into his hand. "I assume this is Charlie?"

She stared at the photos, her mouth slowly dropping open as worry bracketed her eyes. "Yes, that's Charlie. At school. Who delivered these?"

"No idea. They showed up on Birdie's desk when she ran out to the Shop & Save."

Ivy stiffened, her body suddenly wound like a coil. "Why would someone do that?"

"To cause trouble. There's no other reason."

She cursed softly. "I don't like the idea of being watched like that."

"I can imagine." It was a violation of her privacy, although not an actual crime. "Do you think Charlie's in danger?"

A dark shadow passed through her gaze before she shook her head and looked away. "He's with my parents."

But there was no ring of assurance in her tone.

She worried the seam on the leg of her jeans. "You think someone's trying to stop us from getting married?"

"Maybe. Who stands to gain if the truce is called off?"

"No one, really. It benefits both families, the way I see it. Mine more than yours. Not that I think anyone on your side is behind this."

He nodded, happy she'd said that. "I see it that way, too, but think about it, and if you come up with any names, let me know."

"I will." Her mouth bunched to one side. "I don't like this at all."

He tossed the pictures on the desk, then reached out, took her hand and gave it a squeeze. "I've already told you I'm in. Nothing's going to make me change my mind."

She stared up at him. "Same for me." Her words were hesitant.

"Why do I hear a 'but' in that answer?"

She sighed out a long breath. "My family and my

pack have a lot of...less than honorable sorts in them."

His hackles went up. "You think you're in danger? Who stands to benefit from hurting you or Charlie?"

She shook her head and smiled, but it looked forced. "No one I can think of. I'm sure it's nothing. I'm sorry this happened. Probably just someone being foolish."

"It's definitely that. And if anyone tries to hurt you, they're going to find out pretty quickly what a bad idea that is." He pulled her to her feet and tugged her close so that she stood between his legs. "No one is going to hurt you, and no one is going to stand in the way of this marriage, so long as that's what you want."

Her smile softened into something genuine. "It is."

He teased a gentle kiss across that smile. "Good. Now let's go have lunch where the whole town can see us. I'm sure Birdie's already told everyone she can think of and posted it on her Facebook page, so prepare yourself for table visits."

"Small towns," she said knowingly.

He grabbed his hat. "That and also there's going to be a lot of curiosity about the woman who thinks I'm a good catch."

She laughed as he opened the door, a happy sound he was glad to hear again. If these pictures were the beginning of something bigger and Ivy ended up in danger, he would very easily leave his badge behind to deal with her tormentors in a permanent fashion.

And if they thought otherwise, they were fools.

Ivy was surprised at how right Hank had been about the table visits. All sorts of people stopped by, proving that Howler's was a very popular choice for locals and tourists alike. The array of supernaturals present was pretty amazing too. After the ninth interruption, Bridget started running interference, which made Ivy like her even more.

Bridget's buffer also finally allowed them to eat. Better still, Ivy had Hank to herself. Which was the best part of the meal. They were tucked away in a booth in a private corner and he'd sat on the same side as her, meaning she could almost hide behind him if she wanted. Maybe that had been his plan. Keep her hidden in case there was some kind of danger.

She thought about the pictures for a moment, about what they might mean and who they might be from, but she couldn't come up with much. Someone wanted Hank to know about Charlie, that was plain, but who? Was there a chance Charlie was in danger? That caused her mother's instinct to clang in alarm and her ache for her son grew stronger. She pulled out her phone and sent her brother, Sam, a text.

Check on Charlie when you get a chance? Make sure he's all right? Thanks.

Didn't mean Sam would do it, but she had no one else to ask. As far as being in immediate danger, it was hard to be afraid of anything sitting next to a werewolf Hank's size.

He pointed at her food with a French fry. "How's your steak salad?"

She laughed. "You mean that half pound of sirloin with the two lettuce leaves and the slice of tomato? Your sister doesn't skimp on the meat, does she? It's great." And almost gone. Being happy gave her an appetite, and it was hard not to be happy around a man who was crazy about her. The only piece of the puzzle that was missing was Charlie. Her heart ached with his absence.

"Pretty sure you got the friends-and-family deal."

"Which one does that make me?"

"Both." He smiled before popping the last of his French fries into his mouth. "You okay?"

She nodded. "I'm great." She just wanted her son by her side. Safe. And where he belonged.

Bridget came to the table and set two bowls of peach cobbler in front of them. A hearty scoop of vanilla ice cream melted into each one. "Still hot from the oven, so be careful."

"More food?" Ivy leaned back, wondering if she should unbutton her jeans. "I'm not sure I can."

"At least try it." Hank handed her a spoon. "The peach cobbler here is legendary."

Bridget leaned against the side of the booth. "I can box it up to go if you want."

But the aromas of peach and cinnamon already teased Ivy's nose, making her mouth water. "I'll soldier through."

"That's the spirit." Bridget grinned. "You guys need anything else?"

Hank looked at Ivy.

She shook her head. "Everything was wonderful, thank you."

Bridget backed away, pointing at her brother. "Don't forget. Dinner at Titus's tonight."

Hank groaned. "Yeah, all right." He stuffed down a spoonful of cobbler.

As Bridget went back to the bar, Ivy questioned him. "Titus is your brother, right?"

"My brother and the fire chief. We all get together at his house the week of the full moon for dinner and a run. There's no getting out of it. Not with what's going on with us. He'll want to meet you in person, because I'm sure Bridge has told him everything."

The tiniest bit of anxiety played along Ivy's nerves. She ate some cobbler in an attempt to stifle that feeling. The cool ice cream and the sweet, hot peaches and sugary flaky crust made her pause for a moment to enjoy it. "Wow, you weren't kidding about the cobbler being legendary." She took another bite just to make sure it wasn't a fluke, then she answered. "We don't need to get out of it. I'm sure it'll be fun. And I should meet your brother. I have to meet him sooner or later anyway. You think he'll like me?"

"You have nothing to worry about. He's been after me to find a woman for years."

"I should get home soon then. I'll make a dessert to take over, although I'm not sure I can compete with your sister's cobbler."

Hank shook his head. "She didn't make that cobbler. She just pays the salary of the chef who did. Anything you want to make is great. Or you could buy something. There's a new shop on Black Cat Boulevard called Delaney's Delectables. They sell all kinds of sweets. The woman who runs it is fairly new to town, like you. She's a vampire."

Ivy stared at him. "It's one thing to know Nocturne Falls is pretty open about supernaturals, it's another to hear them discussed as regular citizens."

He shrugged. "The tourists think we're all playing parts. It makes life a lot easier than trying to hide who you are."

"And what if a visitor realizes you're not playing a part?"

"Remember the waterfall we drank from on our run?"

"Sure."

"That water comes from an enchanted spring. Humans think drinking the water from that spring has the power to grant wishes. What the water actually does, thanks to the magic involved, is blur the edges of reality a little."

"How can you be sure everyone drinks it?"

"That spring feeds the town's reservoir and it's the bottled water you'll see being sold in all the shops. It's everywhere."

"And it only affects humans?"

"Supernaturals are immune."

"Wow." This place was unreal.

He nodded and took another bite of cobbler.

She lifted her spoon, then paused. "How do you know it's enchanted?"

"The family who started this town did it. Actually, the witch who works for them. It's a big part of what makes this whole place work."

"That's not the Merrow family, is it?"

He snorted. "No. Nocturne Falls was founded by the Ellinghams. Vampires. The woman who runs Delaney's? She just married the middle son, Hugh Ellingham."

"I might go down there just to see a vampire in person." She'd never seen one before, and her curiosity was strong. She shrugged. "I guess I'll have to wait until after dark."

He finished his cobbler and put his napkin on the table. "You can go anytime. The Ellinghams also have some kind of magic that makes them immune to the sun."

"Wild. I'll head down there when we're done." She rested her spoon on the table. "The Ellinghams sound powerful."

"They are. But they don't abuse it." He put his arm around her, drawing her in. "Enough about them. It's time for your surprise."

She settled against his warmth. "You mean it wasn't the cobbler?"

"Hardly." The spark in his eyes was a mix of happiness and anticipation. "You ready to find out what it is?"

She smiled, unable to help herself. She had no idea what he could be up to. "Let the wooing commence."

HANK FIGURED when they walked into Illusions, Ivy would know they'd come there to get her an engagement ring and the surprise would come to an end.

He'd assumed wrong.

She leaned into him and whispered, "Is this about getting me a job? This would be a very cool place to work."

"A job? No." He led her to the diamond case. "It's about getting you a ring."

Ivy's lips parted, disbelief etched in her gaze. "What?"

"Is that question because you think I should have picked it out on my own or because you didn't think I was getting you a ring?"

"I..." She shook her head and looked like she was trying to blink away tears. "I didn't expect a ring is all."

"Even better." He gestured toward the case. "See anything you like?"

Willa, the owner and one of the fae citizens in town, met them on the other side. "Hi, Sheriff."

He'd called ahead to let her know what he was coming in for. "Willa Iscove, this is Ivy Kincaid. My fiancée."

Willa smiled at her. "Hi, Ivy. Congratulations to both of you on your engagement."

Ivy nodded and squeaked out a, "Thanks." She cleared her throat, then spoke to Willa again. "Could you give us a minute?"

"Sure. Give me a wave when you're ready." Willa left to help another customer.

"Hank, I don't know about this."

He frowned. "Having second thoughts about marrying me?"

"No!"

Her emphatic response pleased him but left him more confused. "What's wrong then?"

She kept her voice low. "You shouldn't be spending your money on—I mean, you're taking on me *and* my son. I just don't want you to think I'm..." She sighed. "This isn't coming out right. I don't need anything but a plain band."

"My wife needs more than a plain band. I want other men to *know* you're married. And don't worry about the money. Or the added cost of your son. I'm good when it comes to finances. Not Ellingham good, but well off. Besides being sheriff, which pays well in this town, I have my stipend." All pack members did, but as an immediate member of the alpha's family, his was about double that amount.

Her frown had yet to leave her face. "But I'm not bringing anything to this marriage but debts. I still have some student loans."

He didn't understand. "Your parents didn't pay for your college?"

"My father didn't want me to go to college, so no, he didn't pay. And cutting hair was barely enough to live on after making the minimum payments."

Something wasn't adding up. Hank hoped Ivy

wasn't one of those women who shopped themselves into debt. An image of her Harley flashed in his head. "What about your stipend? I'd think the whiskey business brings in enough to keep you in good stead. Unless you're not spending it wisely."

Her frown turned angry, and he could tell he'd hit a nerve. "What little money I have, I'm very careful with. And *if* I got a stipend, maybe things would be different, but I don't. The Kincaid stipend only goes to males."

"Are you serious?" Clemens Kincaid was a low-life piece of garbage. How could he not provide for his daughter? Or the rest of his female pack members? Sharing the stipend was standard operating procedure. All packs did it. It created loyalty and stability.

She nodded. "My brothers are in high cotton. Me? Not so much."

That still didn't explain the Softail. "How did you afford that motorcycle?"

She snorted. "I inherited that from my grandfather. And if he hadn't had an iron-clad will, I'm not sure I would have held on to it, either."

"Your father is a horrible man."

"You have no idea," she muttered.

He kissed her, as much to soothe her as to soothe himself. Clemens Kincaid was enough to make anyone see red. Hank couldn't imagine how Ivy had survived having him as a father. It only fueled his desire to spoil her. "Then you should give me an idea. When you feel ready. Because there's no reason you need to bear all that yourself. But this moment is not about him. You're about to be a Merrow. Time to live like it. Pick out a ring."

"You're sure?"

"Pick out a ring or I'll buy the gaudiest one in the case."

She grinned. "Okay. No pressure."

He laughed and waved Willa back over.

Ivy immediately pointed to the smallest diamond in the case.

"Don't even play that game," he said. "Try the one next to it."

"But that's twice the size."

"And still not big enough." He leaned in to whisper in her ear. "Think like a Merrow."

She gave him a look he interpreted as a plea for patience.

He took the hint. "I need to step outside and make a call. Be right back."

She nodded, her interest fully seated in the tray of rings Willa had just taken out. He left the shop, slipping his phone out as he went.

He called Birdie. "Any messages?"

"I heard you had a nice lunch."

Honestly, how did the woman find this stuff out?

She was probably just fishing. He wasn't going to bite. "Not *about* me. *For* me."

"Deputy Cruz got himself a date for the Zombie Prom."

Hank pinched the bridge of his nose. "These are not the kind of messages I'm referring to."

Birdie clucked her tongue. "There's nothing else going on. No crime, no vagrancy, not even a speeder. What do you want me to say?"

"*That there are no messages.*" He took a breath and tried to think patient thoughts. "I have to go."

"How's the ring shopping coming?"

Hank pulled the phone away to stare at it. Maybe Birdie was part witch. "Goodbye." He hung up and went back inside.

Three rings sat in a velvet tray between Ivy and Willa.

"Have you narrowed it down already?"

Ivy nodded.

Willa smiled. "The woman knows what she likes."

"I can appreciate that." He'd thought this might take hours. More proof Ivy was the right woman for him.

Ivy looked up, eyes soft and sparkly. "Which one do you like?"

The rings all looked alike to him. "Try them on."

She obliged, and he watched her face and the

light in her eyes. The middle ring made them sparkle the most. He glanced at the tags. It was the most expensive, but still well within his budget.

He kept his expression neutral. "Which one do *you* like the best?"

"They're all pretty." But her gaze stayed fixed on the second one.

"That doesn't help me. I'm a guy. They might as well be the same ring to me."

With a slight hesitation, she touched the first and least expensive. "This one is very nice."

He looked at Willa. "The ring will have to be sized, won't it?"

She nodded. "I can do that for you today."

"All right. Hang on to those three and I'll call you when I get back to the station, let you know which one we're getting."

Ivy stared at him, her sweet mouth bent in a half-grin. "You dirty dog."

He smiled. "There has to be some surprise." He grabbed her hand. "Thank you, Willa. I'll be in touch."

Ivy waved goodbye as he led her out of the shop. "She's nice. Fae, right?"

"Mm-hmm."

"This town is pretty cool. People are nice, for the most part, and—"

A warning bell went off in his head. He stopped

in the middle of the sidewalk, letting tourists flow around him. "Was someone here unkind to you?"

"No. Yesterday at the Shop & Save some woman wanted to know what I was doing getting out of your car." She shrugged. "Small-town stuff. No biggie."

He started walking again. She fell into step beside him. Town gossips weren't an actual threat. "Anyone sets off your sixth sense, you let me know."

"I will."

"Where's your bike?"

"In the free lot by the library."

"I'll walk you over there. Park at the station from now on."

She stared at him. "You're scaring me. Stop that."

They crossed the street and walked toward her bike. Traffic stopped for him instantly. The power of the uniform. "I want you to be safe. That's all."

She linked her arm around his. "I know. It's nice. I'll be fine, though. It's not like I can't protect myself. I've got all the same shifters strengths you do."

He nodded as they came to a stop beside her motorcycle. "That alpha possessiveness is built into me. I can't help it."

She combed her hair back with her fingers and started braiding it. "Hey, I meant to ask. What are all those posters for the Zombie Prom?"

"It's the town's June event. There's one big thing

that happens every month. It's why there are so many people around right now."

"Do you go?"

"Not always, but this year, yes. We rotate the security shift. I picked the short straw this time."

"Not your thing, huh?" She tied off the braid and unlocked her helmet.

"I did prom in high school. That was enough. And putting on zombie make-up? Not for me."

She nodded, helmet on her hip. "I can't imagine it would be."

He caught the wistfulness in her eyes and realized how dense he was. Again. "You...want to go with me this year? I'll be on duty, but there's no rule that says I can't bring a date."

Her smile was answer enough. "I would love that. It's this weekend, right?"

He nodded. Seeing her all dolled up would go a long way toward making the night bearable. "The night after the full moon. You have a dress?"

"No, but I'll figure something out." She pulled her helmet on. "And just for the record, I don't think your possessiveness has anything to do with you being next in line for alpha. I've never known a shifter who wasn't."

"Too much?"

She smiled and kissed him. "Nope. But I'll let you know."

He kissed her back. Not as deeply as he would have liked to, but they were practically in the middle of town. "We'll leave for Titus's around six thirty."

She climbed on the motorcycle. "Then you need to be home by five thirty."

"It doesn't take me that long to get ready."

She revved the engine and her eyes went gold with desire. "It's not about you getting ready."

A bolt of need shot through him, and his mouth opened, but he was too dumb-struck with happiness to answer. Instead, he just nodded as she rode off, grinning and wondering how he'd gotten so damn lucky.

11

The look on Hank's face had been everything. She'd practically giggled all the way home, but that giggling had pretty quickly turned into fantasizing about all the things she was going to do to him. That man was *amazing*. And then there was the surprise of the ring. She'd never thought a ring would even be a part of the equation, but the fact that he was insisting on it really made it feel like he was taking this marriage seriously.

If she wasn't nuts about him already...but it had gone far beyond being nuts about him.

Her only option now was to figure out how to survive the inevitable broken heart.

She pulled into the driveway of his house—their house? No, she couldn't quite make that leap yet. It was still his house and would be for a while. Maybe always, once he found out about Charlie's troubles.

But for now, she was going to pretend that everything was fine and that the man she was *most definitely* falling in love with was going to magically accept her child, shortcomings and all.

She got off her bike and walked up to the keypad on the side of the garage to punch in the code he'd given her when something on the front porch caught her eye. Hank had gotten some packages. Well, not *exactly* packages.

She climbed the steps to investigate. One was a vase holding a beautiful bouquet of flowers, all wrapped up in a cloud of tissue paper. A business card-size envelope was taped to the front. And her name was written on it.

She pulled the note off and opened it.

You're prettier than the GTO. -Hank.

She laughed, not only because he'd sent her more flowers but the message was so...him. That man.

The second package was a basket covered in a gingham dish towel. She lifted the towel. Inside was a plate of cling-wrap-covered cookies. A note dangled from red ribbon tied to the basket's handle. Had Hank sent her cookies, too? Maybe it was a thing the florist did.

Hank had just mentioned that new shop. Delaney's Delectables. Maybe these had come from there? She took a long look at the cookies. They seemed pretty normal. Could they have actually been made by a vampire baker? Talk about a first.

She glanced at the note. The writing was a

strange combination of flowery and shaky, like an old woman's penmanship, which could totally belong to a vampire. Weren't they all like a thousand years old? Ivy just barely made out what it said.

Welcome to the neighborhood, Ivy.

Hmm. If they weren't from the florist, they might be from one of Hank's neighbors. Wasn't that nice? She glanced around at the other houses. To think someone had made cookies for her. She'd never in her life lived in a place where the neighbors did things like that. Maybe it was because Hank was the sheriff? Whatever the reason, it was sweet. She couldn't wait to show Hank when he got home.

She fixed the dish towel over the cookies, then snagged the basket by the handle and grabbed the vase of flowers in her other hand. She went into the house through the garage, putting the cookies and the flowers on the kitchen counter, then went back to wheel her bike inside and shut the garage door.

She went to work making an orange pound cake. The recipe was her mother's, except for the orange bit, which Ivy had added on her own. The simple ingredients—butter, flour, sugar, eggs and the orange zest—were about all Ivy had on hand unless she made another trip to the Shop & Save.

When the batter was mixed and poured into a Bundt pan, something Bridget had no doubt added to Hank's kitchen, Ivy slid the cake into the oven, then cleaned up. Job done, she went to her bedroom to study her slim clothing options and figure out what she had to wear that was presentable for a family dinner.

As the aroma of the cake wafted upstairs, her stomach started to rumble.

She glanced down at her torso. "Seriously? Lunch was enormous."

But that was the blessing and the curse of a shifter's metabolism. After settling on the jeans she was currently wearing with the nicest top she'd brought, a simple silky tee in deep cobalt blue, she grabbed her phone off the bed and ran back downstairs to check on the cake.

She set her phone on the counter and peeked into the oven. The cake was coming along nicely and making the whole house smell incredible.

She turned around to grab her phone and found herself face to face with the basket of cookies as her stomach rumbled again.

Hard to deny cookies. She pulled the dishcloth off. The note said welcome to the neighborhood, *Ivy*. Not Hank. He already lived here, he didn't need to be welcomed. That meant technically the cookies were hers.

They looked like chocolate chip. She took the plate out of the basket, lifted the cling wrap and sniffed. Definitely chocolate chip. Hard to go wrong with a classic.

Her stomach growled in agreement.

She checked the time. The pound cake had another forty-five minutes in the oven. Hank would be home in an hour and a half. Dinner wasn't for another hour or so after that.

Plenty of time to eat some cookies and not ruin her appetite.

She put the plate down, then poured herself a big glass of milk and took a seat at the counter.

She slipped one of the cookies from underneath the cling wrap and took a big bite. Crispy, chocolatey and...she stopped chewing. There was an odd after-taste. Nothing she recognized.

Numbness spread over her tongue and mouth.

She ran to the sink and spit out the remnants of the cookie, but she'd already swallowed some.

The numbness sank into her muscles. Her knees buckled. She reached into her back pocket for her phone, realizing she'd left it on the counter by the basket.

The kitchen phone was closer. She just made it, collapsing onto the floor as her hand closed over the receiver and yanked it from the cradle. Her muscles were seizing, turning her fingers into stiff, useless digits, but she managed 911.

"Hello, this is 911. What's your emergency?"

She opened her mouth and nothing came out, her vocal cords frozen as the poison anesthetized her. She banged the phone on the floor, hoping that would be enough. A second later, the phone dropped out of her useless hands.

Darkness swept in around the edges of her consciousness, clawing at her. She clung to the will to live, focusing on the faces of the only two people who'd ever brought her happiness, Charlie and Hank.

Then the poison took them, too.

Hank!" Birdie's shrill cry filled the reception area.

He leaned around the side of his desk so he could make eye contact with Birdie through his open office door. "That phone has an intercom feature."

She pointed at him with the phone. "But you're right there."

"Do I have a call?"

"Yes." She leaned the phone against your shoulder. "The com center just called with a possible prank 911 dialed from your address."

Hank jumped up. "Like hell it's a prank." Ivy wouldn't do that. "I'm on my way, but radio Deputy Cruz and send him, too." He grabbed his hat and raced to his duty car. Nothing in his gut said this was a prank call. Whatever was going on was intentional, he could feel it. The hang up call at his house, then the pictures of Charlie, now this? It wasn't a coincidence.

He made the drive to his house in record time. Nothing looked amiss. He opened the garage and went in just as Cruz pulled into the driveway behind him.

Cruz jumped out of the car. "What's going on?"

Hank shook his head. "Do a perimeter check. I'll secure the inside."

Cruz nodded and started around the house.

Hank went through the laundry room and checked both directions before proceeding toward the kitchen. The house smelled good. She must have been baking. Had there been a kitchen fire? He didn't smell smoke. "Ivy?"

No response. Where was she? He put his hand on his duty weapon as he rounded the corner.

And saw a body.

Ivy was sprawled on the floor, the phone near her right hand.

He yelled for Cruz as he went to his knees and scooped her into his arms. She was breathing. Barely. "Ivy, can you hear me?"

Nothing.

He squeezed the radio on his shoulder. "Get an ambulance here now."

The radio crackled with the dispatch's affirmation.

Foamy spittle dotted the corner of Ivy's mouth. He leaned in and sniffed, then recoiled in recognition. Sweet and bitter.

The bitter he recognized. Wolfsbane, an herb fatal to werewolves.

Cruz came charging in. "What did you—I'm calling an ambulance right now."

"Already called in."

"I'll get the first aid kit," Cruz said.

"No point," Hank told him. "It's wolfsbane." He held her close, rage spiraling through him like a storm.

Cruz sucked in a breath. "That's fatal for your kind, isn't it?"

"Can be." But not this time. Please not this time.

Cruz knelt beside Hank. "There's got to be something we can do."

"Get her to the hospital so they can pump her stomach, but that's about it. Pray she didn't ingest too much and wait it out." Then he would find out who did this and kill them.

"Any idea how this happened?"

"Someone did this to her, that's how." Hank

forced himself to look at Cruz. "Find anything suspicious around the house?"

"I was only halfway through when you called. I'll go finish." He stood and took a few steps but didn't go very far. Hank couldn't see enough of him to know what he was doing. Didn't matter. Only Ivy's survival mattered.

"Boss, you might want to look at this."

Still holding Ivy, Hank got to his feet.

Cruz pointed at the counter. "Was that stuff here already?"

"I sent her the flowers, but I don't recognize the rest of it." Beside the bouquet from the florist was a red dishcloth-draped basket with a handle. Beside it sat a glass of milk and plate of cookies. The cling wrap was disturbed, and one partially eaten cookie lay next to the plate amidst a scattering of crumbs.

Ivy's phone was there, too. He grabbed that and stuck it in his pocket. "Get the crime scene kit. Bag the basket, the towel and the cookies."

Sirens wailed in the distance. Help was on the way.

"You got it, boss." Cruz ran out to the car to get his things.

Hank bent his head to whisper in Ivy's ear. "Stay with me, sweetheart. Fight it. Be strong."

Wolfsbane was deadly. Whoever had done this knew exactly what Ivy was. They had to also know that killing her would mean no marriage, and no marriage would mean no truce.

But if Ivy didn't make it, no truce was going to be a minor concern for whoever was responsible.

Being number one on Hank's hit list? Now that was something to worry about.

12

Despite being joined by Bridget and Titus, Hank couldn't sit. He paced the hospital waiting room, his body present, his mind elsewhere. Cruz had found a note attached to the basket when he'd bagged the evidence. The lab was running tests on the cookies and the note, but Hank had a feeling that, other than the presence of the wolfsbane they already knew about, nothing else would be found.

It made him want to punch something. Repeatedly.

"Sheriff Merrow?"

Hank stopped pacing and turned. Ivy's doctor stood before him. The man's face was unreadable, sounding new alarms in Hank's head. "How is she?"

"Resting comfortably. We've pumped her stomach and given her a mild sedative, so she'll most likely sleep until morning."

"I want to see her. And I'm putting a deputy on the door to make sure there's not another attempt on her life."

"That's fine, but as for seeing her..." The doctor

shook his head. "She's in no state to answer questions—"

"I don't want to question her, you idiot, I want to *see* her."

Bridget jumped up and grabbed Hank's arm. "Maybe we could have this conversation outside of the waiting room?"

Without waiting for an answer, she hustled them both out the door. "Doctor, what my brother is trying to say is he's madly in love with that woman so if you could just give him a few minutes with his fiancée, he'd feel much better."

The doctor nodded slowly, like he was dealing with the slightly insane. "Five minutes. That's it."

Bridget smiled broadly. "Five minutes. Awesome. Thank you."

The doctor left. She punched Hank in the arm and hissed, "Dude, you cannot get all wolfy like that in front of the humans in the waiting room. The doc might know we're weres, but those people in there don't. It's one thing on the street, but no one thinks you're pretending to be a character in here."

Hank glared after the doctor as Bridget dragged him back into the waiting room. "Like he can keep me away from her."

Bridget punched him again. "Are you even listening to me? Breathe, Hank. "

Titus snorted and dropped the magazine he'd been looking at. "Does he ever?"

"I'm listening." Hank took a deep inhale and shot Bridget a pointed look. But breathing didn't help. Nothing would help but seeing Ivy. "Stay here."

He went down the hall to the nurse's station. "Ivy Kincaid's room?"

"Three twenty, down and to the left."

"Thanks." He found her room and slipped in. The lights were dim, some monitor was beeping softly and the whole place smelled of disinfectant.

Ivy lay in the bed closest to the window. The other bed was empty. For the first time since he'd met her, she looked fragile.

It was a harsh reminder that for all their shifter strength and abilities, they were still vulnerable.

He went to her bedside and took her hand, careful of the protruding IV. Her skin was hot and dry. Her fingers twitched, but her eyes stayed closed. "Can you hear me?"

She nodded, a slow almost imperceptible movement, but a nod all the same. She followed it up with a soft murmur that might have been his name.

He tightened his grip on her hand. "I'm here."

"Sorry," she whispered.

"Don't apologize. None of this is your fault. You didn't know."

A weak smile curved her mouth. Then the smile disappeared and her lids flickered halfway open. "Wolfsbane," she muttered.

He nodded. "I know. I'm going to figure out who did this to you."

Her eyes closed. "M'kay." Then her breathing evened out and she was asleep.

He bent and kissed her forehead, pressing his lips to her feverish skin. The need for justice pierced him like an iron rod, stiffening his resolve to find whoever had done this to her and make them pay.

He left her to sleep and headed back to the waiting room, pinching his radio and calling Cruz. "I'm setting up a rotation in front of Ivy's room. I'll take the first shift. You and Blythe decide who's next."

"You got it, boss," Cruz answered.

As Hank walked in, Bridget and Titus stood. Bridget spoke first. "How is she?"

"Groggy and feverish. Asleep now. She knew it was wolfsbane. Obviously too late to do anything about it."

Titus growled softly. "Who the hell does that to someone?"

"I plan on finding out." Hank's pocket buzzed. Ivy's phone was going off. "Hang on."

The name Sam came up on the screen. He answered it. "Hello?"

Silence for a second, then, "Sorry, I must have the wrong number."

"Were you trying to reach Ivy?"

"Yes. Ivy Kincaid."

"Then you have the right number."

More silence. "Are you the Merrow she was sent to marry?"

"I am. Who are you?"

"I'm her brother. Where is she?"

"Unable to come to the phone right now." Her brother had interesting timing. "Is there a message?"

"I'm in town. I need to talk to her."

In town. How convenient. "In that case, we'd better meet."

Hank gave Sam the address of the station, then hung up. He looked at Titus. "Can you stand guard on Ivy's door until I get back? That was her brother. He's in town. I need to go meet him and explain what's going on. And find out why the hell he just showed up."

Titus nodded. "You got it."

Bridget wrapped her arms around herself. "I feel like I should be doing something, too."

Hank tipped his head. "Just keep your wits about you and your phone on in case I need you."

"You know it."

"I'll walk you to your car." He nodded at his brother. "Be back as soon as I can."

Hank saw Bridget safely to her vehicle, then took off for the station. Birdie was gone for the day and Cruz was at the front desk.

He frowned as Hank came in. "Something change?"

"Titus is standing guard. Ivy's brother is in town. I told him to meet me here."

Cruz stood. "I can take over for Titus if you want. Give you some privacy."

Hank thought about it. "Okay."

Cruz grabbed his things and left. Sam showed up ten minutes later. He had Ivy's coloring but not her delicate features. He was almost Hank's size. Apparently, the Kincaids were getting bigger.

Sam looked Hank up and down as he came in. "You're Hank Merrow."

Hank nodded, but didn't move from where he stood in front of the reception desk, one hand on the desk, the other casually on his duty belt near the handle of his service weapon. "What brings you to town all of a sudden, Kincaid?"

Apprehension tightened the muscles in Sam's jaw. "What makes you think it's all of a sudden? What's going on? Why couldn't Ivy come to the phone?"

"Because someone tried to kill her with wolfsbane."

Sam's mouth opened, and genuine shock registered in his eyes, giving Hank the sense that Sam might not be as bad as his father. Sam swore and glanced away. "I'm too late. Those mutt bastards. Is she going to be okay?"

"Should be. What are you too late for?"

Sam sighed. "Is there somewhere more private we can talk?"

"My office." Hank pushed off the desk and led the way.

Sam closed the door behind him and sat as Hank settled into his chair. The other shifter eyed him warily. "When was she poisoned?"

"Late this afternoon."

Sam nodded. "Anything else happen?"

"Yes. Earlier. Some pictures were dropped off in an envelope with my name on them." Hank watched Sam's face. "Pictures of her and Charlie."

Sam's brows lifted. "I guess you know now that's her son."

"I already knew. She told me about him yesterday."

Sam frowned. "She told you about him?"

"Did you think she wouldn't?"

Sam hesitated. "Our father made her swear she wouldn't."

"Why?"

Sam snorted. "Isn't it obvious? He thought it would sour the deal."

Hank stared at the man as his opinion of the Kincaids and their tactics worsened. "It didn't."

Sam sat back. "You like her."

"You sound shocked. You shouldn't be. Your sister is a good person. But maybe that's a rare breed of Kincaid."

Sam started to say something, but Hank interrupted. "Let's get back to why you said you were too late. What do you know?"

Sam sighed. "The night the truce was announced, word of the marriage leaked. It wasn't supposed to get out, but you know how packs talk."

"Not really. Go on."

Irritation edged Sam's voice. "I overheard two of our pack members talking in the meeting hall parking lot. The Jenkins brothers. They're distant relatives. They've always felt like they deserved more respect in the pack. A higher ranking. A bigger share of the stipend."

"That only the men get."

Sam made a face but continued. "They weren't happy about the truce. They said as much in the meeting, but they disagree with ninety percent of the things my father does or the way he does them. Based on their conversation in the parking lot, they were steamed."

He shrugged. "I didn't think they'd do anything about it. They're big talkers. But when my father called another meeting to confirm the marriage rumor, they didn't show. They never miss a meeting. Or their chance to be heard."

"So you thought what?"

Sam sighed. "That they'd come here. To make trouble. To disrupt the truce."

"They stand to gain from that?"

"Maybe. If the truce falls through, my father will bear the shame of that since he initiated it. One of the brothers could challenge him. They're younger and stronger."

"Pack leadership has changed over lesser issues than failed agreements." Though, not in the Georgia pack. A Merrow had been alpha for the last century. But, then, Merrows didn't rule the way Kincaids did, in that all or nothing style. Merrows allowed some compromise. And treated all pack members equally.

"I may not agree with everything my sister's done in her life, but she's still my sister, and I don't want to see her hurt. I'd like to stay and help you keep an eye out for the Jenkins boys."

It was saying something that a Kincaid was asking permission to be in Nocturne Falls, but these were extenuating circumstances. Hank could keep an eye on Sam that way, too, because even if he was Ivy's brother, he was still a Kincaid and Hank didn't trust him. "I don't plan on keeping an eye out for them."

Sam's brow wrinkled. "You don't?"

"I plan on hunting them down. Starting tonight." Hank slid a notebook toward Sam. "Full names and descriptions."

"I can do better than that." Sam reached into his jacket and pulled out a sheet of folded paper. "Here are their pack registrations."

Hank unfolded it and looked at the photos on the registrations, memorizing the faces of the men who'd most probably hurt Ivy. It was unlikely they'd registered at any hotel under their real names, but it was a start.

Sam jotted a number on a piece of scrap paper, then stood. "I'll visit Ivy in the morning, but after that I'll come straight here. Call me if you find them before that."

"Will do." Hank pushed to his feet. "I'll let my deputies know you're allowed into her room. You can see her, but you can't be alone with her."

Sam grunted. "I don't like it, but I get it. You don't trust me."

"No, I don't. You could be pushing blame on the Jenkinses to hide your own guilt."

"I would *never* hurt Ivy."

"You were raised by a man who didn't have a

problem with it. Why should I think you're any different?"

Sam frowned. "Point taken. I'd do the same thing if the situation was reversed. So while I still don't like it, I understand. Trust is earned."

Hank walked the man to the door. "I couldn't agree more."

13

Ivy woke up feeling like a slice of crap between two pieces of crap bread. Sun streamed through the hospital window, digging into her brain and making her cringe. She turned away from it to face the door and was greeted with a familiar silhouette.

"Sam?" He wasn't the last person she expected to see, but it was still a shock. Albeit a pleasant one. One of Hank's deputies moved from the hall to stand inside the door.

"Hey there." Sam came over to the bed. The deputy stayed put. "How are you doing?"

"Achy, but not bad, considering. How did you get here so fast?"

"I was already here. Got your text when I was on the road. I had no idea what had happened to you until I called and Hank answered your phone."

"You met him, huh?"

Sam nodded. "Seems like a good guy. Although he might not be all there."

She frowned. "Why do you say that?"

Sam's eyes were full of mischief. "He's marrying you, isn't he?"

"Says the man who can't find a wife." She turned onto her side, trying to find a comfortable position. Her whole body ached, and her muscles were as sore as if she'd been beaten.

"I'll settle down when I'm good and ready." He brushed a piece of hair off her forehead, a rare gesture since they'd grown more distant. "You look like crap, by the way."

"And somehow, your visit isn't helping." She swatted at his hand. Her relationship with Sam was definitely the usual sibling love/hate. If only she could get him away from the influence of their father. "Why did you come to Nocturne Falls if not because of what happened to me?"

"Because of the Jenkins brothers. Overheard some of their conversation at the meeting where Dad announced the truce, and they didn't like it at all. Gave me a bad feeling. I figured I'd better get down here, make sure they weren't up to something stupid. Looks like I was too late."

She smiled. At least he still cared. "Thanks. It was sweet of you to look out for me that way."

He nodded, but his expression was serious. "Look, about you and Hank, it's great that you like each other and all, considering you're getting married, but you shouldn't have told him about Charlie."

She froze, her pain replaced by fear. "What did you say to him?"

Sam shrugged. "Nothing, really. I did tell him you weren't supposed to say anything. Why did you?"

"All I told him was that I have a son. I had to. He overheard me on the phone."

"So he doesn't know about—"

"No. And I plan to keep it that way until after the wedding. I'm in a no-win situation. There's no way anyone will marry me if they know about Charlie's condition. But I'm also not going to risk Charlie's life over this." She knew exactly what her father would do to Charlie if the truce fell through. He'd told her in very plain terms.

The memory sent a shiver through her.

Sam was quiet a moment. "Hank might hate you for it."

She stared past Sam, the truth of his words another knife in her chest. "I know. But what choice do I have? I'd rather have a husband who hates me than lose Charlie. That would kill me. Hatred I can live with. I've had plenty of practice."

"He'll divorce you."

"And nullify the truce? I don't think so. Neither of us has a choice. Because Clemens has made it that way." She glared at Sam. "How you can stand by and let our father treat your nephew this way—"

Sam straightened. "Don't put this on me. You're the one who insisted on going to college."

"That's Dad talking, not you." Clemens had never wanted her to go to college, never wanted her to do anything but what he told her to do.

Sam held up his hands. "Hey, you're the one who wanted a life beyond the family businesses. Look where it got you. Now you're living with the consequences."

"My son is not a *consequence*. He's a good kid and an innocent child."

"He's a mutt."

Her heart constricted. "Get out."

He sighed. "I didn't mean—"

"Get out or I'll call the nurse and have you removed." She struggled to sit up in bed.

The deputy took a step forward but Ivy shook her head.

With a look of frustration and regret, Sam left. The deputy walked out behind him, leaving Ivy alone. She collapsed and began to weep, too hurt in body and soul not to. Hearing that word out of her father's mouth was bad enough, but from Sam, the brother who'd been her ally growing up? She covered her face with her hands and gave in to the pain she'd been pushing down for too long.

"Hey, what's wrong?"

Hank's gravelly voice was like a balm. His warm

arms embraced her, and she relaxed into his touch. She took a breath and forced the tears away. "I just... hurt all over."

Not a lie. But not the truth that would take this wonderful man away from her either. That would come soon enough.

He kissed the top of her head and released her, but took hold of her hands. "It takes twenty-four hours to get all the wolfsbane out of your system so you've got a few more hours. Until then, you're not going to feel so hot."

She nodded. "I already feel better now that you're here."

He smiled. "Good. But if you want to postpone the wedding—"

"Tomorrow's the full moon." Panic seized her. "We're supposed to get married tomorrow night. I know it's just a civil ceremony, but I haven't done a thing to get ready."

"Sweetheart, there's still the rest of today and most of tomorrow. But there's really nothing for you to do. The Justice of the Peace is a friend. I set things up for five tomorrow, but he's willing to perform the ceremony whenever we need him. I know the full moon is traditional, but the bride isn't usually recovering from a near fatal poisoning. We can absolutely postpone to give you a chance to get back on your feet."

She relaxed a little. There was *some* time left. Enough maybe that she could at least plan a nice wedding meal for them. "No postponing. It has to be the night of the full moon. Postponing would mean waiting another month." There was no way Charlie would survive staying with his grandparents that long or she could keep from telling Hank the truth. If only her mother could be counted on to stand up to Clemens, but Ivy wasn't holding her breath for her mother to grow a backbone anytime soon. "I'll be fine by this afternoon. Really, I'm already so much better."

"You're sure?"

"Positive." Even so, a JOP ceremony meant they weren't going to have a cake or flowers or anything. But then, she'd never really expected any of those things. *Cake.* She grabbed his arm. "I hope you turned off the oven. I had a cake in there."

"Deputy Cruz did."

She nodded and slumped back into the bed. At least she wouldn't be responsible for burning the house down, too.

Hank let go of her hand and hooked his thumbs into his belt. "I passed your brother in the hall."

She smoothed the sheet out. "It was nice of him to come." Too bad he'd brought so much of their father's attitude with him.

"He told you why he came?

"Mm-hmm. The Jenkins brothers."

"He's going to help me track them down. I have a lead on them at a motel on the outskirts of town. Cruz is staking the place out right now. Sam and Titus are going with me. Should be a simple operation. Deputy Blythe will keep watch at your door."

"What will you do with them after you arrest them?"

Hank shifted, his expression resolute. "This is a pack matter. They'll be dealt with at a tribunal. Which also means I need to change out of my uniform before I head over there. I can't appear to be representing the local law."

She stared at him. "Speaking of appearances, I just realized something."

"What's that?"

"The night we went out for a run, when we stopped at the waterfall, there were two black wolves on the other side. They were staring at us, but they were gone before I could tell you."

"The Jenkins brothers?"

She shook her head, her mouth twisting in frustration. "I don't know. I've never seen them in wolf form. Men and women don't run together in our pack. And women aren't allowed at the meetings, so I barely know what they look like in human form."

"That's some serious misogynistic thinking going on."

"Have you ever met my father?"

Hank frowned. "No."

And hopefully, he never would. "You'd understand if you had."

"How did he end up with such backwoods nonsense?"

"We're a backwoods pack. But his father taught him everything he knew."

Confusion clouded Hank's handsome face. "I thought you inherited your motorcycle from your grandfather. Seems like an odd thing to leave a granddaughter if you think of women as second-class citizens."

"It came from my maternal grandfather, not Clem's dad. Harlan Kincaid was as big of a bastard as his son is." She pushed up a little more on the bed. Already, the achiness was half of what it had been. Which only made her antsy to do something besides convalesce.

"You need anything?"

"Yeah, to get out of here. I have a wedding to prepare for and lying in this bed isn't helping."

"Maybe I can get you released, take you home."

"I'd rather you get those Jenkins boys locked up. I can get myself home. Plus, then your deputy can go back to real police work."

"No." He narrowed his eyes. "Until they've been dealt with, I don't want you alone."

"Hank, I'll be fine—"

Knocking interrupted her.

They both turned to see Birdie standing in the door

"Trouble in paradise?" Birdie trotted around to the other side of Ivy's bed. "How are you, dear?"

Ivy smiled at her. "Your timing couldn't be better. I feel fine, I want to go home and Hank won't let me."

Birdie frowned at Hank. "You're not a doctor. You can't dictate these things just because you're the sheriff."

"I don't want her alone until I know she'll be safe."

Birdie set her enormous turquoise purse on the bed and crossed her hands over top of it. "She won't be alone. I'll be with her."

"I fail to see how that's going to keep her safe."

Birdie leaned toward him. "I'm still a werewolf, sonny. I can hold my own."

Hank snorted. Birdie looked like she might swat him.

Ivy held up a hand. "Hank, if anything happens, anything, I'll call you immediately. Promise."

Hank's radio went off before he could answer. "Sheriff, we have a visual and can confirm the two men at the hotel match the photos Ivy's brother provided."

He squeezed the radio and responded. "On my way." He pointed at Birdie. "You can take her home, but I expect your best behavior. Actually, better than that."

He looked at Ivy. "And you take it easy. Keep the house locked and let no one in until I get back." He leaned in and kissed her. "I'll see you soon with good news."

She kissed him back. "Be careful."

"You, too." And with a nod, he was gone.

Ivy took a breath, then turned to Birdie. "Thank you. I owe you."

Birdie waved a hand at her. "We're about to be family. Speaking of, do you think I could get a peek at your wedding dress when we get back to Hank's?"

"Oh. Uh...I don't have a wedding dress. It was such short notice and..." She shrugged. She wasn't about to drop all that money on a dress she was only going to wear once for a marriage that had little chance of being anything but contemptuous once the truth came out. "I just brought a dress I already had."

Abject horror masked Birdie's face. "Oh, that will not do. Who's making the cake?"

Ivy shrugged. "We could get cupcakes from the Shop & Save, I guess—"

Birdie clutched at imaginary pearls and gasped like she'd just taken a hit to the solar plexus. "What about the flowers? The music? The reception afterwards? A photographer?"

Ivy took a breath, wondering how she was going to explain that there was no point in spending all kinds of time, effort and money on a marriage that was only going to dissolve into the thinnest of unions. "I just thought we could keep things simple. No muss, no fuss."

"Oh, my word, you can't be serious."

"I'm totally serious."

"This marriage represents the union of two very important packs. Not to mention, it's my nephew's first and *only* wedding. Simple will not do."

"You know I'm lying in a hospital bed, right?"

"You told Hank you felt fine. Is that the truth?"

"Yes." Ivy wouldn't say she was a hundred percent, but she was at least eighty. Maybe eighty-five.

Birdie's hands starting flopping through the air like she was trying to organize dust motes. "Then get up, girl, get up! We have work to do. *Lots* of work to do."

14

With its tucked-away location, the Pinehurst Inn had once been the county's favorite "No tell motel," but time had worn the place down, and now its guests fell into three categories: cheapskates, the unfortunate, and delinquents.

Whether or not Dalton and Wade Jenkins were cheapskates remained to be seen, but they were definitely delinquents, and they were about to be very, very unfortunate.

Hank raised his hand and chopped it forward to indicate to Titus and Cruz that it was time to move into position.

Titus put two fingers to his forehead in a salute that said he understood, and he and Cruz moved out.

Keeping his voice down, Hank looked at Sam. "Let's go."

Sam nodded.

They crept past Titus's pickup truck and around the side of the building, making their way through weeds littered with trash and an old mattress. Once upon a time there had been a pool back here, but it had been filled in a long time ago. Hank glanced at his watch. Three minutes to get into position at the back door of the Jenkinses' room. The doors that had once led to the pool area still remained, and were probably a big part of the Pinehurst Inn's reputation as a good place to make a fast getaway.

If the Jenkinses tried it, they were going to run right into him and Sam.

Hank wasn't keen on executing this kind of operation in the middle of the day, but Ivy's safety was paramount.

These lowlifes needed to be dealt with.

Hank ducked as he passed beneath the room's open bathroom window. The sounds of a daytime TV game show and the acrid scent of cigarette smoke wafted out. The Jenkinses must be biding their time until night fell and they could make another attempt on Ivy's life. They had to know by now that she'd survived the wolfsbane.

Hank flattened himself against the wall as Sam did the same on the other side of the window.

Hank checked his watch. *Thirty seconds.*

This wasn't going to be some slick undercover op. Hell no. This was going to be a little taste of shock and awe. Brute force and the element of surprise. It was their only option to keep things neat and tidy, because if anyone shifted, they'd all shift, and having five wolves and a panther battling it out at the Pinehurst Inn was unacceptable.

Fifteen seconds.

Adrenaline coursed through his system, narrowing his focus until time seemed to slow. It had been like this in his Army Ranger days, too. The rush calmed him. He reached for the door knob, the sound of his pulse ticking in his head like a metronome keeping him on pace.

Ten seconds.

Sam crouched, ready to charge through.

Five seconds.

Hank's fingers curled around the knob.

Go time.

He yanked the door off its hinges just as Cruz and Titus burst through the front. Chaos ruled. The Jenkins brothers leaped off the bed and lunged, going into half-forms.

Hank and his crew did the same, sprouting elongated fangs and sharp nails, while Cruz shifted into his partial panther form and unleashed a lethal set of claws.

The Jenkins closest to Hank swiped at him, catching him on the shoulder, but the momentum left the man open.

Hank rammed his arm back and clocked the

man in the head with his elbow. A solid hit. The man slumped to his knees and fell forward, the gold in his eyes blinking out like a plug had been pulled.

Titus, Sam and Alex Cruz had the second brother well in hand. Hank grabbed the brother who was moaning at his feet, pinned him against the wall and held him there by his throat.

The man's lids fluttered open.

"Good. You're awake. We need to talk."

He blinked. His pupils were slow to focus. "'Bout what?"

Hank snarled. "You tried to kill my fiancée."

Realization filled Jenkins' eyes. He clawed at Hank's hands, trying to free them from his neck. "It's...not...your business...Merrow."

Blood welled in the cuts made by the other man's scratching, but Hank held fast, squeezing a little harder. "She's about to be my wife. That makes it my business."

Jenkins started to go blue. He opened his mouth, but no words came out. His eyes went buggy.

With a growl, Hank dropped Jenkins to his feet. He couldn't kill the man. Yet.

The second Jenkins touched down, he took a breath. Then he swung.

Hank dodged the man's talons and rammed his shoulder into the man's chest. The air left him with an audible woof, and he collapsed to the ground again, heaving in air.

Hank rolled him over and cuffed him before he got his wind again. "You don't know when to give up, do you?"

With the battle over, Hank went back to his full human form as the rest of the crew did, too.

"Found it," Cruz yelled.

Hank looked up to see his deputy holding a small red and white cooler by the handle. "Wolfsbane?"

Cruz nodded. "Two vials and a syringe. Probably shot the cookies full of the stuff. We could get the lab to match the strain if need be."

Hank flipped his captive over, who'd also returned to human form. "The presence of it in their room ought to be enough. Plus, Billy Bob Idiot here is going to confess. Aren't you?"

"Name's Wade, you stinkin' Merrow, and I'm not confessing to anything."

Hank grunted. "Suit yourself. It's not really necessary anyway."

Wade's eyes went gold, like he was about to go full wolf.

Hank stared at him and shook his head slowly. "Attempt to shift, and I'll put you in silver-plated cuffs. Right after I knock you out."

Wade snarled, but stayed human. Titus let out a low whistle from the other side of the room. Hank straightened.

"Lookie here." Titus took a hunting rifle with an electronic scope out of the closet.

Hank grabbed Wade and tossed him on the bed beside his brother, who was now also in handcuffs and sporting a bloody lip thanks to whoever had tackled him. "Loaded?"

Titus racked the slide open. "Yep. And that's not all…"

He plucked out one of the bullets, lifted it to his nose and sniffed. He grimaced, making the scratch on his cheek wrinkle. "Silver. They meant to make another attempt at killing her. Or you."

Sam, who'd come through the fight unharmed, grabbed the other brother, Dalton, by his shirt, hoisted him to a sitting position and got in his face. "You tried to kill my sister. The daughter of your alpha."

Dalton's lip curled. "Your father's old and out of touch. It's time for a new alpha to run the Tennessee pack. This truce makes us look weak."

"Yeah," Wade agreed.

"You're both idiots," Sam said. "You have no idea what's at stake."

Hank's ears perked up. What did Sam mean by

that? Something more than peace between the two packs?

Dalton laughed. "I should've taken that rifle to your old man when I had the chance."

Sam slugged Dalton, knocking him back onto the bed and rendering him unconscious. Wade shut up. Sam shook his head and looked at Hank. "These mutts make me ashamed to be a Kincaid."

Hank could think of a few more reasons to be ashamed of that lineage, but held his tongue. "Let's load them into the truck and get them to the holding site." There was a place just an hour outside of town. "I'll call my father, tell him what's going on, then he can send his men to pick them up. Sam, you'd best fill Clemens in, too."

"I will." Sam's hands clenched at his sides as he stared at the two brothers. "He's not going to like this. At the very least, he'll kick them out of the pack."

"As he should, but there's still going to be a tribunal. It's pack law." Which meant the Jenkinses would get a chance to tell their side. No doubt something that would upset Clemens, too. He probably wouldn't like having his dirty laundry aired so publicly.

Sam nodded, but the expression on his face was unreadable. Anger, definitely, but whatever else was there, Hank couldn't tell. Was he worried what the

Jenkins brothers would say? That wasn't Hank's problem. And so long as Ivy's brother didn't decide to go rogue and mete out whatever punishment he thought fit, everything would be fine.

The last thing Hank wanted to do was add to Ivy's troubles by arresting her brother for murder.

15

"It's perfect." Birdie clasped her hands and tucked them under her chin, her eyes shining with tears, just like they'd been with every other dress Ivy had worn out of the dressing room. "You look beautiful. That is definitely the dress you should get married in."

Ivy stared at her reflection. The dress *was* amazing. White lace with cap sleeves and a simple A-line skirt that fell to the floor in a sprinkling of crystals and beading. There was just enough to make the dress sparkle and add a hint of vintage. Ivy had always dreamed about a dress like this.

But she didn't deserve it. Not with the scheme to deceive Hank. Thinking about that while wearing such a beautiful gown made her heart break a little. The white dress seemed such a stark contrast to the horrible thing she was about to do to the man she was falling in love with. If only she could get Charlie to safety.

"Gathering wool, dear?"

Ivy shook herself. "Sorry. I just..." She took a breath. "Birdie, I can't afford this." Not financially or emotionally. Having a nice wedding with all the pretty trappings was only going to highlight how much of a sham the whole thing was.

Birdie clucked her tongue. "How about this is my gift to you?"

"No, I can't possibly—"

"Corette, can you come here?" Birdie waved at the owner of the shop, an attractive older woman who, Birdie had informed Ivy, was one of the town's better-known witches and currently dating Hugh Ellingham's valet. Birdie had insisted that Ever After was the only bridal boutique worth shopping at in town. Seemed to Ivy it was also the only one, but what did she know?

Not much about bridal shops, and not that much about witches. Just like vampires, she'd never met one personally, but it was cool to be in a shop owned by one. Not so cool that she was about to let Birdie get away with buying the dress. The woman would hate her when she found out the truth. "That is a sweet gesture, Birdie, but it wouldn't be right—"

"Hush, now. It would be absolutely right. I never had a daughter so let me do this."

Corette joined them, smiling broadly at Ivy. "You're the perfect height for a gown like that. You look stunning."

"Thank you."

Birdie touched Corette's hand. "We're going to take this dress, but we need it for tomorrow."

"That soon? Oh my. There's no way I can order one with such short notice." Corette frowned and looked at Ivy. "Are you okay with taking the floor sample? You're the first person to try that on, so it's not like it's been worn by anyone else. Still, it *is* the sample dress."

Ivy was about to say they weren't taking the dress, when Birdie spoke up.

"That's fine. I imagine there's a little discount that will go along with that?"

"Of course. I'll sharpen my pencil."

"Good." Birdie smiled like she'd won something. "Now, about alterations. Since we need it so quickly, can you…" She waved her hands. "Do your thing?"

Corette looked around. "Since we're all alone, I don't see why not."

She walked up to Ivy, who stood on a small platform in front of a large bank of angled mirrors. Corette pinched the dress in a few spots, checking the fit and taking up excess fabric. She lifted the shoulders and let them drop. Next, she spanned Ivy's rib cage with her hands front and back. Finally, she took a few steps away and squinted. "Doesn't need much."

She stretched out her hands and waved them through the air with a flourish.

The dress moved, fitting itself to Ivy as though it was being tailored right on her body. Ivy gasped. "What was that?"

Corette gave her a wink. "Just a little magic. But then you shifters know all about that, don't you?"

Ivy smiled. "I guess we do." Every supernatural had their own kind of magic.

"I'm so glad you're taking Sheriff Merrow off the market. He needs a woman in his life. Someone to take care of him, you know?" Corette shook her head. "He works too much. But then maybe that's because there's no one to go home to."

"I agree," Birdie said. "My nephew's been married to his job for far too long. Time he has a good woman to spend his days with. And nights." Birdie twittered and blushed a little.

A good woman. Ivy did her best to keep a smile on her face, but inside her happiness faded at the reminder of what she wasn't.

All because of her father.

Birdie shooed her back into the dressing room to change. After Corette folded the dress into tissue paper and boxed it up, Birdie took hold of Ivy's arm, and they were off again. This time they went several streets until they turned down one that rang a bell for Ivy.

Black Cat Boulevard. She looked up at the sign. "Delaney's Delectables. Hank told me about this place." She leaned in toward Birdie and whispered, "He said the woman who owns it is a vampire."

"She is." Birdie nodded, eyes sparkling. "And she owes Hank a favor. C'mon."

She took Ivy's arm and marched them both in. "Hello, Delaney, dear. How are you?"

A cute woman with chestnut waves and a smattering of freckles who looked nothing like any vampire Ivy had ever imagined put her hands on her hips and grinned. "Hey there, Birdie. I'm just fine. How are you?"

"Oh, I'm in a panic." Birdie shuddered and clutched at her throat like the panic was choking her. "I am *desperate* for your help."

How Birdie hadn't won an Oscar was astonishing.

Delaney's brow puckered. "What's the matter? I'm happy to do whatever I can."

Birdie put her arm around Ivy. "This is Ivy Kincaid. Ivy, meet Delaney Ellingham, the owner of this very fine establishment and the baker of all these delicious things. She's won awards."

Delaney rolled her lips in, an effort meant to stop herself from laughing at Birdie's hyperbole, no doubt. Ivy liked her immediately. She gave her head a little shake. "I actually haven't won any." She stuck her hand out. "Nice to meet you, Ivy."

Ivy shook her hand. "Nice to meet you, too." For

a vampire, she was surprisingly warm. Maybe they all were. Ivy wasn't exactly an expert on that particular brand of supernatural.

Delaney's hands went back to her hips. "Now, what seems to be the trouble?"

"Hank, you know Hank, my nephew. The sheriff."

"Of course. I owe him one." Delaney looked at Ivy. "He helped save my life once."

"That's a story I'd like to hear," Ivy answered.

Birdie cleared her throat. "If I could just bring us back to why we're here," she said. "Ivy and Hank are getting married."

Delaney clapped her hands. "How wonderful! Congratulations. I didn't even know Hank was seeing anyone."

"He wasn't. This is an arranged marriage. It's a pack thing." Ivy saw no reason not to be honest. It was a nice change of pace.

Delaney's mouth rounded to an O. "You and I have a lot in common. We really should get together and have lunch."

"That would be great. I didn't know vampires ate real food." Ivy's mouth puckered up, but it was too late to pull the words back. "Sorry, was I not supposed to know you're a vampire?"

Delaney laughed. "Only if you're human. Which I assume you're not?"

"Werewolf. Just like Hank. Which is why our marriage is about to bring *peace*"—she used air quotes around the word—"between our respective packs."

Delaney nodded. "Cool. So what can I do to help you guys with this?"

"They need a cake." Birdie leaned in and whispered conspiratorially, "We just got her a wedding dress thanks to Corette. You tell Stanhill he's got a real keeper there."

Delaney laughed. "I will. As for this cake, how many people does it need to feed?"

"A hundred," Birdie said at the same time that Ivy said, "Ten."

The two women looked at each other. Ivy barely controlled the urge to walk out. "Birdie, no one even knows we're getting married. Why on earth would we need a cake to feed a hundred people?"

"I was planning on inviting some—"

"No." Ivy gave Birdie a sharp look. "I want this to be a quiet, simple affair. Our parents aren't even going to be there." She turned her attention back to Delaney. "I'll compromise and say twenty, but that's it. Is that even doable?"

Delaney wiggled her brows. "I don't have Corette's magic, but yes, I can swing that. Especially if you like simple. But complicated is fine, too. As long as I have the time, I can do just about anything."

"That's the thing," Birdie said. "We need this cake by tomorrow."

"Wait, when?" Delaney leaned forward like she hadn't heard correctly.

Ivy sighed. "Tomorrow. I know it's super short notice. We're getting married the day of the full moon. It's a traditional werewolf thing."

Delaney made a face, then nodded. "Okay, forget complicated. Simple is going to have to work."

Ivy let out the breath she'd been holding. "I'll go you one better. The cake design is completely up to you."

"In that case, I can definitely do this." Delaney squinted. "You don't want to have *any* input? Colors? Flavors? Anything?"

Why should she? She hadn't had any say in the marriage. Ivy shook her head. "I can see by the stuff in the cases you do beautiful work. Whatever you come up with is fine. Chocolate, vanilla, I don't care." She held up a finger. "Actually, there is one stipulation."

Delaney smiled like she'd been expecting something. "What's that?"

"Budget. I don't have a lot to spend on this so—"

"Oh, please. I owe Sheriff Merrow a big thank-you. Cake's on me. It's my wedding gift to you guys."

"Really?" The people here were so nice. Too bad they were all going to end up hating her when they found out she was pulling one over on their beloved sheriff. Ivy tried not to lose it right there. "That's just...thank you."

"Yes, thank you. That's lovely of you, Delaney," Birdie said. She pointed toward the note pad Delaney had pulled out. "You can deliver the cake to Howlers."

"I'll have it there tomorrow afternoon."

Birdie and Ivy said their goodbyes and added another round of thanks before heading out.

Ivy put her hand on Birdie's arm as they left. "Birdie, I appreciate all your enthusiasm for the wedding, but I'm exhausted. I'd really like to go home."

"Of course. You've had quite a day. I'll stay with you until Hank returns." The older woman raised her brows in a very motherly fashion. "I'm sure you're capable of taking care of yourself, but I'd rather not hear it from him because I left you alone."

Ivy dropped her hand and nodded. "I understand."

"He loves you, you know."

Ivy stared straight ahead as they walked to Birdie's car. "We've only known each other two days."

"Doesn't matter. That's how it is with the

Merrows. When you know, you know. And he knows."

Ivy hiked the wedding dress box a little higher. Thinking that Hank might be in love with her was amazing. Although it only made things worse. "I'm not sure Hank feels that way. I know he likes me, but love...love takes time."

Birdie squinted at her but didn't say anything else about it the rest of the way to the car. As Birdie was pulling out of the parking lot, Ivy's phone chirped with an incoming message. She pulled the phone out and saw a message waiting from Hank.

Mission accomplished. See you at home.

She smiled. "You won't have to wait with me. Hank just messaged to say everything's taken care of and he'd see me at home. Or he's headed home. Either way, you won't have to wait long."

"Glad to hear it." Birdie drove with both hands on the wheel, firmly planted in the ten and two positions. "I mean, glad to hear he took care of those hoodlums. Not that I won't have to stay. I'd be happy to do that."

"I know."

But she didn't have to. The squad car was parked outside the garage.

Birdie dropped Ivy off in the driveway. Ivy thanked her, scooped up the wedding dress box and went in. As sweet as Hank's aunt was, it was a relief to be away from the constant wedding chatter.

Hank met Ivy at the door with a smile, but his eyes held an endearing amount of concern. "Did she wear you out?"

A little, but Ivy wasn't about to disparage the woman who'd just gifted her with a wedding dress. "No. Your aunt is lovely."

He snorted as he stepped out of the way to let her inside.

"Really, she is."

"Looks like you did some shopping."

"We did." If only he knew what was in that box.

"So did I."

She frowned at him. "You went shopping?"

He dug a little velvet box out of the pocket of his jeans and handed it to her. "See for yourself."

She set down the box she was carrying and opened the one he'd given her, even though she already knew what was in it. The ring. She sucked in a breath when she saw how wrong she'd been. It was a ring all right, but not the little one she'd picked out. It was the expensive one she'd loved but known was too much. "You crazy man. You bought the big one."

He nodded. "You like it?"

She swallowed and swiped at her eyes, feeling

the heat of building tears. "It's beautiful. But it's not the one I pointed to."

He took the ring from the box and slipped it on her finger. "It's the one I thought you should have. You seemed to like it best."

She had, but it had been so expensive she hadn't dared let him know. Apparently, she'd failed at that. She glanced at the ring, but her gaze came up to stare at his handsome face a second later. "You're really something, you know that?"

He smiled. "So are you."

She leaned in and kissed him. He wrapped his arms around her and held her tight.

"I'm so glad you're okay."

"I'm so glad you caught those guys." She leaned her head on his shoulder. There was so much pleasure in being in his arms, safe and protected. It was such a rare feeling in her life that she almost started weeping for real.

Reluctantly, she broke the embrace and picked up the wedding dress box. "I'm just going to run upstairs and put this away, then I'll be back down and I want to hear all about how you took down the Jenkins brothers."

"You want a beer?"

He really was the man of her dreams. "More than words can say."

With a grin, she jogged up the stairs to her

bedroom and shut the door. She put the box on the bed and freed the dress from the wrappings, her heart fluttering a bit as she shook it out. Up until Hank had given her the ring, it had been the most beautiful thing she'd ever owned.

She hoped neither one became the symbol of a horrible day. The ring could be returned, but the dress, she wasn't so sure about. She sat on the bed and clutched the gown to her, the lace soft and perfect in her hands.

Hank was amazing. So much more than she'd dreamed of. Maybe...more than she deserved, although after life with her father, maybe Hank was her reward for not killing Clemens.

Whether or not Hank loved her, Ivy knew she loved him. How could she not? For all his gruff exterior, he'd warmed up fast and shown her a side of himself that was caring and concerned and fiercely protective.

One thing after another and he'd proved what kind of man he was.

When she'd almost died at the hands of the Jenkins brothers, Hank had gone after them and taken them out of the picture.

She'd told him about Charlie and he hadn't blinked an eye. She could only imagine what kind of amazing father he would be. Someday.

He was a generous lover. He'd made her breakfast. Bought her flowers. And then there was the ring he'd picked out. The ring he'd thought she should have. She stuck her hand out and splayed her fingers, not quite able to enjoy the glitter of the diamond now seated there.

All that when she'd expected him to judge her for her last name and treat her like something to be endured.

He did not deserve the trap Clemens was setting for him. Nor did the Merrow pack deserve the war that would follow if Hank refused to marry her, which would be perfectly within his rights if he found out the truth before they were married.

Her cell phone rang, snapping her out of her head. She let the dress fall limp over her lap as she checked the screen. Her mother's number. Which meant Charlie. Her heart leaped. She swiped to answer. "Hey, baby! It's so good to hear your voice."

Sobs answered her. "Mom, you gotta come home."

Pain stabbed her in the heart. "What's wrong, sweetheart?"

The crying increased, and all her son could manage was, "Grandpa."

Rage rose up in Ivy. A lifetime's worth. But it was her mother's instinct that drove her to her feet. The dress fell to the floor, forgotten. Enough was enough.

Whatever the consequences, she was *done* abiding by her father's rule at her son's expense.

She stared out the window, seeing nothing but her own, golden-eyed reflection. "I'm coming, baby. I'm coming."

16

Hank popped the top off Ivy's beer, set it next to his, then leaned against the counter while he waited on her. He'd changed into a fresh shirt and tossed the old one out as soon as he'd gotten home. He might have healed from Wade's nails slicing him, but his T-shirt was a lost cause.

He also didn't want Ivy to worry that he'd gotten hurt. Shifters healed fast, but if she'd seen the dried blood and the torn shirt, it would have upset her. Poor woman had enough to deal with after nearly being poisoned to death.

Those damn Jenkins brothers should be counting their blessings she hadn't died. It was the only reason they were still breathing.

He glanced out toward the street. The sun was about an hour from setting. Maybe they'd sit on the back deck and have their beer out there. It would be nice to unwind with someone like that every day. Especially someone like Ivy. He smiled. Thinking about her did that to him. Thinking about life with her made it impossible not to smile.

Ivy stormed down the steps, her saddlebags over her shoulder. His smile vanished at the anger dancing in her eyes.

"What's wrong?"

She didn't stop moving. "I have to go."

"What?" He stopped leaning and stood up straight. "Where?"

"I have to get Charlie. He just called me crying. I don't know what my father's done, but I'm not leaving my son there a second longer." She bit the words out, her emotions visible in her face and stiff movements.

"It's almost a seven-hour drive."

"I'm not asking you to go." She headed for the garage.

"Hold on a second, will you?"

She paused, her hand on the door handle. "Why? My father is terrorizing my son. I'm not waiting another second. I've already waited long enough."

"Because I might have a better solution." He pulled his phone out and dialed.

Her mouth opened, but she said nothing and closed it firmly, popping her jaw to the side. Visible tension held her ramrod straight as her lips thinned to a hard line. She was trembling the slightest bit. Hank guessed that was rage.

Hugh Ellingham answered on the third ring. "Sheriff Merrow, what can I do for you this fine evening?"

"I need a favor."

"Name it."

"I need the Ellingham plane."

Less than two hours later, they'd landed at McKellar-Sipes Regional Airport. Ivy had thanked Hank profusely before they'd left, but had gone quiet on the flight, pulling into herself. Introspective, but never without losing the fire in her eyes. He'd seen that in soldiers about to go into the field.

He understood and left her alone.

She was preparing to go to war.

He just hoped she understood she wasn't going alone. He wasn't about to let his fiancée face Clemens Kincaid by herself, even if the man was her father. *Especially* since the man was her father. Ivy didn't seem to have much love for the man, and Hank had a pretty good idea of why that was, based on what Ivy had told him and what Hank had inferred.

Clemens ruled his pack and his family with an iron fist and an outdated sense of place. None of that made too much difference, except for how it affect Ivy and Charlie. And if the man had hurt Charlie, Hank was going to kick his ass. Alpha or not, consequences be damned, Hank was not going to let the man harm the child who was about to be Hank's son. No way in hell.

The poor kid must miss his mother beyond words.

Hank had only known Ivy a few days and already couldn't imagine being away from her. How much worse was it for a little boy with Clemens looking after him?

As soon as they deplaned, Hank rented a car from the lone rental agent and got them on the road.

"It's a little tricky in the dark. Country roads aren't well marked either." Ivy plugged the address into the GPS and went quiet again.

Occasionally, she'd glance at her engagement ring, then frown and stare out the window for long uninterrupted periods. Mostly she seemed lost in thought, her mouth bent in a permanent frown.

Whatever was going on in her head made him hurt for her. He glanced over, wishing there was something he could do to help. To fix things. "You all right?"

"No. But I will be."

"Once we get Charlie."

She nodded and rubbed at her eyes.

"You want to give me some recon? What are we walking into here?

"My father is a mean SOB who believes his word is law."

"Is he armed?"

She glanced at Hank. "It's Tennessee."

"So yes."

She stared through the windshield. "He prefers his fists."

Hank could handle a little hand to hand. He nodded. "It's going to be okay."

She barked out a harsh laugh. "I wish I could believe that, but I know better. I'm a Kincaid. I know how these things play out."

"Except this time, you're not on your own."

Ivy put her hand on the door handle and turned to face him. "Hank, if I don't get another chance to tell you this, I just want you to know that you're the best man I've ever known. Thank you for everything."

That sounded like goodbye. Hank stared at her. "What do you mean if you don't get another chance—?"

"Hank, my father is a conniving, manipulative man. In place of his soul there's an empty, black pit." She was shaking. "There is nothing good in him, and there never will be. I only left Charlie with him because he forced me to."

"Just like he forced you into this marriage. I get it.

But I did a tour in Iraq and a tour in Afghanistan. It takes a lot more than an alpha werewolf with an overblown sense of importance to scare me."

"Well, he scares the hell out of me. Has for most of my life." She turned away and stared out the window. "But I'm done with that now. Done with his threats. I don't care what he does to me, but if he's hurt Charlie—"

"You really think he would hurt his own grandson?"

The sharp, bitter laugh came back only to be choked off by a sob. "You have no idea what this man is capable of." She bent her head. "Or what he's capable of getting others to do."

"You think he was behind the Jenkins boys?"

"No. Getting me married off to a Merrow was his number one plan. Killing me would ruin everything and leave him stuck with Charlie." She sniffed and took her hand off the door handle.

"Stuck? With his grandson?" Hank's hackles went up as he followed the GPS instructions to turn right. "What aren't you telling me?"

She swallowed and a single tear spilled down her cheek. "I'm really, really sorry, Hank." Her voice had the soft, deflated tone of guilt. "It was never my intent to deceive you, but my father said he'd leave Charlie out alone in the middle of the woods on the night of the full moon if I told you the truth. I couldn't risk my son's life for the feelings of a man I had never met." She glanced at him. "I wouldn't risk my son's life for anything."

"I can understand that." His hatred for Clemens grew a notch. Arranged marriages weren't untypical in pack life. Hank's jaw tightened. "But not how your father could threaten his own grandchild. That makes him more of a monster than I'd imagined."

"You're starting to understand." She seemed small. Like she was trying to pull away from him.

"Why didn't you take Charlie and run?"

"Too dangerous. My father would have hunted us down and made an example out of us. No one shames Clemens Kincaid. It's bad enough that Charlie..." She swallowed the rest of her words and went quiet.

Hank wanted to touch her, but kept his hands on the wheel. "Bad enough that Charlie what? I know you're keeping something from me. There has to be more. Like why leaving Charlie alone in the woods on the night of a full moon is such a threat. Whatever it is, I'm not going to be mad. Just tell me."

"I don't want to. Because I don't want you to hate me."

"Would you rather I hear it from your father?" He couldn't guess what she thought was so terrible.

She clasped her arms around herself and

retreated against the door, cringing a little as she spoke. "Charlie...can't shift."

The words punched Hank in the gut. A kid who couldn't shift? He knew immediately why she'd pulled away from him. Why she'd kept this from him. Clemens must think he was really about to get one over on the Merrows. Hank kept his voice calm, even though that wasn't what he was feeling inside. "I thought you said Charlie had gone through his first turning."

"No. You asked if he's just had his first moon. I only said that he had, right after his May fifth birthday. Not that he'd actually turned." She tucked a strand of hair behind her ear. "I didn't want to lie to you, Hank. I thought a vague answer was better than a lie."

"Except I took it to mean—never mind." Ivy didn't need him adding to her guilt. He understood her reasoning and her deep-seated desire to protect her child. "Why can't Charlie shift?"

She shrugged, her eyes bleak with misery. "I don't know. His father was a wolf. There's no real reason. It just happens sometimes."

"It does." It was rare, but it occurred every few generations. In the old days, those children were considered cursed, a blight on their packs. They were turned out. Left to the elements. Which was exactly what Clemens Kincaid was threatening if he couldn't pawn the child off on the Georgia pack. Hank looked through the swath of light created by the headlights, embarrassed by the history of his kind and barely able to control his anger. This wasn't something a mother should have to deal with.

"I get that this changes things," she said softly. "I'm really sorry to have led you on, and I want you to know I understand why you won't be marrying me. I have no hard feelings toward you. I just hope you don't hate me."

He felt her hand on his leg. He looked down from the road. Her palm was on his thigh, face up. Her engagement ring squarely in the middle.

"Hate you? For something your father forced you to do? I'm in love with you, Ivy. Don't you know that? Put that ring back on." He glanced at her. "It's time to get Charlie."

Her eyes rounded. "You...don't care...that Charlie can't shift?"

"No. I mean, I care, but only because it must be making the kid's life miserable. Especially with Clemens for a grandfather."

"But it means you'll never be able to be alpha. Not with a firstborn son who can't succeed you. It means you'll be known as the father of a...*mutt*."

Anger stirred within him. The slur held more derogatory meaning than any other a were could be called. "Anyone calls Charlie a mutt in my presence, there's going to be hell to pay."

He pulled into the driveway at her parents' house and turned the car off. The place was big but artless. The goal of the house seemed to be size, not class. It was a two-story brick monstrosity with white columns and arched windows and a front porch that ran the length of the house. Sort of a plantation manor without the charm. He twisted on the seat to face her. "Do you care if I never become alpha?"

She gave him a strange look. "Of course not, but don't you care?"

"No. I can live without it." He realized he could. He already had a great life. Being alpha wasn't going to change that. "So long as I have *you*, that is. *And* Charlie. Okay? I love you."

Eyes liquid with emotion, she nodded. "Okay," she whispered. "I love you, too."

He nodded, feeling the fire in his belly building to a dangerous crescendo. "Good. Let's go get our kid."

IVY STOOD ON HER PARENTS' front porch, Hank at her side, wondering what she'd done right in her life to end up with a man like this. If she let herself think about it too much, she'd probably break down and have a good long cry, but there wasn't time for that. Not when Charlie needed her.

Hank rapped his big fist on the Kincaids' front door. The brass knocker, a wolf's head, was in need of polishing.

"Patsy, get the damn door." Clemens' shout reached beyond the house walls to scrape down Ivy's spine like the tines of a sharpened fork.

Hank reached out and squeezed her hand as Ivy's mother answered the door. She looked gray and worn. The smell of roasted meat and vegetables wafted out.

"Hello?" She dried her hands on the apron tied at her waist. "Oh. Ivy. I didn't know you were coming."

"Where's Charlie?" Ivy asked. The time for pleasantries was long gone.

Patsy's eyes went blank with fear. "He's-he's on restriction."

"Where is he?" Ivy repeated. She was past being gentle with her mother. Ivy loved her, pitied her, really, but if Patsy wasn't going to protect her grandchild, then she was as bad as Clemens.

Patsy glanced inside the house.

Ivy was done waiting. "If that man did anything to hurt him—"

Hank stepped forward. "Mrs. Kincaid, *where* is Charlie?"

She dropped the apron. "You must be the Merrow boy." Her gaze flickered from Hank to Ivy and back to Hank. "Never thought we'd see you."

"Well, here I am. And I want to see Charlie. Now."

Patsy leaned back into the house. "Clem, you better come here."

He answered with another shout. "Why the hell for?"

"Ivy's here," Patsy yelled back.

Ivy shook her head, disgust coating her tongue with a sour, familiar taste. "Nice way to stick up for your daughter, Mom."

"Ivy, hush now before your father—"

Clemens stormed up to the door, nudging Patsy out of the way. He had a can of beer in one hand. "What are you here for? I see you brought your new boyfriend with you."

"Charlie," Ivy repeated.

Clemens' broad grin revealed his yellowed teeth. He shoved his free hand through his too-long salt and pepper hair and ignored Ivy to talk to Hank. "Come to meet your new kid, huh, Merrow?"

Hank nodded. "Where is he?"

Clemens stared at Hank for a second, maybe hoping to intimidate him. When Hank didn't respond, Clemens' smile faded. "He's out back in the shed. I locked him in there for lying to me. Rotten little mutt."

Hank turned to Ivy, rage simmering gold in his eyes. "Shed. Now."

She shot a curse at her father, then ran for the backyard, Hank on her heels. Clem's laughter echoed through the trees as they looped around the pool. She pointed at her father's storage shed at the edge of the tree line. "There."

Hank barreled past and ripped the door off.

Charlie screamed. He was curled in a ball near the back, his skinny arms over his head, clothes grimy from the dirty floor.

Ivy rushed into the dark, damp space and cradled him in her arms. "It's okay, baby, Mama's here. It's all right now. I'm so sorry. I'm so sorry."

He wept against her, clinging to her and mumbling *Mama* over and over. She picked him up and took him out of the shed, her hand covering his little head. "Shh," she murmured in his ear. "I've got you, baby."

Hank looked like he could chew nails. "Is he all right?"

"Charlie, are you hurt?"

He lifted his head, eyes wet, nose red, and sniffled. There was a bruise on his cheek.

Ivy wanted to vomit. Memories of her own childhood came boiling up. She asked a question she already knew the answer to. "Did Granddad hit you?"

Charlie nodded, his wary gaze landing on Hank. "Who's that man?"

Hank lifted his hand. "I'm Hank. You and your mom are going to come live with me now."

Charlie clung to her. She kissed his temple. "We're going to a great place, kiddo. You're going to love it."

Clemens lumbered out of the back of the old brick house. The beer was gone. He stood on the edge of the pool deck and called out to them. "You better be taking that kid with you."

"I am," Ivy shouted back. "You're never going to lay a hand on him again."

Clemens laughed and walked into the yard to stand face to face with Hank. "You two still getting married?"

"As soon as we get back," Hank answered.

Clemens shot a look at Charlie. "Good luck with that."

Hank stood his ground. "You think you're pulling one over on me. That I don't know the truth about Charlie. But I do."

Confusion clouded Clemens' ugly mug. "And you're still going to marry her?"

"Yes."

"Damn, you Merrows are dumber than I

thought. Suit yourself. You want that worthless kid, you can have—"

Hank's fist closed Clemens' mouth and knocked him to the ground. "He's a *child*. He's not worthless."

Clemens propped himself up on one elbow and swiped at the blood trickling off his lip. Gold edged his pupils. "You think that's a good idea? Coming on my property and laying hands on me? Son, you got no idea the world of hurt you just put yourself in."

"Hank, don't," Ivy pleaded. "He's not worth the trouble."

Hank snarled. "You're lucky I didn't kill you. Cross me again and I might yet."

Clemens pushed to his feet. "You dumb son of a—"

Hank punched him again.

"Hank!" Ivy's sharp cry echoed through the surrounding woods.

Clemens rocked back on his heels and fell hard. He moaned and shook his head. When he opened his eyes, the gold was gone.

Hank pointed at him. "Stay down." Then he snagged the chain attached to Clemens' wallet and gave it a tug. A black leather billfold popped free of her father's front pocket. Hank opened it, lifted a fat wad of cash out and handed it to Ivy. She took it, unsure what to do with it. Hank let the wallet fall onto the ground near Clemens. "That's for the stipend you owe your daughter."

Then Hank put his hand on Ivy's back. "Let's go."

She tucked the money in her front pocket, walked around her father's sprawled form and headed for the car, hugging Charlie tight.

Hank went ahead of them and opened the door to the back seat. "You two sit here until we get to the airport."

"Thanks." She couldn't manage more and not break down. She put Charlie in the car and told him to scoot over, then climbed in beside him. Hank shut the door and went around the driver's side just as Patsy came running out of the front of the house with a brown paper grocery sack.

Ivy opened the back door to see what she wanted, but kept one arm firmly wrapped around Charlie.

Patsy held out the bag. "I put some of his clothes in there for him."

Ivy took the bag but said nothing. Patsy looked like she was on the verge of tears. *Good. Let her cry.* Ivy was tired of being the only one.

"I hope it helps," Patsy mumbled. "I'm sorry."

"Me, too." Ivy shut the door.

Clemens bellowed for Patsy again, and she went running to him.

Hank got in, started up the car and took off for

the airport with the kind of speed Ivy appreciated. When they were clear of her parents' property, he glanced at her and Charlie through the rearview mirror. "You okay? You want to stop for anything?"

"Nope." She hugged Charlie tight and smiled at Hank. "I have everything I need."

17

Despite Ivy's answer, Hank stopped at a drive-through burger joint near the airport and placed a large order, making sure to get milkshakes. Charlie deserved one. And Hank wasn't above using ice cream to get the kid to like him.

It was a good plan.

Charlie spent his first fifteen minutes on the plane devouring two cheeseburgers and a large order of fries with more ketchup than was probably healthy. After takeoff, he carried what was left of his milkshake around with him as he explored every inch of the plane, including the cockpit, which the pilot and co-pilot were nice enough to give him a tour of.

Ivy glowed with joy. She'd spent the first fifteen minutes in the car with Charlie checking him for other injuries and asking him a thousand times if he was okay. She leaned forward in her seat. "Charlie, don't touch anything."

"I'm not, Mom."

The co-pilot gave them a wave. "We'll keep an eye on him."

"Thanks." Ivy sat back as she turned to Hank and slipped her hand into his. "You shouldn't have hit my father. I'm glad you did, but I worry what the repercussions will be."

"There won't be any. Not unless he wants to open this whole business up to pack scrutiny."

"I hope you're right." Her mouth turned up in a half-smile. "I owe you more than I can repay you. Thank you. From the bottom of my heart. And later, when Charlie's asleep, I'm going to do my best to show you just how much I appreciate everything."

"I'd say you don't owe me anything and that repayment wasn't necessary, but I'm not about to turn down an offer like that." He definitely owed Hugh Ellingham, though. Without the plane, they'd still be on the road and Charlie would still be locked in the damn shed. Fresh anger welled up in him.

Then she leaned in and kissed him, and he forgot all about Clemens Kincaid. "I love you, Hank Merrow."

He smiled and kissed her back. "I'm happy you're happy. Charlie's a great kid." His smile flattened. There was only so long he could stop thinking about what Clemens had done. "Your father ought to be brought to tribunal for the way he's abused Charlie."

She frowned. "Good luck with that. He's been alpha for almost fifty years. He's too powerful."

"He's not above the law, pack or human. What he

did to Charlie is inexcusable. I'm not going to let it slide."

"No one ever cared how he treated me when I was kid."

"I'm sorry about that, Ivy, I truly am. Did anyone ever try to do something about it?"

She shook her head sadly. "No."

"So maybe this time it could be different."

Charlie came racing back. "Mom, Mom, you can see the whole earth from the front windows."

"That sounds pretty neat, baby."

"It is." The excitement left his face when he saw her and Hank cozied up. He studied them for a moment, his gaze lingering on Hank before turning curious. "Are you going to be my new dad? Grandpa says you won't want to because I'm not a wolf. Are you a wolf?"

Hank tried not to let his amusement at Charlie's questions show. He nodded seriously. "Yes, I am a wolf. And I would love to be your new dad, if that's okay with you."

Charlie's little mouth bunched up like he was thinking it over. "Why did you punch my grandpa?"

"I was mad at him for what he did to you. But I would never hurt you or your mother. And just because you can't turn into a wolf doesn't mean there's anything wrong with you. It just means you're different. And that's okay. You were born exactly the way you were supposed to be."

Charlie frowned, hurt clear in his eyes. "Grandpa says it's not okay. Grandpa says I'm no good."

"Grandpa's the one who's no good." Ivy put one hand on Hank's arm and reached out to Charlie with the other. "And, baby, no one's going to say mean things to you anymore. Your grandfather was wrong. He's not a nice man and I'm so sorry you had to stay with him. So sorry. From the bottom of my heart. That's never going to happen again. I promise, okay?"

Charlie nodded and climbed into her lap, turning so he could lean against her and see Hank at the same time.

Hank shifted in his seat. "You know, Charlie, the town where you're going to live is pretty cool. We celebrate Halloween all year round. You can trick or treat every Friday night if you want to."

Charlie's body went taut with excitement, and he looked up at Ivy. "Really?"

She laughed and shot Hank a look before returning her attention to her son. "Yes, but that doesn't mean you can eat candy all day long."

"I *know*," he replied with the kind of world-weary exasperation only a seven-year-old could manage.

Her head lifted, and she gazed at Hank. "I know we've got the wedding tomorrow night, but I have to get him to a doctor first thing. I need to know he's all right."

"There's a walk-in clinic in town. You should be able to get in there. Then afterwards, Birdie can watch him if you need time to get ready for the wedding."

"I don't know." She hated the thought of being away from Charlie again, but Birdie was a far cry from Clemens Kincaid.

"Just warning you," Hank said. "That woman will spoil him rotten. Charlie will be her first grandnephew."

Ivy smiled. "That might be a nice change of pace for him. You sure you don't need her at the station?"

Hank snorted. "I've *never* needed her at the station, trust me." His gaze drifted down to Charlie. Hank smiled. "He's asleep."

She glanced down. Charlie's eyes were closed, and his breathing had gone soft and even. "Poor thing. He's exhausted."

"He had a rough time."

"A horrible time. He needs a shower and clean clothes and soft bed." She bit her lip, fighting tears. "I feel like the world's worst mother."

"You did what you had to do in a situation where your choices were taken away, but it's over. Put it behind you. There's no point wasting time and energy on the past."

"I know."

But he also understood that was easier said than done. "Are you still worried about your father?"

She nodded. "There's no way he won't retaliate for you hitting him."

"We'll deal with him when and if he does something. Until then, we have bigger things to deal with."

"You're right." She rested her chin on the top of Charlie's head, closed her eyes and soon joined her son in sleep.

But Hank couldn't get that relaxed. He knew Ivy was right. Clemens wasn't about to let a physical confrontation go, not when Hank had made him look like a fool in front of his family. But if Clemens started something, he had to know Hank would bring to light his awful treatment of Charlie.

A tribunal wouldn't care if Charlie could shift or not once they heard what Clemens had done to him.

But that would mean putting Charlie in front of the tribunal. He'd have to relive everything that had happened to him and tell his story. All while standing in the presence of the very man who'd tormented him. Hank couldn't see putting Charlie through that.

Maybe some kind of special circumstance could be allowed for. Or maybe Ivy's sworn testimony of her childhood would be enough to spare Charlie from having to testify.

Or maybe if Clemens attempted any kind of revenge, Hank would just deal with it off book. It wasn't his preferred way, but then he'd never thought he'd have a kid to protect.

IVY STARED down at her son, now asleep in the guest room. She hadn't had the heart to force him into a bath. Instead she'd stripped him down to his underwear and tucked him in. He'd been half asleep the whole time.

Hard to believe she'd gotten her wish. A new start for her and Charlie. Freedom from Clemens. A life with Hank, a man who wanted her *and* her son, despite the baggage they came with. She didn't know how she'd gotten so fortunate, but she'd take it.

She just couldn't help but pray there wasn't another shoe waiting to drop.

She kissed Charlie on the head and pulled the cover over his narrow shoulders, then quietly picked her wedding dress off the floor and hung it up before tiptoeing out of the bedroom.

Hank waited in the hallway. "Is he still asleep?"

She closed the door, turning the knob slowly

until it clicked. "He woke up when I was taking his jeans off, but went right back to sleep."

Hank nodded. "He's a great kid. I like him."

"He likes you, too." She draped her arms around Hank's neck. "I think you're pretty amazing myself."

He settled his hands on her hips, sending a thrill through her. "Tomorrow's your last day to change your mind about marrying me. Not even a full day. We'll be in front of the justice of the peace by five."

She leaned into him, a sudden surge of desire making her knees go weak. "Same goes for you."

He walked her back against the wall and held her there with the length of his hard body. "I'm not changing my mind." His mouth went to her neck.

She sighed and arched against him, welcoming the friction between them as he trailed kisses down her throat. The full moon was one night away and it sang in her blood like a siren's song, its pull intensifying every feeling until her body was one giant needy ache.

A soft groan left her throat, and his hands slipped under her shirt, hot and insistent. They traveled up her rib cage until his thumbs brushed the undersides of her lace bra.

Her nails dug into his shoulders. "It's too bad we can't go for a run."

"Mm-hmm," he murmured without taking his

mouth off her skin. "We'll have to think of another way to use up all this energy."

The vibration of his words sent a shiver through her skin, and all she could manage in response was a mewl of pleasure.

He slid his hands down under her thighs and lifted her, wrapping her legs around his waist. "Lucky for you, I just had an idea."

She hung on to him as he walked them into his bedroom, tangling her hands in his hair and kissing him. "I bet I know what it is."

"I bet you do, too." He laughed and nudged the door shut with his foot, then he dropped her on the bed and yanked his shirt off over his head, the gold gleam in his eyes pure lust.

Holy nakedness, the man was unbelievably hot. She grinned.

"What's that look for?"

"How crazy sexy you are." She pulled her T-shirt off, too, leaving herself in just a black lace bra and jeans.

"I think crazy sexy is your department." He nodded as she tossed her T-shirt onto the floor. "Keep going. All of it. The only thing I want you wearing is that smile and that ring."

She laughed out of sheer happiness.

Tomorrow she would be Mrs. Hank Merrow.

Tonight she would be anything he wanted.

18

It was a rare day that Hank slept in. He chalked it up to extreme contentment. He rolled over to find the sun in his eyes and his bed empty, but the sounds that carried up from downstairs were happy ones. Ivy and Charlie, fixing breakfast no doubt by the aromas of coffee and bacon that were wafting up. He threw his arm over his head and grinned up at the ceiling.

Amazing how your life could change so quickly. In such a great and unexpected way.

What hadn't changed was his need to get to work. He got up, grabbed a quick shower and headed downstairs in his uniform. "Morning."

Ivy smiled at him with the sort of knowing look that told him she'd been very happy with his performance last night. Not a bad way to be sent off to work at all. "Morning, tiger."

Charlie looked up from a plate of scrambled eggs, his eyes going big at the sight of Hank in his uniform. "Are you a cop?"

"I'm a sheriff."

"Is that a real gun?"

"It is."

"Do you arrest bad guys?"

"I do. And sometimes bad women." He shot a glance at Ivy, who gave him the don't-you-dare-tell look.

"Wow." Charlie's eyes hadn't left the gold star on Hank's chest.

"You want to come down to the station later and take the secret tour?"

He whipped around to look at Ivy. "Can I, Mom?"

"You bet." She raised her brows at Hank. "Around lunch?"

"Sounds great."

"That'll give me time to take him to the walk in clinic for a quick check up. How about some breakfast?"

"Love some, but I don't have time."

"Already thought of that." She passed him a wax-paper-wrapped bacon and egg sandwich and a travel mug of coffee.

He shook his head. "You're something else, you know that? I could get used to this."

She winked at him. "Just taking care of you."

"I love it." He lifted the sandwich and the coffee. "I'll make sure Birdie's free in case you need her."

"I think I can manage. Besides, Birdie will probably have wedding fever today. I'm sure she thinks there are still a million things to do."

"In that case, Charlie can hang out at the station with me until it's time to go." He started for the garage door, then paused. "Why would there be a million things left to do? We're still doing the justice of the peace thing, right?"

"About that..."

"That sounds ominous."

"Do you own a tux?"

He frowned. "Do I look like a guy who owns a tux?"

"Then you need to get over to Corette's and get one." She tapped a finger on her chin. "Hmm. Charlie might need one, too."

"What's a tux?" Charlie asked.

"A monkey suit," Hank answered.

"I'm not wearing one of those," Charlie said.

"Hank." Ivy narrowed her eyes.

Hank nudged Charlie with his elbow. "Hey, if I have to, you have to. Besides, your mom wants us to look nice. Plus, we can be monkeys together."

"Can I have a badge like yours?" Charlie asked.

"I can arrange that." Hank pushed the stopper back on the mug and took a sip of coffee. The kid was all right.

"Fine, I'll wear one. But I probably won't like it." Charlie went back to eating his eggs.

Ivy laughed and shook her head. "Why do I feel

like you two are forming some kind of alliance against me?"

Hank swallowed. "We're wearing the suits, aren't we?"

"Thankfully. Do you really have to go right now?"

He looked at his watch. He could skip checking in on Bridget one morning. "I could stay another fifteen minutes if you need me."

"I do. I haven't had a chance to get a shower. Can you hang out with him until I'm done?"

"Sure." He'd wanted to talk to Charlie alone anyway.

"Great. I'll be fast." She put down the dish towel she was holding and ran upstairs.

When he heard the water start running, he turned to Charlie. "You know your mom and I are getting married today."

The little boy nodded. "I know."

"What do you think about it?"

"I think it's good."

"I'm glad you approve. That's important to me." He hesitated, not exactly sure how to phrase his next question. The last thing he wanted was to upset Charlie. "Can I ask you some questions about the night you were supposed to turn?"

Charlie frowned. "I guess."

"I just want to know what happened. How you felt."

"I didn't turn, you know."

"I know. How did that make you feel?"

Charlie put his fork down and stared at his plate. "I felt bad. And scared."

"Because you couldn't turn? Or something else?"

He shrugged and went quiet for a long second. "I asked Grandpa what to do, and he said no one in his family needed directions." His little shoulders rounded. "Then everybody else but Mom turned into wolves, and they were really big and all around me, and Grandpa's wolf growled at me."

Poor kid. Hank stayed quiet and let him talk.

"Mom picked me up, but Grandpa turned back into himself again and told me to stop being a baby and just shift." Charlie sniffed. "I couldn't. I didn't know how."

Being able to shift wasn't really something that could be taught. It just happened. But Hank was starting to question Charlie's inability to shift. Getting growled at by his grandfather couldn't have been a very encouraging environment. "Do you ever feel different as the full moon approaches?"

Charlie looked up at him. "I dunno."

Hank took another sip of his coffee. "The full moon makes me want to run around. I feel like I have extra energy."

Charlie nodded. "Yeah, I feel like that some-times. Like...now a little bit."

"You want to run around now?"

He lifted one shoulder. "Kinda."

"You want to play a little game with me?"

He perked up. "Okay. What is it?"

"Follow me." Hank put the coffee and sandwich down then jogged up the stairs.

Charlie raced alongside, following Hank into the room that held his gym equipment. Time to see if Hank could get a clue about what was going on with Charlie.

"I'll do something, then you do it." Hank grabbed the chin-up bar and knocked out five pull-ups, counting them out as he did, then dropped to the floor. "Your turn."

"No fair." Charlie crossed his arms, a mini-version of Ivy. "I can't reach it."

"That's okay, I'll lift you up."

Charlie stuck his hands up, ready to be lifted. Hank picked him up, and the little boy grabbed hold of the bars.

"I'm letting go."

"Okay."

Hank took his hands off Charlie, and the kid did five without blinking an eye. "Wow. Good job, Char-lie. Can you do more?"

Grinning broadly, Charlie did another five reps.

Hank smiled. The kid definitely had the strength of a shifter. "You won that one. Do you want me to lift you down?"

"No." Charlie glanced at the floor but didn't let go.

"It's not far," Hank said. "You can do it."

"I know." Charlie took a breath and dropped, landing lightly on his feet.

Hank stuck his fist out. "Nicely done, kiddo."

Charlie bumped his little fist against Hank's. "Now what?"

"We'll play the rest of the game this afternoon."

"What game is that?" Ivy walked in, towel-drying her hair and wearing jeans and a T-shirt.

"It's guy stuff." Hank winked at her.

"Yeah," Charlie said. "Guy stuff."

Amusement sparkled in her eyes. "All righty then." She looked at Hank. "Don't you need to get to the station?"

"I do."

"And you." She pointed at Charlie. "You need a bath, son."

"Aw, Mom, do I have to?"

"Yes. Bathroom. March."

Charlie dragged himself out of the room like he suddenly weighed a thousand pounds.

Hank snorted out a laugh, then gave her a quick kiss before heading out. "See you at lunch."

"See you," she called after him.

Birdie was already at her desk when he got in. "What are you doing here?" she asked "You have a wedding to get ready for."

He stopped to pick up his messages. "I'm getting a tux from Corette this afternoon. Other than that, I just have to show up."

"Men." She shook her head. "You haven't done a thing to help with this wedding."

"I called the J.O.P. That was a thing." He gave her a sharp look. "You're talking about it like it's the event of the year. We're going to the courthouse at five o'clock. There's nothing to prepare for."

"What about the reception afterwards?"

His eyes narrowed. "What reception?"

"For your *guests*."

"We haven't invited anyone."

"Not even Titus and Bridget? And if you think you're keeping me away—"

He raised his hand. "Okay, I get it." He pinched the bridge of his nose. "What do we need to do?"

"I've already done it. The reception is in the back room at Howler's. Bridget is setting up a buffet dinner, so nothing fancy, but it is what it is. Delaney Ellingham is making the cake, so of course she and Hugh are invited. And with Corette helping with the wedding attire, it only made sense to ask her and Stanhill to attend as well. And isn't

Ivy's brother still in town? Plus a few other people."

For the first time in his life, Hank was slightly afraid of his aunt. "How many is a few?"

With the most challenging expression she'd ever given him, she answered, "Fifty. Ish."

He held his hands up in defeat and walked toward his office. "As long as you're handling it, fine."

"I've already made you an appointment at Corette's this afternoon for your tux. You're welcome."

He paused at the door. "Call her and tell her I'm going to need a second one."

"No need. Titus got fitted for his this morning. I assumed you'd want him for your best man."

"Good. Yes." Actually, he hadn't figured he needed a best man, but if anyone was going to fill that role, it would be Titus. "But I wasn't talking about him. I need to get a tux for Charlie, Ivy's son. And your soon-to-be great-nephew."

A little gasp escaped Birdie and she lit up in the most female of ways. "He's here?"

Hank nodded. "He'll be coming in with Ivy for lunch."

She clapped her hands together in front of her heart. "My first grandnephew. Oh my stars."

He gestured at the phone. "Corette?"

"Yes! Right on it! How old is he?"

"Seven."

Another gasp. "Seven. How precious."

"Corette."

"One more thing," Birdie started. "I called Belinda."

Hank eyed her suspiciously. "My parents already know I'm getting married. My father started it, remember?"

"Yes, but I invited them. I figured they had time to make it after all, so—"

"Where are they staying?" In theory, it wasn't fair to Ivy that his parents were coming and hers weren't, but he was certain she'd be fine with it.

"Bridget's. They should be here just in time to make the ceremony." She made a slightly apologetic face. Wasn't one he was used to seeing. "I hope that was okay."

"It's fine." He pointed at the phone again. "Corette."

As soon as Birdie actually made contact with the receiver, Hank closed his office door and started going through the day's paperwork. Sadly, his brain had been infected by Birdie, and he couldn't stop feeling like he was forgetting something.

He went back out to the reception area.

Birdie frowned. "If you're going to argue this wedding thing with me again, I swear I will quit."

"Would that be your wedding gift to me, then?"

"You're a horrible child."

He sighed. "I feel like I've forgotten something. Is there anything the groom is supposed to be doing?"

"Yes, but we've opted to leave you out of the planning because of your *attitude*."

He closed his eyes for a moment, trying to find the fortitude to get through this conversation. "Everything is done? You don't need me to do anything? Pick anything up?"

"Get your tux this afternoon, and we're good. Assuming you got the rings?"

"I got the engagement ring."

"You need wedding *bands*, too."

He groaned. "On it."

He went back to his office and called Willa.

"Illusions, Willa speaking."

"Hello, Willa. It's Hank Merrow. Thanks again for delivering the ring to the station."

"Hi, Sheriff. You're welcome. Was she surprised?"

"Very. She loved it."

"Wonderful. What can I do for you today?"

He stifled a sigh. "I need wedding bands."

"I can fix you up with that no problem. I already know Ivy's size, but you'll have to come in so I can measure you. When do you need them?"

"By five."

"Oh. In that case, you'd better come now in case I have to size yours."

"I'll be right down." Wasn't like he was going to get any work done today anyway. "Would you like to come to the reception? I know it's short notice, but seeing as how you helped us with the rings and all..."

"I'd love to, but I have a meeting with a customer for a new custom piece this evening. I'd move the appointment, but they drove all the way up from Florida. I told Birdie it was sweet of her to ask."

"Birdie already invited you?"

"Mm-hmm," Willa answered.

"Of course she did." The sigh slipped out. "I'll be down in ten minutes."

Getting rings took longer than Hank anticipated once Willa showed him all the different styles to choose from. He ended up with a plain one for himself and a diamond one for Ivy that Willa said would match her engagement ring nicely.

Then he asked Willa for one more very special thing, explaining the situation. Fortunately, she was happy to oblige and had just the thing whipped up for him in about ten minutes. He took that gift with him as well and headed back to work.

As he reached the station on his return, Ivy and Charlie were coming from the other direction. Charlie ran up to him, looking less than happy. "What's wrong, kiddo?"

"I start school on Monday."

Ivy laughed. "It's not school, it's camp. The receptionist at the clinic told me about a three day summer sports camp that starts on Monday, so I got him registered. She said it's all the same kids Charlie will be going to school with so I thought it would be a good way for him to make some friends. Maybe meet some kids he can hang out with over the summer."

"Good call. How was his check up?"

"Other than the bruise, he's fine."

"Even better." Hank reached for the station door. "You ready for that tour, Charlie?"

Charlie's face brightened. "Totally."

"First, there's someone who's dying to meet you. Your new aunt, Birdie. C'mon." Hank pulled the door open, and Charlie took a few tentative steps inside with Ivy and Hank right behind him.

Birdie looked up from her desk, saw Charlie and smiled. "Is this the new deputy you hired, Sheriff?"

"It is."

Charlie grinned but stood close to Ivy's leg. "I'm not a deputy."

"Not yet," Hank said. "We'll get you that star and swear you in right after the tour."

Birdie stuck her hand out to Charlie. "Hi, Charlie. I'm going to be your new aunt. It's very nice to meet you. You're very handsome."

He shook her hand and retreated to Ivy's leg, hiding his face against her jeans.

Hank put his hand on the boy's shoulders. "Birdie, would you mind taking the rest of the day to help Ivy with—"

Birdie was out of her seat, purse in hand. "Wedding things? I'm on it. But you have an appointment at Corette's. There won't be anyone on duty."

"Blythe and Cruz are coming in."

Deputy Blythe stuck her head out from the back room. "I'm already here. And Cruz is right behind me clocking in."

Hank gave Ivy's hand a squeeze. "I guess I'll see you at the J.O.P's office. Five o'clock. Don't be late."

She laughed and kissed his cheek. "Same goes for you and Charlie."

"We'll be there. So will my parents."

Ivy smiled and nodded, the slightest bit of shock and stiffness in her face. "I have to meet them sometime."

"They'll love you. Don't worry about it."

"Let's hope."

Before Hank could say anything else, Birdie took Ivy's arm and led her out of the station, keeping up a constant buzz of wedding conversation that Hank was happy not to be a part of.

He introduced Charlie to Blythe and Cruz, then took him for a tour of the station, which didn't take long because there wasn't that much to it. From there, they walked down to Corette's, where she worked her magic, literally and figuratively, to get them fitted for their suits and out the door in less than thirty minutes.

Hank carried the garment bags back to the patrol car. "You ready to go home? We have a little time before we have to get ready."

Charlie pointed eagerly at the car. "We're gonna ride in that?"

"Yep. And we're going to play the second part of our game when we get there." Hank had a theory about Charlie's shifting that he wanted to test. If he was right, and he had a pretty good feeling he was, then Charlie was about to have a very interesting afternoon.

Ivy wanted to sink through the floor of Howler's and disappear. With each person Hank's aunt ticked off the guest list to Bridget, Ivy cringed. Birdie had apparently invited everyone she knew to the reception. It was worth repeating that that included Hank's parents. No pressure there.

What had started as a simple reception was becoming a party for at least seventy-five people. Maybe a hundred with the plus ones. It was asking a lot for Bridget to accommodate all of them, not to mention the costs they were incurring. Her gaze settled on her ring, a beautiful reminder that Hank didn't seem worried about money, but still. Asking for so much always left her feeling guilty.

And undeserving.

That was her father's doing, and Ivy hated it. She took a breath and tried to remember the Merrows weren't like that.

To her credit, Bridget seemed to be taking it in stride. The woman had a clipboard, for Pete's sake.

"Are you sure this is all okay?" Ivy asked for the third time.

Bridget grinned. "It's great. Let me show you what we've done so far."

Then she nudged them toward the back room. The entrance was shielded with white drapes. As Ivy stepped through, she understood why the woman was so calm. Some kind of magic had been worked, and the whole place had been draped in white tulle, fairy lights and strands of silk ivy. The pub tables and chairs were covered with white damask. The three pool tables had tops on them and pristine white tablecloths.

Bridget pointed at the three. "These will be the food islands with all kinds of hot and cold dishes, but the prime rib carving station will be closer to the kitchen."

"Prime rib?" Ivy chewed on her lip. "That sounds expensive."

"It's not nearly as pricey as you think. Plus, it's one of Hank's favorites."

Birdie smiled. "Men like their steak, don't they?"

Bridget nodded. "Name a shifter who doesn't. Now, the guys will be bringing the cake table out any minute. That will go in that corner. There's a spotlight I'll put on over it, really makes it look nice."

Birdie put a hand on Ivy's arm. "I know you ordered a small cake, but I bumped it up a bit."

Ivy was too overwhelmed by how much these two women had done for her to be anything but practical. "That's good. Otherwise, we wouldn't have enough."

Bridget waved a hand. "I do at least a wedding a month in here. Nocturne Falls is a very popular place to get married. Mostly with the Goth crowd, but even that's changing. Delaney's done a few cakes for us now, and she's always generous when it comes to serving sizes. You should have plenty."

Bridget glanced at her clipboard. "I forgot about the bar. Forgot to tell you about it, that is. We'll set that up on this wall. There's three cases of champagne so the toast is covered." She looked up at Ivy. "Is there anything specific you like to drink? I know Hank's a beer guy, but if you want something special..."

"No, I'm good. Great, actually. I can't believe how much you've done. You've really got this under control."

Hank's very capable sister smiled while Birdie preened. Bridget scanned her list one more time. "Like I said, we do at least a wedding a month here. It's a well-oiled machine now."

"It still seems like a lot of work."

"Nah, not that much." Bridget hugged the clipboard to her chest. "You know my parents are coming, right?"

"I do." Ivy tried not to look freaked out.

Bridget smiled. "They'll love you. Don't panic."

The back door opened, and a pretty brunette peeked in, giving Ivy a break from that line of thought. "Y'all ready for flowers?"

Bridget and Birdie both turned and said, "Hi, Marigold."

Birdie leaned in toward Ivy. "That's Marigold Williams. She's one of Corette's girls. She's a witch just like her mother. All the girls are. Marigold's got a girl about Charlie's age. Saffron. They'll probably be in the same grade."

Ivy looked at Birdie. "Well, that's...good."

Birdie put her hand on Ivy's arm. "Feeling a little overwhelmed, dear?"

"More than a little. But I'm so impressed that you took care of getting flowers."

"What's a bride without a bouquet to throw?" Birdie smiled proudly. "I hope you like them. I got mostly roses and hydrangeas. All white. With ivy. Very Southern. Too much? I figured if I stuck with white, I couldn't get the colors wrong."

"Sounds perfect. Really, you could have gotten weeds and I'd be thankful." She put her arm around the woman. "Thank you so much. I've never had anyone look after me so well." And that included her own mother.

Birdie blushed. "Thank *you* for making Hank so happy. I'd never have thought I'd have a Kincaid for a niece-in-law, but I couldn't ask for anyone better. Welcome to the family, Ivy."

"Thank you." Ivy's phone buzzed. She pulled it out of her purse and saw Sam's name on her screen. "Excuse me a moment, Birdie." She stepped a few paces away before she answered. "Hey, what's up? I wasn't sure you were still in town."

"I am. Where are you?"

"Howler's. It's on Main Street."

"I've seen it. I'll be there in a few. We need to talk."

"Okay. See you in a bit." She hung up. By now her father surely had told Sam what had happened with Hank when they'd gone to get Charlie. That had to be what he was coming to talk to her about. Or, more likely, yell at her about.

There was too much to do to worry about Sam until he got here. She and Birdie went to work helping Marigold carry arrangements in and set them where they were directed. The flowers were gorgeous, and once again, Ivy was swept away by Birdie's generosity.

They were all busy with the flowers when Bridget suddenly straightened and let out a low whistle.

"Hello there," she purred. "You lost, honey? I'm pretty sure I can help you find your way."

Ivy turned to see Sam standing in the midst of

the wedding decorations with a befuddled look on his face. She gave Bridget the side-eye. "Bridget, that's my brother."

But Bridget just shrugged and kept staring. "So he's a Kincaid. I can overlook that. Introduce us."

Ivy put down the centerpiece she was holding. "Bridget, this is my brother Sam. Sam, this is Hank's sister, Bridget."

They shook hands, then Ivy peeled Bridget off her brother and sent her to help Birdie and Marigold with the flowers on the other side of the room. She led Sam to the booth farthest away. "What's going on?"

He frowned. "Dad told me what happened. I want to hear your side of it."

She crossed her arms. If Sam thought their father was even a little bit right, they were done as brother and sister. She wasn't willing to have that kind of backward thinking anywhere near her son now that she had a choice about it. "It's simple. Charlie called me, crying and scared. We flew up to get him and found out Dad had locked him in the shed out back. We got him out, Dad threatened us and Hank punched him. Twice."

Sam's jaw notched to one side, and he looked away for a second. "Dad locked Charlie in the old shed?"

She nodded. He'd done that to Sam at least once too.

His eyes went gold with anger. "That son of a— I'm so sorry, Ivy. About everything. I haven't been a great brother to you lately or a great uncle to Charlie and...I'm sorry."

"That's nice to hear. I have to admit, I kind of felt like I'd lost you. We were always so close and then, I don't know. You started siding with Dad. And against me."

Sam sighed. "Yeah, I've been an ass. I admit, I drank a little of his Kincaid Kool-Aid, but this whole thing with Charlie has cured me of that. I'm sorry I said he was a mutt. I didn't mean it. And I will *never* say it again. And I will lay out anyone who says it about Charlie."

She hugged him. It was good to have her brother back. "Thanks for saying that. And for apologizing."

"Hank punched Dad, huh?"

"Twice."

"Damn." Sam whistled. "He's not just going to let that go."

"He does anything to retaliate and Hank will bring him before a tribunal for his treatment of Charlie. And me, when I was a kid."

Guilt clouded Sam's eyes. "You haven't had it easy, have you, sis?"

"No, but that's all different now." She smiled,

ready to put the past behind her. "You going to stick around for the wedding?"

"Does that mean I'm invited?"

"Yes! You're my brother."

He looked at the room again. "Are you getting married in here?"

"No, this is for the reception. The wedding is at the justice of the peace at five."

He glanced at his watch. "I didn't exactly bring any nice clothes."

Ivy grinned. "Go see Corette at Ever After. It's a little bridal boutique about four blocks away. Tell her you're my brother and I can pretty much guarantee she'll fix you up."

He gave her a curious smile. "You're really all in for this wedding stuff, huh?"

"Now that everything is out in the open, yes. I love Hank. He's a great guy. His family is pretty awesome, too." She threw her hands up. "So why not go a little crazy? It's not like I'm ever going to do this again."

"Good point." He gave her a wave as he headed out. "See you at the wedding."

She watched him go, unable to stop smiling. She'd been so worried he'd come to tell her about some new wrinkle of bad news, but instead, she'd gotten her brother back. Maybe she could talk him into staying. He'd have a hard time of it if he went home and didn't toe their father's line.

She looked over her shoulder and realized Bridget was watching Sam leave, too. Ivy laughed softly. Maybe she wouldn't have to talk him into anything.

HANK AND CHARLIE walked through the woods behind the house, the soft earth quiet beneath their feet. For once, Charlie seemed content just to observe and not ask a thousand questions. Hank took that as a good sign that the boy felt at home in the woods.

When they were far enough that there were no other houses visible, Hank stopped. "What do you think, Charlie? It's nice out here, huh?"

Charlie nodded, his face turned toward the sun, eyes slightly closed, his expression peaceful. "I like the woods."

"Me, too." Hank smiled. "You know that besides today being the day your mom and I are getting married, it's also the day of the full moon."

"I know."

Hank bridged into a more delicate subject. "After the ceremony and the big party, there's going to be a run. You know what that means, right?"

Charlie scowled and kicked at the ground. "I guess."

Hank put his hand on Charlie's shoulder. "No one's going to try to make you shift again."

Charlie looked at him. "They're not?"

Hank shook his head. "But you know what I think?"

"What?"

"I think you *can* shift." Hank sat cross-legged on the damp ground, glad he'd changed into jeans.

Charlie sat down beside him. "You do?"

"Mm-hmm. I just think you got so scared and confused during that last full moon that your instincts shut down. It's been a month since that night. You're probably even more ready to shift than you know."

Excitement lit his eyes, then blinked out. "What if I still can't do it?"

Hank shrugged. "No big deal. You're still you. Awesome Charlie."

A little grin bent his mouth. "Really?"

"Really."

"Can you teach me to do it?"

That was the opening Hank had been waiting for. "I can try, but you might not be ready yet."

He sprang up to his knees. "No, I wanna do it."

"I mean, your body might not be ready. I just

don't want you to be disappointed if nothing happens."

"I won't be."

Except he would. There was no way Charlie wouldn't feel let down if he couldn't go wolf. This was dangerous territory, and Hank knew it. If the kid failed twice, he might never shift. Which was exactly why Hank had brought some insurance.

"Just in case, I have something to help you." Hank pulled the leather cord and pendant he'd gotten from Willa out of his pocket and held it up so Charlie could see the silver disc with the engraving of a wolf's head.

Charlie jerked back. "Is that silver?"

"No. Nickel plated with rhodium." Hank realized that probably wouldn't mean anything to the kid. "It's safe, I swear. It's just silver colored." Willa had assured him the metal was safe for all kinds of weres. He laid it flat on his palm. "See? Nothing."

Relief filled Charlie's eyes. "What is it?"

"It's an amulet that has magic built into it."

Charlie's mouth fell open. "Real magic?"

Hank nodded. "One hundred percent real."

"What kind of magic is it?"

"The kind that's going to help your wolf come out." Willa had done a quick spell on the piece as she'd engraved the wolf, promising Hank it would rid

Charlie of all his grandfather's stifling, negative energy and open him up to his animal side. She swore that if Charlie had a wolf in him, this would set it free.

Grave seriousness rounded Charlie's eyes. "Really?" he whispered.

Hank held it out. "You want to put it on?"

"Yes," Charlie said solemnly.

Hank adjusted the cord and slipped it over the little boy's head.

Charlie kept his head down and his eyes on the pendant. He held it between his fingers. "I don't feel any different."

"Not even a little bit?"

Charlie shook his head, his gaze still firmly fixed to the amulet.

"That's okay. Let's try something. You ready?"

Charlie nodded with such sincerity that Hank's heart ached for the kid. To be unable to shift in a family of shifters...he couldn't imagine what that felt like. "Close your eyes and think about being a wolf. Picture one in your mind. Think about running as fast as you can through the woods. About how your muscles move when you jump over a fallen tree. About feeling the earth under your feet and the breeze ruffling your fur. Sniff the air. You *are* a wolf. How does that make you feel?"

A smile appeared on Charlie's face. "I want to howl."

"Howling is great. Focus on that. Imagine tipping your head back and letting out the biggest howl you can as the light of the full moon bathes you."

Charlie's head fell back as if he was doing just that. His mouth opened a little.

Hank swore the kid's canines had grown.

"Look at me, Charlie."

He opened his eyes.

They were bright gold.

By the time Ivy made it to the justice of the peace, she felt like she'd been overhauled from head to toe. Which she kind of had been.

After Howler's, Birdie had taken her to a salon, where Ivy had been swarmed by attendants. Her hair was curled and coifed, her toenails and fingernails polished, and her makeup done, a rare and wonderful treat.

Then Birdie had bustled her home and helped her change into her wedding dress, veil and satin slippers. Hank's aunt had sniffled through the whole thing in the most endearing way. Then she'd given Ivy a pair of diamond and sapphire earrings to borrow as her something blue.

Ivy had sniffled a little bit too.

In the end, the woman staring back at Ivy in the mirror was someone new.

And Ivy was okay with that. This was, after all, a fresh start. A big one, but a good one. The last time she'd been this overwhelmed by change was the day Charlie was born, and he was the light of her life.

Now she'd have two lights. Charlie and Hank.

She couldn't stop smiling as Birdie led her to a little room inside the courthouse. "You wait here. I'll go make sure Hank is ready."

As Birdie sailed out, Ivy faced the window and took a deep breath. This was really happening. The door behind her opened and closed.

"Is he ready?" She turned to see what Birdie had found out.

She sucked in a breath. Hank and Charlie stood in front of her. "Hank! You're not supposed to see me before the wedding."

"I couldn't resist." He shook his head, his eyes gleaming gold as he took her in. "You look...like I am a very lucky man." He swallowed. "You're *beautiful*."

He chucked Charlie on the shoulder. "Doesn't your mom look pretty?"

Charlie nodded. He'd been staring at her the whole time. "You look like a princess."

She laughed. "I'll take that."

Hank cleared his throat. "We did come in here for a reason. Charlie and I have a surprise for you."

"You do?"

Hank nodded and reached back to lock the door before his proud attention was aimed at Charlie. "Show her, kiddo."

He stuck his hands in his pockets, making his tux pants pleat across the front. "What if I can't do it again?" His voice came out in a loud, strained whisper.

Hank tapped his bow tie, a gesture Ivy didn't understand, but Charlie nodded.

He looked up at her. "Watch, Mom. Watch what Hank taught me."

She nodded. "I'm watching." She had no idea what he was about to do.

He backed up to the farthest corner of the room, then adopted a very exaggerated runner's pose before taking off toward the other corner. A few steps in, and he jumped into the air.

And landed as a wolf.

Ivy's heart pounded. She flattened her hand to her chest and shook her head. Charlie made a handsome silver and black wolf. She couldn't stop staring at him even as she spoke to Hank. "How is this possible?"

Charlie wagged his tail and smiled at her, his tongue hanging out.

Hank stuck his hands in his pockets. "After everything with your father, then talking to Charlie and spending time with him, I started to think his inability to shift had been brought on by other reasons. We...figured it out."

"I can't believe it." She went to her knees and wrapped her arms around the little wolf. "Oh, Charlie, I'm so proud of you, baby."

His tail wagged harder.

She buried her face in his fur for a moment, then kissed his muzzle. She was crying, probably ruining her makeup, and didn't care. There were no words for what Hank had done for her son.

"Hey," Hank said softly as he knelt beside her. "Don't cry."

"I can't help it. This is just so amazing." She sniffed, laughing even as another tear trickled down her cheek. "I've never been much of a crier—living with Clemens has a way of beating that out of you— but being around you and your family has kind of changed all that. I'm so overwhelmed by everything you've done for us..." She hugged Charlie closer, oblivious to the formerly pristine state of her wedding dress. "I have no words."

"Well, I do." Hank kissed her temple, then ruffled the fur on Charlie's back before he stood again. "That's enough, kiddo. You'd better shift back before your mother ruins her pretty dress."

With a little woof, Charlie wriggled free from Ivy and jumped into the air, landing on two human feet. He was red-faced and grinning. "Pretty cool, huh, Mom?"

"The coolest, Charlie. I'm so proud of you."

His smile lit up his face. "Take my picture and send it to Grandpa. Show him I can shift."

"I don't know if that's a good idea."

"Please, Mom." Charlie's little brow furrowed.

She understood his motivation. Clemens had made Charlie's life hell when he hadn't been able to turn. Charlie wanted vindication. And he deserved it. She looked at Hank as she got to her feet. "What do you think?"

Hank nodded slowly. "I say if Charlie wants his biggest doubter to know what he's capable of, so be it. In a few minutes, we'll be married and pack law will officially make him my son. Anyone who wants to come after Charlie will have to come through me."

"Yeah," Charlie said. "I'm gonna be a Merrow."

Ivy laughed and shook her head. "Okay, back to wolf form, but quickly. We have a wedding to get to."

The door handle jiggled. Knocking followed. "Ivy, unlock the door. It's me, Birdie. I can't find Hank anywhere."

Birdie sounded a little panicked. "It's okay," Ivy replied. "He and Charlie are in here with me. We'll be out in a little bit."

"What?" she screeched. "The groom isn't supposed to see the bride. Hank, get out of there right now."

Hank huffed out a breath. "Birdie, five minutes. Now leave us be."

"But I—"

"Five. Minutes." Hank's voice was a sharp, stern growl.

With an audible *hmph*, Birdie went silent.

Hank gave Charlie a nod. "Go ahead. Shift."

While Charlie shifted, Ivy dug through the bag of supplies Birdie had brought until she found her phone. She pulled up the camera and focused. Wolf Charlie sat proudly in front of Hank. She focused, took the picture and attached it to a quick text.

Charlie wants you to know he can shift after all. Looks like you underestimated your grandson. Your loss.

She tapped the send button, then put the phone away. "Okay, Charlie. Back to being a boy."

She looked at Hank, so crazy in love with him she couldn't stand it. "We've got a wedding to go to."

AFTER MORE SCOLDING FROM BIRDIE, Hank and Charlie took their places next to Titus in front of the justice of the peace, who'd cleared his schedule to accommodate Hank's request. Bridget stood in as Ivy's maid of honor. Hank's parents and Birdie made up the entire audience.

The door to the courtroom opened and Ivy entered, escorted by her brother Sam. Even though Hank had already seen her, she took his breath away a second time. She had a short veil covering her face and something about that wisp of white between them made the idea of marriage very real.

She was about to be his wife, and the little boy at his side, his son.

Contentment filled him, melding with the sense of purpose and clarity that this was what he was meant to do with his life. Be a husband and a father. To protect and love these two. There was peace in that sudden swell of understanding, and his chest expanded with the emotion of the moment.

Whether or not he ever became alpha was inconsequential.

Soft music began to play, and Sam walked Ivy down the short aisle to Hank.

The justice asked, "Who gives this woman to be wed?"

"I do," Sam said. Then he kissed Ivy's cheek, patted Hank on the shoulder and went to stand with Birdie.

"Hi again," Ivy whispered.

Hank smiled. "Hi."

The justice cleared his throat and began. "We have gathered today to celebrate the love that Ivy and Hank have declared for each other, and to recognize and witness their decision to blend their lives as partners in marriage and in the raising of their son, Charlie."

"Their marriage represents more than the union

of the heart and body and of the mind and spirit. It signifies their wish for peace for their families and their packs. It seals the truce between the Kincaids and the Merrows and shines a light of love and possibility on the future."

"Knowing this, Ivy and Hank do not enter into this agreement lightly, but with the understanding of all they represent. To that end, they invite those present to witness this union and ask them to become a part of that union. What say you?"

Everyone in attendance responded with, "We will."

The justice nodded. "Hank, do you take Ivy to be your wife and your mate, promising to protect her and cherish her?"

Hank kept his gaze on Ivy. "I do."

"Do you also agree to accept her son as your blood and raise him with the love and care due a child of your own flesh?"

He looked down at Charlie. "I do."

Charlie smiled a lop-sided grin even as tears shined in his eyes.

The justice turned slightly. "Ivy, do you take Hank to be your husband and your mate, promising to protect and cherish him?"

Her eyes gleamed bright with tears as well. "I do."

"And do you accept him as the father of your

child, understanding that he will raise your son with the love and care due a child of his own flesh?"

"I do."

The justice looked at Charlie. "And Charlie, do you accept Hank as your father, understanding that his line becomes your line and that he will love and care for you just as he would any child of his own flesh?"

Charlie nodded with great seriousness. "Yes."

"Very good." The justice smiled at Charlie. "May I have the rings please?"

Charlie dug them out of his tux pocket and handed them over, his pride at being charged with such an important task evident.

The justice held up the rings. "Let these rings be a symbol of your love, seamless and unending, faithful and true. Let them also remind you of the moon that commands your spirits and when it calls to you, may it also call to mind the vows you have made here today."

He handed Ivy's ring to Hank. "Repeat after me. With this ring, I take you as my wife and mate, to love and honor all the days of my life."

Hank repeated the words as he slipped the ring onto Ivy's finger. She was trembling slightly.

The justice then handed Hank's ring to Ivy. "Ivy, repeat after me. With this ring, I take you as my husband and mate, to love and honor all the days of my life."

She spoke the words as she wiggled the ring onto Hank's finger.

The justice smiled. "It gives me great pleasure to be the first to wish you a lifetime of happiness and love. By the power of the great state of Georgia, I pronounce you husband and wife. You may kiss the bride."

Hank lifted Ivy's veil and embraced her, planting a big kiss on her as their family cheered. Charlie jumped up and down and clapped.

The justice held his hands up. "Ladies and gentlemen, I give you Mr. and Mrs. Merrow and their son, Charlie."

As Birdie wept, Bridget pumped her fist in the air. "Let's get this party started."

21

Another round of applause greeted Ivy and Hank as they walked into the back room of Howler's and the DJ announced them again as husband and wife. The number of people assembled was slightly over-whelming, but Ivy kind of figured Birdie deserved to invite whoever she wanted since she was the reason this celebration was even happening. Ivy recognized only a handful of people, but the happiness and affection that radiated off the gathered crowd was obvious.

And now that she'd met Hank's parents and they'd met her and Charlie, she could relax and enjoy herself. They were good people, which was not that surprising, considering the amazing man Hank was. They'd even brought Charlie a gift of a toy racecar.

As the evening wore on, she lost track of how many hands she shook and how many people she was introduced to, wondering if she'd ever remember them all. A few stood out: Hugh Elling-ham, Delaney's husband, because Ivy knew even before meeting him that he was a vampire so that immediately made her curious. Nick Hardwin, a gargoyle shifter who had been in the Rangers with Hank and was almost as new to town as she was. Lastly, there was Corette's boyfriend, Stanhill, who was also Hugh Ellingham's butler of sorts.

But the thing that amazed Ivy the most was the diversity of the group helping them celebrate their wedding. Besides the expected wolf shifters, there were feline and avian shifters. And probably some species she hadn't recognized. In addition, they were joined by witches, vampires and fae.

Never in her life as a Kincaid would she have thought such a gathering possible. Not only had marriage to Hank given her new hope for the future, but she saw such possibility in the harmonious existence of this town.

When she'd returned home from college, pregnant and unable to finish her education, life had seemed so small and closed off. Now, it felt enormous and wide open.

Not only did these diverse groups live together in peace, but because of the way Nocturne Falls was set up, they rarely had to pretend they weren't what they were. She watched the couples dancing and the clusters of people talking and laughing and shook her head in amazement. Did they know how lucky they were? Would she take all this for granted after a few years of living here? She hoped not.

Hands slipped around her waist, and Hank's voice whispered in her ear, "You look lost in thought. What's going on in that sexy head of yours?"

She turned, planted her hands on his face and kissed him. "I just can't get over everything that's happened and how wonderful you and this town are. I feel like anything is possible. And it's all so good. And almost more than I can wrap my head around. It's crazy how happy I am. I don't ever want to lose this feeling."

He smiled. "This place does that to you." He looked over her shoulder and laughed. "Speaking of crazy, have you seen our son?"

Our son. She almost melted from the joy of those two words. She turned to see what Hank was looking at and started laughing. Birdie and Charlie were dancing. Well, Birdie was sort of rocking back and forth, while Charlie was jumping up and down and gyrating like he'd eaten too much sugar, which was a very distinct possibility since Delaney had brought three additional trays of sweets besides the stunning wedding cake.

Ivy giggled and covered her mouth. "That kid. It's after ten PM and he's carrying on like he's got all the energy in the world. I couldn't love him more if I tried."

"He's exactly what Birdie needs. Someone else to fuss over. I'm pretty sure we've got a lifetime babysitter in her. You want to join them? I think I've got one more dance left in me."

"No, I'm happy right where I am." Besides, there would be more slow dances with Hank. A lifetime of them.

Hank's arms encircled her waist again, and he tucked his chin into the curve of her neck. "Today is a good day."

She nodded. "It is."

He grunted softly. "It's more than that. It's...the best day."

"I agree."

He kissed her neck. She closed her eyes and sank into the moment, trying to imprint the sounds of the music and the laughter, the aromas of the food and flowers, and the warmth of Hank's embrace and the gentle caress of his mouth on her skin. She wanted to remember this for the rest of her life, this flawless slice of time when everything in the universe was perfectly aligned.

"I love you, Ivy Merrow."

She laughed at the happy sound of her new name. "I love you, too." She opened her eyes, scanning the crowd with no real focus until her gaze tripped over a tall figure standing near the door. A figure she recognized. Her smile disappeared, and she uttered a soft curse.

"What's wrong?" Hank stepped out from behind

her to stand at her side. "That's not a word I expected to hear out of you on our wedding day."

She couldn't take her gaze away from the man who'd just appeared at her wedding reception. After all these years, how had he ended up here? And why? Her heart thumped with anger and anxiety as her spine went rigid. Hell, she knew why. She forced herself to look at Hank.

He looked around, then back at her. "Ivy, what's going on? Your eyes are gleaming, but based on your change in body language, it's not out of love."

Trying not to cause a scene, she responded in a calm, rational manner. Mostly. "You see the man standing by the door?"

Hank turned to look. "What about him?"

Ivy glanced that way again, but the man had moved. He was almost upon them. Bile rose in her throat as he approached, his haughty demeanor exactly as she remembered it, although the last time she'd seen him, he'd been walking away. The same direction she wished he was going in now.

He stopped in front of her, his gaze tapering into something that screamed judgment. "Ivy."

His smarmy tone made her hands clench. "What the hell are you doing here?"

A toothy smile greeted her. "And to think I was just about to congratulate you."

"I'm so sure." Painful memories and the bone-deep instinct to protect her son cramped her ability to be civil.

Hank stepped forward, his voice quiet but firm. "What's your business here?"

"The kid's my business."

Hank's lip pulled back in a snarl. "What the hell is that supposed to mean?"

The smile returned, this time with a threatening bent. "It means I'm about to do you a favor."

"What favor is that?"

"I'm going to get the kid out of your hair."

A vein throbbed on Hank's temple. "The hell you are—"

Ivy stepped between them. "Outside. Now."

Neither man budged.

Hank looked at her. "Please tell me this idiot isn't who I think he is."

Hank's parents were watching. Aware something was wrong. Ivy ground her teeth together. This was *not* how this day was supposed to go. She swallowed, but nothing could remove the bitter taste coating her tongue. "I wish I could, but I'm pretty sure you've already figured out he's Eric Prescott. Charlie's biological father."

∼

THE FRESH AIR in Howler's parking lot did nothing to clear Hank's head. He stared across the lot at the man who'd not only dared to show up at their wedding and disrupt it, but actually thought he was going to leave with Charlie. Prescott was leaning against his rental car, taking a phone call.

Hank wanted to shove the phone down the man's throat. Or possibly into a different body cavity.

Ivy came out. "Birdie's keeping an eye on Charlie."

"What did you tell her?" The last thing Hank wanted was for his aunt to get involved in this. He wanted it over and done with quietly.

"Same thing I told your parents. Enough to make sure she didn't let Charlie out of her sight."

"Good."

She sighed, looking as deflated as she sounded. "I can't believe Eric showed up here. On today of all days."

"I can."

Ivy blinked, squinting. "What do you mean? How?"

"Your father, that's how."

"You think he had something to do with this?"

Hank grunted. He thought Clemens had a hand in most of the trouble in Ivy's life. "This guy shows up five hours after you text your father a picture that proves his grandson can shift after all? That's damned convenient. Where's this guy from?"

"Mobile, Alabama. His mother is a Hayden."

Hank looked at her. "As in William Hayden? Alpha of the Alabama pack."

"That's his uncle." She looked away, anger sparking in her eyes. "When we started dating, I used to think my dad might finally be proud of me for landing such a great catch. Little did I know what an ass he'd turn out to be."

Prescott joined them. "What was that?"

Ivy glared at him. "I was just telling Hank what an ass you were. *Are*."

Prescott smirked. "And I see you still haven't matured."

She stiffened. "I'm not the one who walked away from my child."

Hank straightened. Ivy and Eric rehashing the past wasn't going to get them anywhere. "What do you want, Prescott?"

Prescott took a second before he answered. "I told you. I want my son."

Hank shook his head. "Doesn't work like that."

"Sure it does." Prescott smirked with the kind of self-confidence that made Hank want to punch him just for the sheer enjoyment of it. "I'm his biological father."

"As of the ceremony that took place five hours

ago, I'm now his father. By pack law, that's as good as blood."

Irritation thinned out Prescott's smirk. "I'm the nephew of the Alabama alpha. I don't really think you want to get into this with me."

Hank laughed. "Apparently, Clemens didn't tell you who Ivy was marrying. My *father* is Griffin Merrow, alpha of the Georgia pack. And I'm his firstborn. He also happens to be inside, if you want to confirm that in person." Hank had never played the rank card before, but this was a special situation.

That took a little of the shine off of Prescott. He shrugged. "So we're equal in rank."

"Not even close, but I'll let it slide since you're about to leave. In fact, I'm willing to forget all about this as long as you disappear in the next sixty seconds."

"Not without my kid."

Hank could feel Ivy bristle. He reached out to hold her hand. "His name is Charlie. Which you'd know if you'd been even the slightest bit a part of his life."

Eric waved a hand. "Great. Charlie. Bring him out here, and I'm gone."

"You're gone *now*," Hank said. "Or I will remove you bodily. Besides being the alpha's next in line, I'm also the sheriff of this town." Not to mention a decorated Army Ranger. Hank wouldn't even break a sweat removing this guy.

"You lay a hand on me, and I'll get my uncle involved."

Hank was about to respond when Ivy squeezed his hand, and he realized he was getting nowhere with Prescott, just wasting words.

The door behind them opened, letting out a burst of noise. Titus and Griffin came out. Griffin stayed by the door, but Titus walked up to stand beside Hank. "Everything all right?"

"It's about to be," Hank answered.

"That's right," Prescott said. He tipped his head at Titus. "Why don't you run back inside and bring Charlie out here?"

Titus gave him the hairy eyeball. "And why would I do that?"

Ivy made a disgusted noise. "Eric, you're not going to win this one. Just go home. Leave us alone."

Titus leaned toward Hank. "Who is this guy?"

Prescott answered. "I'm Charlie's father."

"Biologically only," Ivy corrected.

Titus crossed his arms and stood shoulder to shoulder with Hank. "Yeah, you're not getting my nephew. He's a Merrow now."

Griffin nodded, silent but watching.

Prescott took a step closer. "You Merrows sure have a big feeling about yourselves, don't you?"

Hank opened his mouth, but Titus beat him to the reply. "Well, we are Merrows. That alone makes us hard to beat."

Confrontation crackled in Prescott's gaze. "*Beating* you sounds like a great idea."

Hank scowled. He was well and truly done with this interruption. "Go away, Prescott. Leave us alone."

"You want me to leave? Fight me."

"You've got to be kidding."

Prescott stared at Hank. "I challenge you to decision by combat. Winner takes Charlie. Loser gives up all rights to him."

Ivy's grip tightened on Hank's hand like a vise, but she said nothing. Hank spoke to his brother while keeping his eyes on the shifter he wanted to put his fist through. "Titus, stay out here and watch our guest, will you? I need to talk to my wife inside for a moment."

"Sure thing," Titus answered.

"You do that, Merrow," Prescott spat. "See what wifey has to say."

Hank escorted Ivy back toward Howler's, speaking to his father as they went inside. "Watch him, Dad."

"I will." Griffin's eyes never left Prescott.

They went into Bridget's office where they could talk. Their guests knew something was going on, but he didn't want to share more than necessary. He closed the door. "This needs to happen."

She twisted her hands together. "We could force it to a tribunal. You are technically Charlie's dad."

"But Prescott still has a blood claim to him. I don't know what the precedence is, but I don't want to take that chance. Besides, it would take too long. I don't want this guy interfering in Charlie's life. The kid's been through enough. I want this dealt with now."

"Okay. I agree, but...is there any chance you could lose?"

Hank went quiet. "Anything's possible, I guess, but it's not likely. I certainly have a lot more to fight for than Prescott does."

She sat on the desk, closed her eyes and took a deep breath. "I cannot lose Charlie. It would kill me."

"I won't let that happen." No matter what he had to do. "What do you know about Eric? Does he have any kind of military background? Any sports? What sort of fighter do you think he is?"

She shrugged. "As far as I know, he graduated and went into his father's waste water engineering firm as the vice president of structural dynamics or something like that. No military service. He was a frat boy, I remember that much. I think his favorite sport was tailgating."

"Do you think he challenged me in the heat of the moment then? Or because he was planning on it?"

She thought for a second. "Heat of the moment. Eric's always been a bit of a hot head. I'm sure he came here figuring he'd walk in, threaten me and leave with Charlie no problem. And that you'd be happy to see him go. I don't think he had any clue what kind of man I'd married. Which makes me wonder if my father is really behind this. Could be the Jenkins brothers again. Retaliating for being forced to face a tribunal for their attack on me."

Hank shook his head. "It's not the Jenkins. They're locked up. And listen, I take back what I said about there being a chance I could lose."

"You're sure? He's the nephew of an alpha. Wouldn't he have been trained for the possibility of a challenge for pack leader? My brothers all were."

"They're all sons of an alpha, like me. A nephew...I don't know."

"Hank, this is Charlie's *life* we're talking about. I'm not saying I don't trust you—I do. I just want to know you're confident you can defeat Eric."

He took her face in his hands and kissed her firmly on her sweet mouth. "Darling wife, I realize we still have a lot to learn about each other, so I'm going to give you a quick lesson in Hank Merrow. I was an Army Ranger. I served two tours. Led more raids than I can count. I once pulled an insurgent out of his cot and had his wrists secured behind his back before he woke up."

She was finally smiling again. "Are you telling me you don't think Eric's going to be that much of a challenge?"

He nodded. "Office Space out there isn't going to know what hit him."

She wrapped her arms around Hank and pulled him in for a kiss full of heat and promise and gratitude. Then she grabbed his hand and tugged him toward the parking lot. "Let's go tell Eric the good news."

She paused. "You know I only mean that you're going to accept his challenge, right? Because I think we should keep all that Army Ranger stuff under wraps. Element of surprise and all that, right?"

Hank saluted her. "Yes, ma'am."

Hank waited until Titus, Bridget and Sam were seated, then shut the door to the station conference room and took the chair beside Ivy.

She glanced at him. "Is your father not coming?"

He shook his head. "They went home. Having the alpha of the Georgia Pack at the challenge creates too many chances for Prescott to say things weren't handled fairly. Griffin thought it would be best. Besides, he's calling his council together to prepare for the tribunal to deal with the Jenkins brothers."

Ivy nodded. "Okay. Makes sense."

Hank looked at the others. "The challenge is tonight, as you know. Midnight, out in that clearing where the old farm house used to be."

"That's up behind Sebastian Ellingham's estate. His land, too, I think. He know about this?" Titus asked.

Hank nodded. "I've informed him and his brother Hugh. Hugh Ellingham already knew something was up since he was at the reception. They've both agreed to act as adjudicators."

Bridget snorted. "You think Prescott is going to agree to the referees being in your pocket?"

Sam shook his head. "He doesn't have a choice. The challenger can't choose the adjudicators."

"Right," Hank said. "And Sebastian and Hugh aren't in my pocket."

"Then how do we get them on our side?" Ivy asked.

He patted her hand. "We don't need them to be, because I'm going to win. What we need is for this to be a fair fight so that Prescott has no recourse when it's over. Having the man who owns the land be one of the judges makes perfect sense. And the fact that the Ellinghams are vampires and not shifters also makes them seem more likely to be impartial. Prescott doesn't need to know that we're also friendly."

Titus frowned. "He might assume that."

"It's a small town and I'm the sheriff. He has to know that there are very few people here I'm not acquainted with. It won't be an issue."

Sam flatted his hand on the table. "Prescott won't even find out."

"I hope not." Ivy rubbed her temple. She'd been fitful all night, tossing and turning beside him when she wasn't getting up to check on Charlie.

"You want me to stay at the house and watch Charlie?" Bridget asked.

"I could help," Sam said.

"No, Charlie has to be there. He's the subject of the challenge. Rules state he must be present. And I want you both there. I'll ask Birdie to watch him."

As if on cue, Birdie opened the door and stuck her head in. "You have a minute?"

"Only if it's important." Hank had told her not to interrupt unless something was on fire, which technically would be Titus's department.

Taking that as an invitation to join them, she shut the door and sat next to Bridget. She rested the file she'd been carrying on the table, straightened it, then folded her hands on top of it.

Hank frowned. "You're supposed to be watching Charlie."

"Deputy Blythe is entertaining him."

"While you're in here to tell me what?"

She lifted her chin a little. "I ran Eric Prescott's financials."

Hank stared at his aunt. "You did what?"

"Don't look at me that way. I know how to use the computer."

Another shocker. "Then why haven't you done it before?"

"Because you have deputies for that. And this is personal. This is for Charlie." She flipped open the file and put her reading glasses on. "Do you want to hear what I found or not?"

He sat back. "I'd love to."

"We all would," Ivy added.

Birdie gave him a self-satisfied look over the tops of her frames, then aimed her gaze at the paperwork. "At 5:27 yesterday evening, a transfer of ten thousand dollars was wired into Prescott's account. The transferring account belongs to Kincaid Industries."

Ivy swore softly. "How could he?"

Hank's anger simmered on low. "Because we let him know that his grandson could shift with the best of them, so Clemens decided to get him back using the most annoying tool in his arsenal. Eric Prescott."

Sam looked sick. "I'm so sorry, Ivy."

Birdie held up a hand. "I have more."

Hank's brows shot up. "What else?"

"Being that I'm the curious type—"

"Don't you mean nosy?" Bridget asked.

Birdie's gaze narrowed. "Don't start with the sass-mouthing now, Bridget Irene."

Bridget rolled her lips in and smirked. "Yes, Auntie."

"As I was saying," Birdie continued, "I started wondering why this man would come after our Charlie out of the blue like that. Ten thousand dollars isn't *that* much money. Not to the nephew of an alpha. Then I thought, maybe he's willing to do this for Clemens because it's not the first time he and Clemens have done business."

Hank could only stare. He'd never imagined such thoughts took place in Birdie's head. To hear her talk like this was...astonishing.

"So I dug deeper. And found more wire transfers between Kincaid Industries and Eric Prescott. Some dating as far back as nearly eight years ago."

Hank's stomach soured at the thought of what that meant.

Ivy seemed to have a pretty good handle on it, too. Her mouth hung open, her face pale. She held her hand out. "Let me see that."

Birdie slid the paperwork down the table.

Ivy snatched it and ran her finger over the lines of information. A soft, choking sound slipped from her throat. "This can't be right. That SOB." She looked up at Sam. "Did you know about this?"

He shook his head. "I swear I don't know what you're talking about."

Hank put his arm on the back of her chair. The numbers and notations she pointed at meant nothing to him. "What is it?"

She tapped one of the lines. "This shows a deposit seven years ago to Eric's account in late August. I met him at the beginning of the semester. In September of that year."

Her finger skipped down a line. "The next deposit is November. Right before I got pregnant." Down another line. "And here's a third in January. A big one. Right before I had to drop out of school and Eric disappeared."

She shook her head, mouth bent in a grimace. "It looks like my father paid Eric to date me. Maybe even get me pregnant."

Bridget sucked in a breath. "That can't be right. What kind of a father would do that?"

"Mine," Ivy answered. "He never wanted me to go to college. He told me it would only lead to no good. Honestly, I think he only let me go to get me out of the house." She tapped the last line. "Then it appears he paid Eric to go away. Just like he's paying Eric now to try to get his grandson back."

Bridget's brow crinkled. "Would he *really* do that?"

Ivy nodded. "My father is an awful man."

"Why wouldn't he try to get Eric to marry you? An alpha's nephew isn't so bad."

Sam answered Bridget. "Not good enough. Not for my father. And this wasn't about getting Ivy married off, it was about our father making a point. Our father is more than awful. He's...he's—"

Hank put his hand on Ivy's back. "When we went up to get Charlie, Clemens had him locked in the shed in the back yard."

Birdie's eyes beamed gold. "I'd kill that man myself if I had the chance. Anyone who could hurt that sweet child..." Emotion strangled off the last of her words.

Bridget took Birdie's hand as Titus sat back and stared at the paperwork Ivy was holding. "Why would Eric do this?"

"He's got a gambling habit," Birdie volunteered. "Turn to the next page. You'll see the payouts to the casinos and a man I'm guessing is a bookie. The man can't keep hold of a dollar longer than a fish can breathe air."

Titus nodded. "That would do it. He was probably thrilled when Clemens called. Would explain how he got here so fast."

Ivy looked at Hank. "Can you use this against my father?"

He shook his head. "Not without more substantial proof. Right now it's just your father giving Prescott money. And while despicable, paying someone to date your daughter and maybe get her pregnant isn't a crime."

She looked at Sam. "Tell me the truth. Did you know about any of this?"

He shook his head. "No, I swear on my life."

"Thank you. I believe you." Ivy turned back to Hank. "He can't get away with this."

He didn't know if she meant Clemens or Prescott. "Neither of them is going to get away with anything. Starting with Prescott tonight."

Bridget spoke quietly. "Does Charlie know about Prescott?

"He knows his biological father isn't in the picture, but he doesn't know it's Eric or that Eric is here." Ivy cleared her throat. "And I'd like it to stay that way, except I know Charlie has to be there tonight since he's the subject of the challenge. I'm hoping he'll fall asleep in the car and miss the actual fight."

They all nodded in agreement.

Hank reached over and patted Birdie's arm. "Thank you for finding us this new information."

"You're welcome." She stood, her posture rigid. She clearly was not over what had been done to Charlie. Hank knew Birdie well enough to know she'd carry that grudge against Clemens until the day he died. As they all would. "I'll be with Charlie if anyone needs me."

"Would you be willing to sit with him in the car tonight?" Hank asked. "Keep an eye on him while we're dealing with the challenge."

"I'd be happy to." With a little nod, she left.

"She's going to stuff that boy full of sweets to make herself feel better," Titus said, looking at Bridget and Hank. "Remember after Uncle John died?"

Bridget's gaze was distant but her smile was warm with the memory of their late uncle's passing.

"She baked non-stop. Cakes, pies, cookies, you name it. The Shop & Save ran out of sugar."

Ivy was still staring at the paperwork. Hank gently took the file out of her hands and closed it. "This is all going to be over very soon."

Ivy nodded, silent and pensive. He hurt for her. To find out that her father had paid someone to sabotage her life...he couldn't imagine what that felt like.

He leaned in. "Why don't you go see Charlie? We're almost done."

"I think I will." She stood, her fingertips still touching the table as she looked at Titus and Bridget. "Thank you for helping us with this."

Titus smiled. "We're family now. That's what we do."

Ivy returned his smile, then glanced at Sam, but said nothing more as she left.

Hank looked at Sam. "You should go check on your sister."

He leaned back in his chair. "I take it you have more to talk about but you don't want me here."

Hank gave him points for being perceptive. "I don't trust you yet."

"I'm on your side in this. A hundred percent. Give me a chance. Let me earn that trust."

"This is Charlie's life. And your sister's sense of well-being."

Sam nodded. "Those are my priorities too."

Hank checked with his siblings. Both of them gave him a little nod. Hank proceeded. "We need to find a way to remove Clemens from power."

"Good luck with that," Sam said.

Titus snorted softly. "We could call Van. See if he'd like to do a drive-by scorching."

Ivan Tsvetkov was a dragon shifter, and technically still a resident of Nocturne Falls, although he lived here only part time since he'd joined the MMA fight circuit.

Hank barked out a laugh. "If only it was that easy. No, we'll figure something out. I'll discuss it with Dad, see if he has any ideas."

Bridget blew her hair out of her eyes. "In the meantime, what are we going to do about the challenge tonight? Are you sure you can take this guy?"

Hank nodded. "Yes. But on the slim chance things don't go my way..." He glanced at the door. "Prescott doesn't leave here with Charlie under any circumstances."

Sam nodded. "That's for damn sure."

Bridget and Titus both leaned in. Titus spoke first. "What do you want us to do?"

Hank frowned. "This goes against my oath of office, but this isn't something governed by human law. Charlie is a Merrow now, and we protect our own."

"Damn straight." Titus pounded his fist on the table.

"Are you saying what I think you are?" Bridget asked.

Hank looked at her, then Titus, then Sam. "I'm saying Prescott does not leave with Charlie. Stop him by whatever means you think necessary. Including lethal force."

A LARGE CHALK circle marked the clearing where the decision about Charlie's future would be made. With Bridget at her side, Ivy tipped her head back to look at the moon. It had begun its waning cycle, but was still very bright and full. Moonlight usually gave her peace.

But tonight was not a usual night. Tonight was the night that the life of her child had suddenly become a prize to be won. The night when the man she loved was putting his own life at risk to make sure her son remained *her* son. She tried to take comfort in the fact that Hank was strong and tough and trained beyond the average shifter. She also knew that he thought of Charlie as his son too now, whereas Eric just saw Charlie as a paycheck.

But that also meant Eric was willing to do anything for money. And to Ivy, that made him unpredictable. What else would he be willing to do? She'd stopped trusting him the day he'd told her he couldn't be tied down to a kid and had systematically removed her from his life.

She'd never hated Eric exactly. Felt betrayed by him. Considered him a loser. And a jerk. She wasn't the first woman to get pregnant and have a guy ditch her. It happened. And she'd gotten Charlie out of it, so clearly she'd come out ahead. But after Birdie had shared the financial information she'd uncovered, Ivy's feelings toward Eric had hit a solid level of contempt. A man who'd try to take an innocent child away from his mother just to get paid? Eric and her father were a match made in hell.

Delaney Ellingham walked up to her and Bridget. Her eyes held sympathy. "I hope you don't mind me being here. You know I am completely on your side."

Ivy nodded but couldn't muster a smile. "I appreciate the support."

Concern bracketed Delaney's mouth. "How are you doing?"

Ivy took a deep breath and told the truth. "Not great."

"I bet not. I wish there was something I could do to help. I'm sure Hank's going to beat this guy easily."

"Thanks. It was nice of you to come." She didn't

know Delaney that well yet, but the fact that the woman had shown up for moral support meant a lot to Ivy. Granted, her husband was here, but that didn't mean Delaney was required to come.

Delaney didn't leave. "Can I stand with you guys?"

"Of course." Ivy took some comfort in that. Friends were good. "The wedding cake was really great. So were all the extra sweets. Thanks again for that."

"Anytime," Delaney said. Then she laughed. "I mean for regular cake. Not wedding cake. Because there's no reason you'd be getting married again." She cringed as if questioning her own words. "I mean...did you know the Tootsie Roll was the first penny candy that was sold in a wrapper?"

Ivy's brows lifted slightly. "Can't say that I did."

Delaney sighed. "Sorry. I blurt random facts about candy when I'm nervous."

Ivy smiled despite her mood. "It's okay. I really do appreciate you being here. I don't know a lot of people in town."

Delaney's smile brightened. "We'll fix that. Just as soon as we get past this."

Sam walked into the clearing. He gave Ivy a little wave. She waved back. He came toward her, glancing once or twice at her, then Bridget, but stopped several feet away. Like he wasn't sure if he'd be interrupting.

She looked at him, then nodded at the space beside Bridget. He just shrugged and kept his distance.

Bridget nudged Ivy with her elbow. "You want us to leave you alone? So you can talk to your brother?"

"No, he'll come over when he wants to." She threw Sam another look.

He started walking toward them again, looking a little sheepish. Ivy got the distinct feeling it had everything to do with Bridget and nothing to do with any kind of remaining strain between them as siblings.

"Men are such strange creatures." Bridget bent forward to see Delaney. "Didn't happen to bring any candy, did you?"

Delaney shook her head. "Not this time."

"Worth a shot." Bridget straightened.

Delaney lifted her chin toward the clearing. "Did someone come out here today and flatten this all down?"

"No," Bridget answered. "But Nick Hardwin came out and did the chalk circle."

Delaney looked around. "Where is Nick? I thought he'd be here."

Sam finally joined them, standing a few steps away on Bridget's side. "Hey, Ivy. Hi, Bridget."

Bridget smiled. "Hi, Sam."

Ivy introduced Delaney, then answered her question about Nick by pointing skyward. "He's patrolling. Making sure Eric doesn't have any backup we don't know about or that Hank doesn't get ambushed in some way."

Delaney glanced up. "Cool. I'm always amazed that a creature made of stone even exists, but add to that his ability to fly and it's just plain impressive."

"Agreed." And Ivy felt better knowing they had that much extra coverage in case something did happen. There was no way Eric would get away with Charlie. Didn't mean she was looking forward to the challenge, though. She glanced at Bridget. "Have there been a lot of challenges out here?"

"No, this is the first one in years. But the pack members do use this area for sparring sometimes."

Ivy found some peace in that. Hank had the home field advantage. That was something, right?

"Look," Delaney whispered as she pointed toward the center of the clearing. "That's Sebastian, my husband's cranky older brother."

He was a sternly handsome man. A real Mr. Darcy. "Why is he cranky?" Ivy asked.

"Wife troubles. Ex-wife. Or something like that. Long story."

Ivy nodded. Exes never made things easy. "I get the picture."

Sam snorted like he understood.

If Sebastian was in the arena, the start of the challenge couldn't be far behind. Ivy knew Hank was on the north side of the field, which meant Eric was probably on the south. She found him at the edge of the tree line. "I'll be right back."

Before anyone could stop her, she took off toward Eric. He watched her coming, smiling like he'd known she couldn't stay away. "Come to beg me to spare your husband? Just turn the kid over and I won't lay a hand on him."

"Not why I'm here. I've come to give you a chance to walk away from all this. I know about my father paying you. For *everything*. Just leave and you might be able to maintain some dignity."

Eric's eyes narrowed. "You don't know anything."

"My husband's the sheriff. Digging into your financial records wasn't hard. I know about the gambling too. Seriously, this is your last chance to leave and put all this behind you. For once in your life, do what's best for Charlie."

"Ivy?"

She turned around. Hank was standing behind her and the eyes of the crowd were on them.

Hank looked at Eric. "She's right. This is your last chance to end this peacefully."

"Scared?" Eric asked.

Hank's jaw tensed.

Sebastian's voice rang out over the clearing. "Tonight we are here to witness the challenge between Hank Merrow and Eric Prescott."

"Too late now." Hank looked at Ivy. "I'll see you when it's over." He looked at Eric. "When we're taking Charlie home."

Ivy nodded and walked back toward her brother and her friends, giving Hank's hand a little squeeze as she went past him.

Sebastian raised his hand to quiet the small crowd that had gathered at the edges of the arena. He waited until Ivy had rejoined her group before doing anything further.

Then Sebastian pointed his hand toward Hank and Eric and beckoned them into the circle. The men walked to the center of the space, stopping a few feet away from each other. Sebastian held his hand out toward Eric. "Eric Prescott, you enter the ring as challenger. State your challenge."

Eric kept his eyes on Hank. "I challenge in the name of my son, Charlie Kincaid, and I challenge you, Hank Merrow, for his final custody. I'd also like to know where Charlie is. He's supposed to be here."

Hugh Ellingham stepped forward. "He's here. He's asleep in a car at the head of the trail in. I can vouch for that."

Sebastian looked at Eric. "Do you accept the word of the adjudicator?"

Eric hesitated. "I don't know."

Ivy's blood boiled. She jabbed a finger toward him, even though he was at least twenty feet away. "Don't you dare drag Charlie into this any more than you already have. He doesn't need to see this."

"Ivy," Sam hissed. "Don't."

Bridget put her hand on Ivy's arm like she thought Ivy might take off again and attack Eric this time. Which certainly felt like a good idea.

Eric frowned. "Fine. I accept the word of the adjudicator." Then he pointed at Ivy. "He'd better be there."

She glared at him, but held her tongue. Sam was right. Making Eric angrier wasn't going to help Hank.

Sebastian turned to Hank. "Hank Merrow, you enter the ring as the challenged. Do you wish to add to this dispute?"

Hank nodded and spoke, his voice steady and determined. "I want this to be about Charlie Merrow's final custody as well, but also, when I win, I want Eric Prescott to disappear from Charlie's life permanently."

"So be it," Sebastian said. "A winner will be declared when one combatant surrenders or is physically unable to continue."

Then he made eye contact with the small crowd. "Anyone who enters this ring will cause the immediate disqualification of the party with whom they side."

As far as Ivy knew, Eric had no one on his side, which meant Hank was the only one who would suffer if someone crossed into the ring.

Sebastian waited a beat, then brought his hand down and backed away. "May the just win."

Hank and Eric began to circle each other. Bridget leaned forward again to talk to Delaney. "Sebastian did a good job memorizing the words."

"He's a stickler for that kind of stuff." Delaney frowned. "I thought there would be more rules besides 'don't cross into the circle.' What about rules for the fighters?"

"There aren't any," Ivy said, her eyes on Hank.

"Really? Yikes." Delaney shoved her hands in her pockets. "That's hard core."

"That's how shifters settle things," Sam said.

Ivy was too busy mentally channeling all the strength and cunning she could toward Hank to talk anymore. She worried her wedding rings, twisting them around her finger nervously.

Bridget brushed her shoulder against Ivy's and said softly, "It's going to be okay."

Ivy nodded but couldn't respond. Her pulse was speeding, her stomach hurt and the inability to help Hank win this thing was eating at her.

If by some cruel twist of fate, this challenge

didn't go their way, if Hank was hurt and unable to keep Eric from leaving with Charlie, she knew exactly what she'd have to do. Not only that, but she was prepared to do it.

And if that meant she ended up arrested for murder, so be it.

Charlie's life was worth spending hers behind bars.

23

The world outside the clearing fell away. In the human part of his brain, Hank knew Ivy, Sam, Bridget and Titus were out there. But in the shifter part of his brain, the *soldier* part, Hank functioned on a different level. His focus had narrowed to the task before him. Defeating Prescott. His mind became a war machine: calculating distances, anticipating moves, projecting outcomes.

Preparing to attack.

Prescott was close in height, maybe an inch shorter, but he had the soft body of a weekend warrior. Prescott's shifter genetics were probably the only thing keeping him from turning into a complete pile of mush. But if the man thought he could take on Hank and win, he must have some kind of training.

Prescott took on a martial arts stance.

Hank wasn't about to underestimate the man. Maybe he knew some karate or judo but Hank knew his own skills and even if Prescott had been taught to fight by the best shifters around, Hank's Ranger training would make that look like a middle school field day.

His plan was to take Prescott down fast and hard, but he also wanted to teach Prescott a lesson, and for that, he needed the other shifter to make the first move so that he could lull Prescott into thinking Hank was an easy mark. Then he would strike with the kind of speed and force that would paint a picture with pain. He needed Prescott to understand what a mistake it was to take on a Merrow.

Enough so that Prescott never tried it again.

Prescott grinned at him as they slowly moved around each other. "You scared, Merrow?"

Hank said nothing. Kept his expression stern. If Prescott wanted to play mind games, he was about to be sorely outclassed.

Hell, he was already outclassed. He was just about to figure that out. The hard way.

Prescott's fool grin never left his face. "I'll take that as a yes. Look, I won't hurt you too much in front of Ivy, but I plan on putting on a good show so some pain is inevitable. Unless you just want to give up now. I'm cool with that, too."

Hank kept his mouth shut.

"I get it," Prescott said. "You're doing the tough thing, right? Saving face in front of the little woman and all that. You do what you gotta do, man."

Maybe Hank wouldn't wait for Prescott to make

the first move. The desire to deal this idiot some pain was fast becoming more than Hank could ignore. But he really wanted to lull Prescott into thinking this was going to be an easy fight.

Then Prescott lunged, and instead of dodging, Hank fought his instincts and training and let the man connect. A little. Prescott's fist grazed Hank's jaw, succeeding in splitting his lip.

A gasp went up from those gathered, but Hank's only response was to retreat from Prescott and wipe the back of his hand across his mouth. He could hear Ivy's voice asking someone what the hell he was doing. He wanted to tell her to watch and see, but she'd figure it out soon enough.

The idiot went back to grinning. "First blood."

Not as sweet as last blood, Hank thought.

"You ready to give up yet?"

Hank kept circling.

Prescott huffed out a bored sigh. "You're really going to make me do this the hard way, huh?"

Then he shrugged. "Suit yourself. If you want to look like a chump in front of your friends, that's your business." Prescott's brows bent as his eyes lit with confidence. "I'll try not to hurt you too much."

Then he launched.

This time Hank went low, caught him under the shoulder and flipped him into the air. Prescott hit the ground hard.

The breath whooshed out in a strained wheeze. He lay still for a couple seconds, then managed to get back on his feet. Prescott's chest was heaving as he struggled to recover his wind.

Hank let him go long enough to make him think the move had been a fluke.

It worked.

"Lucky"—Prescott sucked in another breath—"shot."

Hank almost laughed. Instead, he charged, fist forward, and landed a blow in the center of Prescott's chest, knocking him to the ground a second time without air in his lungs.

Hank stood over him. "Done yet?"

Panting for air, Prescott rolled to all fours, his eyes golden. He bared his teeth in a half-hearted snarl. "Maybe," he wheezed, "I'll hurt you after all."

Hank shook his head slowly, let his wolf into his gaze. "I don't think you know what pain is." He rolled his head around, cracking his vertebrae and loosening himself up for the real work. "But here comes lesson number one."

With a snarl, Hank attacked. Prescott retaliated by going into his half form and slicing wildly with his claws. He made contact with Hank's upper arm but only managed to cut through his shirt.

Hank threw him off but stayed in human form. The half form had its limits, like not being able to make a fist without digging your claws into your palm, and this wasn't the kind of fight where a backhand was going to suffice.

Prescott had regained his breath, but his eyes were round and gleaming with the realization that Hank wasn't the easy mark he'd thought.

Building on that, Hank punched Prescott across the jaw. His eyes rolled back in his head as he staggered, trying to stay upright.

Hank put another fist in Prescott's gut, doubling him over, then Hank swept his leg around and brought Prescott to the ground.

He went fetal, gasping for breath as he returned to his fully human state.

"Do you give?" Hank asked as he stood over the man. No point in fighting more than he had to.

"Hell, no," Prescott rasped. He put a hand on the ground and pushed to a sitting position. Blood trickled from his lip.

"Really?" Hank raised his brows. "So you're only a quitter when it comes to fatherhood."

Prescott glowered at him. "Why aren't you attacking me? Why are you letting me recover?"

"Because you're not a threat to me. I want you to realize what a bad decision challenging me was so that you never do it again. Just remember how completely unprepared you are."

Prescott cursed. "You think you're better than me, don't you?"

"From a fighting standpoint, I know I am." Hank backed up a step to give the man some space and gestured for Prescott to rise. "Get up and let's finish this."

Prescott shook his head, eyes glowing gold, and with a growl, he launched toward Hank, shifting into a wolf as he came down. He took Hank to the ground. Hank jammed his arm up to shove Prescott off, but Prescott sank his teeth into Hank's arm.

Pain shot through Hank, and he howled in anger, the pain driving him harder. He drew his feet up, planted them on Prescott's body and shoved, flipping the wolf into the air and giving himself a chance to roll free.

The wolf landed with a yelp as Hank got to his feet. He checked the bite. Blood oozed from the punctures on his right arm, but it would heal. Right now, he had more important things to deal with. Like Prescott charging at him on all fours, jaw gaping, muzzle red with Hank's blood.

Hank put his head down and ran toward Prescott, shifting into his wolf form on the move. He collided with Prescott in a chaotic tangle of teeth and claws. They rolled over the ground, biting and snarling.

Prescott clearly needed the payday because he'd

finally started making an effort to win, but Hank was done playing. Time to bring this challenge to a fast close. Prescott threw his head back to wriggle free, giving Hank the opening he needed. He clamped his jaw over Prescott's throat. The other shifter wheezed and whimpered and went still.

Prescott had to know he'd been beat. Any second, Hank expected to hear the fight called. Then cries went up from the crowd, and Sebastian Ellingham's voice rang out. "Hold."

Hank released Prescott and backed away, knowing he'd won. But when he looked around, the crowd wasn't focused on him or Prescott, but on a small figure running toward them, about to cross the chalk line.

Charlie.

Birdie trailed after him, yelling for him to stop.

Hank opened his mouth to yell, too, but he had no voice as a wolf. He quickly shifted back to his human form and put his hands out. "No, Charlie. Stay where you are."

Charlie skidded to a stop, looking at Hank with questions in his eyes. But it was too late. His sneakers were dusted with white, and the line behind him blurred in two spots. Hank's stomach dropped. He sank to his knees, the cold hand of defeat squeezing him.

Charlie had crossed the line.

IVY WANTED to run to Charlie, to scoop him up, but fear held her back. She was *definitely* on Hank's side whereas Charlie could possibly be seen as belonging to either. She didn't want to be the reason Hank was disqualified and Eric won. She laced her fingers into a begging pose. "Charlie," she pleaded. "Get out of there."

On the edge of the circle, just feet away from Charlie, Birdie wrung her hands, her eyes tearing up. "I'm so sorry. He got out of the car before I knew what he was doing." She looked at Sebastian as he walked toward Charlie. "He didn't mean anything—"

Sebastian held his hand up. "The damage is done." He stepped over the chalk line and into the circle to speak to Charlie, his role as adjudicator letting him cross the line without consequence.

A few feet away from Hank, Eric shifted into his human form. Ivy found some happiness in the fact that he was bleeding in far more places than Hank. Maybe he'd get an infection and die.

Sebastian crouched down to speak to Charlie. "Why did you come into the circle, son?"

Uncertainty bent Charlie's mouth. Ivy understood that look. He knew he'd done something wrong, he just didn't know what. He looked at his hands when he spoke. "Aunt Birdie told me they were fighting."

"So you came to see them?"

Charlie nodded.

Sebastian leaned down farther, trying to make eye contact. "Who did you come to see?"

Charlie pointed behind him at Hank and Eric. "I wanted to see my dad."

In any other moment, Charlie calling Hank dad would have melted her into a puddle of mush. But in this moment, the word cut through her like a blade. Charlie had just sealed their fates.

Sebastian stood, and Ivy braced herself for the inevitable announcement that would disqualify Hank and rip her son from her life forever. The vampire stared at the two men, then pointed at Eric. "Is this your son?"

Eric glanced around as if realizing what was being asked of him. He hesitated, then shook his head, his smirk horrifyingly victorious. "No."

Sam swore softly.

Ivy's heart hurt to hear Eric's denial, but it was exactly what had she expected.

Sebastian pointed at Hank. "Is this your son?"

Ivy held her breath. There was no way to answer the question without Charlie getting hurt. She grabbed hold of the women on either side of her and prayed for a miracle.

Hank looked at Charlie. A muscle in his jaw twitched, and his gaze went oddly liquid. He smiled at the little boy. "Yes, he is."

Then he opened his arms. Charlie ran to him, and Hank wrapped him in a hug.

Pain tore through Ivy, erasing the joy at seeing them together like that. For a moment, she felt light-headed, then the dizziness passed, and she focused on her two men. She wanted to run to them, to hold on to both of them, to fight to the death to keep Charlie at her side.

As if sensing that, Bridget and Delaney took her hands and held her in place.

"Not yet," Bridget whispered.

Sebastian raised his hand. "I rule that the boy has crossed the line and is on the side of Hank Merrow."

"That means I win," Eric announced. He looked so pleased with himself that Ivy shifted into half-form long enough to snarl at him.

He jerked around to look at her, the smile vanishing off his stupid face to be replaced by a look of uncertainty. And maybe a little fear.

Good. He should be afraid. Because if he tried to take Charlie, the only way he was leaving Nocturne Falls was in a body bag.

Sebastian's gaze landed on Ivy briefly, his eyes full of warning. "By the rules of the challenge, Hank

Merrow is disqualified."

Birdie started to cry.

"However," Sebastian continued. "Eric Prescott's challenge was predicated on Charlie Kincaid being his son. Prescott's words to the contrary invalidated that challenge. Furthermore, as adjudicator, it is within my right to make a judgment concerning the challenge so long as the second adjudicator agrees with me. And I say that there is no rule that can force me to grant custody of this child to the man who is unwilling to claim him as his own."

He looked at his brother. "Do you concur?"

Hugh nodded. "Absolutely."

"Good job, honey," Delaney called out.

Sebastian crossed his hands through the air. "This challenge is over. Hank Merrow is the winner. Charlie belongs with him."

Eric stared, mouth open, body rigid with shock.

Ivy started laughing uncontrollably as chaos erupted around her.

Bridget was jumping up and down. Birdie fainted.

Sam whooped and headed toward Eric. He pointed at Prescott. "You are so done."

Ivy laughed harder, happy that her brother would be the one to deal with her ex.

Hank threw Charlie into the air with a loud, happy howl. Delaney was running toward her husband. That was a great idea. Ivy took off toward Hank and Charlie, reaching them a few seconds later.

Hank put Charlie on his shoulders and pulled Ivy into his arms. "We did it."

She was too happy to speak. She clung to him, one arm around him, her other hand on Charlie's back.

From the edge of her peripheral vision, a burst of movement caught her attention. Sam yelled, "Ivy," at the same time as she moved to get a better look.

Sam was on the ground, his hand on his belly where red bloomed from a long gash. Eric flew toward them, a snarl on his lips and the flash of metal in his hand. *Silver.* It registered as a blade a second too late. He sank the knife into Hank's side and whipped it out again just as fast. Then he grabbed Charlie's arm and yanked him away from Hank.

The impact staggered Hank, but it was the silver that dropped him to his knees. Blood welled from the wound.

Charlie screamed, "Mommy."

Ivy froze as panic, fear and anger incapacitated her. Her brother and her husband were bleeding and poisoned, but her son was in the hands of a maniac.

Eric held on to Charlie, brandishing the bloody

weapon in front of him. "If you think I'm going to accept the ruling of the two vampires you happen to be buddy-buddy with, you're dead wrong. I won the challenge. Charlie's coming with me."

Charlie was in danger. There was no more thought needed. Ivy leaped, shifting into her wolf mid-air, and attacked Eric with her motherly instincts driving her.

Protect Charlie.

Kill Eric.

As Ivy chomped down on Prescott's knife hand and caused him to drop the knife, Hank clamped a hand to his side and urged Charlie to action. "Charlie, shift and bite him."

"I can't," Charlie cried, his gaze stuck on Prescott, who still held him.

Hank pulled his hand away. It was covered in blood. The silver had tainted the wound and kept it from clotting. Breathing took work. Prescott was still trying to shake Ivy loose and refused to let Charlie go. "You can do it, Charlie. I know you can. Just think like a wolf."

Charlie closed his eyes. A second later, he was a wolf.

"You did it!" Hank nodded, his head getting lighter and lighter as blood seeped out of him. He dragged himself toward Ivy, who was still struggling with Prescott. "Now bite him and run as soon as you're free."

Charlie bit the hand that was holding him. Prescott released the boy. Ivy got free too, only to leap on top of Prescott and knock him down. Her teeth snapped inches from his face. Charlie took off running.

Relieved that his son was safe, Hank focused on saving his wife. He wasn't worried she'd be hurt so much as that she'd kill the guy in front of so many witnesses. He found the knife Prescott had dropped. He managed enough strength to drive it into Prescott's thigh.

A cry of pain rewarded him. He smiled as he fell back onto the ground. "Get him, Ivy."

He was vaguely aware of people rushing toward him as his vision wavered. It was hard to focus on anything but the stars overhead. A dark, gargoyle-shaped form swept through the sky. Then keeping his eyes open became impossible.

"Ivy," he managed.

Familiar, comforting voices answered him. "She's fine. And Charlie's with Birdie."

Bridget maybe. Hank couldn't think. So he closed his eyes and drifted into the darkness.

When he opened them again, everything was too bright and his head felt like it was packed with warm cotton. He squinted. Nothing looked or smelled familiar. A dull ache radiated from his side. "Where the hell am I?"

"You're awake! You're in the hospital." An angel appeared in his field of vision. He realized a second later it was Ivy. His wife. He smiled as she peered down at him. "How do you feel?"

"You're pretty." Why was he in the hospital?

He tried to sit, but she shook her head. "I can see the morphine is still working. Now stop moving, you'll open the stitches."

"Stitches?" He blinked, trying to make sense of things.

She nodded. "Eric's knife was silver plated. He meant to kill you."

Hank let his head sink in the pillow as the memory of what happened returned in loose, unconnected scenes. "Where's Charlie?"

"He's fine. He's with Birdie at the house."

"I love that kid. I love you."

She nodded, grinning. "I know you do."

"Is he okay?"

"He was a little freaked out, but I told him how proud of him we are and how nothing like that is ever going to happen again."

"That's for damn sure. You're a good mother. How long have I been here?"

She took his hand, her smile making him feel better. "Not long. About twelve hours. Sam's already been released. His cut wasn't nearly as bad as yours. The silver really knocked you out. And it's slowing down the healing process, so you might be here overnight."

He frowned. Twelve hours. "We missed the Zombie Prom."

"That's okay. There's always next year."

He started to get out of bed. She grabbed his arm. "What part of you might have to be here overnight don't you understand?"

"Like hell. I'm not staying overnight. I might have to arrest someone."

A little trill of laughter escaped her. "Oh, this is fun."

"What?"

"You. You're highly amusing on morphine. I wasn't expecting that."

He peered at her. "Have you been here the whole time?"

"Yes." She kissed his forehead. "Because I love you," she whispered.

"Hey." He put a hand on her shoulder.

She sat back. "What?"

"We're married." He grinned. "We're going to have sex later."

She snorted softly. "Maybe not today."

He blinked at her, feeling a little sad. "Why not?"

"Stitches, remember?"

Stitches. Where had he gotten those again? "What happened to...?" His head was too fuzzy to think right.

"Eric?" she offered.

He nodded. "I don't like him."

"No one does. He's in another room with stitches of his own. When he's capable of leaving, Sam and Titus will be taking him to lockup because, while bringing a knife to the challenge wasn't against the rules, using silver against another shifter violates pack law. He'll be going to tribunal along with the Jenkins brothers."

"You attacked him."

"You helped." She sighed and sat on the edge of the bed. "If only we could link all this to my father, too."

Hank laced his fingers through hers. "We'll figure something out. Maybe I should get to the station."

"Not today, Sheriff."

He closed his eyes as the morphine overtook him.

Her lips brushed his mouth. "Sleep, baby. All I need is for you to heal up. Everything else can wait."

WHILE IT WASN'T funny that Hank had been hurt, his attitude during the whole thing kept cracking Ivy up. First he'd been loopy and sweet on the morphine. Now he was cranky and petulant because hospital regulations meant he had to leave the hospital in a wheelchair.

Ivy tried to keep from laughing as the nurse gave her directions. "If you'd like to pull your car around, I'll meet you at the front with Sheriff Merrow."

"I don't need a wheelchair," Hank groused.

"Hey," Ivy said. "Just be glad they let you put on the clothes I brought you, otherwise you'd be leaving in that pretty blue hospital gown."

He glared at her. "You were a lot nicer when I was on morphine."

She shot him a finger gun. "Right back at you." Then she nodded at the nurse. "See you up front."

She slipped out and headed for the parking lot. Hank would have more to say when he saw she'd brought his GTO, but it wasn't like she could take him home on the Harley. She pulled the sweet machine under the hospital's covered entry just as the nurse was wheeling him out.

Leaving the car running, she hopped out and went to open the passenger door.

Hank's face was screwed up into a mix of incredulous irritation and begrudging admiration. "Nice ride," he said dryly.

"You have no idea," she said. "Well, I guess you do."

The nurse moved the foot rests out of the way. "You're all set, Sheriff Merrow."

"Thanks." As the nurse held the wheelchair, he eyed Ivy and slowly stood, his smirk telling her he wasn't really upset. "You were probably just waiting for a moment like this."

She put her arm around him and helped him into the passenger's seat. "Yes, I was hoping you'd get stabbed so I could drive your car. You figured me out."

She gave the nurse a wave, then shut his door, went around and got back behind the wheel. "Buckle up. This thing is fast."

Smiling, he shook his head. "I have a feeling I know why you married me."

She threw the shift into first and winked at him. "The car's one reason. I'll remind you about the other when those stitches come out."

He laughed, wincing. "That can't be soon enough." He looked over at her. "Charlie at home?"

Ivy pulled out carefully and got them on the highway. "Yep. Birdie's babysitting. She's madly in love with that kid, but she still feels guilty for letting him out of the car. She blames herself for you getting hurt."

Hank shrugged. "Could have happened to anyone. I'll talk to her." He put his head back on the seat.

"Tired?"

"Only of being away from you and Charlie."

She reached over to pat his leg.

"Hey, two hands on the wheel. Unless you want to park somewhere for a while."

Laughing, she managed to get them home without crashing. She pulled the car into the garage, parked it, then helped him out and up the steps with her shoulder under his arm on his uninjured side. "I hate to tell you this, but you're supposed to be on bed rest for another twenty-four hours."

He grunted.

"I'm serious."

"The doctor knows I'm a shifter so he should also know I don't need twenty-four hours. And I hate bed rest. Unless you want to join me in the bed."

"That wouldn't really qualify as rest then, would it?" She rolled her eyes and shook her head as she opened the door to the house. "Where do you want to set up?"

Birdie's and Charlie's voices carried in from the living room. Hank hesitated. "What are they doing in there?"

"Sounds like a video game. I didn't know you had a system."

"I don't." He changed direction toward the living room. "Birdie must have bought one for Charlie."

Ivy helped him to the couch. Birdie and Charlie were too enthralled by the game on the screen to notice until Charlie finally won.

He turned around and saw Hank, and his face lit up. "You're home! Did you see me win Mario Kart?"

Hank nodded. "You drive like your mother."

Ivy laughed as Charlie ran toward Hank, but she caught him and blew a raspberry into his hair. "No jumping on Hank until he's better, okay?"

He sighed with seven-year-old exasperation. "I know."

Shaking her head, she set him down.

"I'm glad you're home." He approached Hank slowly. "Are you gonna be better soon?"

As Hank answered him, Ivy turned to Birdie. "Everything good?"

She nodded, the soft edge of guilt lingering like sadness in her eyes. "I hope you don't mind that I bought Charlie a Wii. I figured it might help distract him from...anyway, I think he likes it."

"Looks like he loves it. That was very nice of you."

Birdie looked at Charlie, who was now sitting next to Hank on the couch and having a serious conversation about something. "I feel so bad."

"Don't. You didn't do anything wrong. And everything worked out, so there's nothing to feel bad about."

Her smile wasn't quite convincing, but she nodded as she put the game controller down. "I should get home. Let you all have some peace and quiet."

Ivy hugged her. "Thank you for watching him. I wouldn't have been able to stay with Hank at the hospital if not for you. I really appreciate that."

This time her smile was genuine. "Anytime you need me, just call." She picked up her purse from the coffee table. "Oh, I almost forgot. Charlie, where's that jump drive you found?"

Charlie put his thinking face on. "I think I left it on the kitchen table."

Birdie nodded. "I'll get it." She headed into the kitchen, coming back moments later with the small black rectangle in her hand. She held it toward Ivy. "I made Charlie take a bath this morning, and he found this in his room when he was getting dressed. I assume it belongs to one of you?"

Ivy took it. "I don't recognize it. Hank?" She tossed it to him.

He looked it over. "Me either." He glanced at Charlie. "This was in your room?"

He nodded. "On the floor."

"Where did it come from?"

Charlie shrugged. "I dunno."

"Did you plug it in?" Ivy asked Birdie. "See what's on it?"

"No." Birdie clutched her purse. "I thought it might be personal information."

"Okay, we'll figure it out later. Right now I think we need to order some pizza and enjoy being home."

Hank smiled at his aunt. "What do you like on your pie?"

Her brows rose. "You want me to stay?"

"Unless you're tired of being here."

"No, I'd love to stay. Thank you." She put her purse down, all smiles. "I can order the pizza. You two visit with your son. Extra cheese okay?"

"Yes. Meat lovers. Get two," Hank called after her. He grinned at Ivy. "Hospital food sucks, and I'm starving."

"Speaking of things to eat..." Ivy joined them on the couch, sitting on Charlie's other side so he was between her and Hank. She ruffled his hair. "How much candy did Aunt Birdie give you?"

Charlie shrugged. "I'm not supposed to say."

Hank smiled. "That sounds like her. Maybe after dinner you can teach me how to play Mario Kart."

"How about tomorrow?" Ivy said. "Tonight you just need to rest."

Hank made a face at Charlie. "Your mother is no fun."

He let out a big exhale. "I know."

25

Sated with pizza, beer and the two pain pills that Ivy had insisted he take, Hank was firmly ensconced on the couch watching Charlie play video games while Ivy and Birdie cleaned up in the kitchen.

He dug the flash drive out of his pocket and turned it over in his fingers. It looked like any other flash drive, but not one he recognized. Curiosity ate at him.

Ivy and his aunt came in, chatting about dessert. Birdie said there was leftover wedding cake, and she happened to have bought ice cream.

Hank held the flash drive up. "Birdie, why don't you use my laptop and open this thing up, see what's on it? Ivy, my laptop's on the counter in the kitchen."

Birdie put a hand to her throat. "You want me to open it?"

"Why not?" He shrugged. "After how you dug into Prescott's bank records, you're clearly the most qualified."

"I'll grab the laptop," Ivy said.

Birdie took the drive from him as Ivy left. "I guess I can try. What if there's a virus on here?"

"I might be on pain meds, but even I don't think someone broke into the house and left a flash drive on the floor in Charlie's room in the hopes of giving me a computer virus."

She sat in the recliner, holding the flash drive in her hand like it was a fragile thing. "I suppose you're right."

Ivy returned with the laptop, set it on the coffee table then fired it up. "Hank, you'll have to log on. I don't know your password."

"Alphawolf." He shrugged, a lazy smile curving his mouth. "You know, 'cuz I am one."

Ivy grinned. "Maybe next time you shouldn't take your pain meds with beer. For a shifter, you have a low tolerance."

She typed the password in, then took the machine to Birdie and set it on her lap. "Here you go. See what you can find."

Birdie put her glasses on, then plugged the drive in. The laptop whirred to life and beeped softly. She hit a few keys, her gaze studying the screen. Light reflected off her glasses as whatever was on the drive popped up.

"What is it?" Ivy asked.

"Files. Not sure what they contain yet." Birdie tapped a few more keys. "This is interesting. Although I'm not entirely sure what it means."

Hank waved a hand sleepily. "Probably nothing."

Birdie looked over the rims of her glasses at Ivy. "Could KI stand for Kincaid Industries?"

She shrugged. "I guess so."

Birdie nodded like she was thinking. "Then KI One and KI Two would make sense." Birdie focused on the screen again, her eyes narrowing behind her glasses. "That would make this years of information."

Hank pushed upright, his interest temporarily sanding off the edges of his drug-induced weariness. "What did you find?"

Birdie lifted her head. "I'm not a forensic accountant, but I'd say this file contains two sets of books for Clemens Kincaid's business dealings. The real one that contains his actual numbers and the fake one he uses for official business. And if that's the case, he could be going away for a long, long time."

A surge of adrenaline zipped through Hank's system, temporarily overriding the effects of the meds. He looked at Ivy, who was sitting very still, then spoke to Charlie. "Hey, kiddo."

Charlie paused his game and turned around.

Hank pointed at the flash drive sticking out of the computer. "Where did you find that flash drive?"

"On the floor in my room."

"And what were you doing when you found it?"

"I was putting clean clothes on."

"Out of the bag your grandmother gave you?"

He nodded.

"Thanks." Hank gave him a smile. "You can play your game."

Charlie went back to crashing his car into those of his opponents and racking up points.

Even over the sound of the game, Ivy's whisper was audible. "My mother."

Hank turned to see her. "You think so?"

Ivy nodded. "How else would it have gotten into the house if not in the bag? She's the only one who could have put it in there. She'd certainly have had access. And when she gave me the bag, she said something like I hope this helps."

"Does she do the books for the company?"

"No, my second-oldest brother, Daryl, does. But my mother works in the office. Filing, answering phones, getting coffee. Stuff like that."

Hank tried to read her face, but all he could really sense from her was shock and concern. "So she'd have access to the records."

"I don't know. I guess." She glanced at Birdie. "Can you tell by looking at the drive who created those files? Or who they would implicate?"

Birdie's mouth bunched to one side. "Let me look closer." She pecked away at the keyboard, finally shaking her head. "There are no names that I can find. Hank, what do you think?"

"If there are no names, then the Justice Department would most likely go after the company and its officers."

Ivy let out a breath. "That would be my father and my two oldest brothers. Which means my mom and Sam would be in the clear." She turned toward him. "Would they, Hank? I'd hate to think of either of them going to prison for my father's crimes."

"What about your older brothers?"

She snorted. "They're his henchmen. If he's guilty, so are they."

Hank thought for a moment, a tough task with the meds in his system. "Do you think Sam and your mother would be willing to testify?"

Ivy made a face. "That's asking a lot. My mother might be too scared. As for Sam...I don't know. I'd have to ask them both."

"Don't say anything yet. Let me work on this in the morning and see what I can figure out to protect them." His lids grew heavy as the drugs started winning. He yawned.

Ivy stood. "Birdie, I'm going to get Hank upstairs and put him to bed. I'll be right back."

"Okay." She hit a key and popped the flash drive out, handing it to Ivy. "Take this with you and put it somewhere safe. I'll keep an eye on Charlie."

Ivy stuck the drive in her pocket, then got Hank to his feet. "Let's go. You need to be in bed."

He draped his arm around her shoulder. "Are you going to tuck me in?"

She smiled as she led him out of the room and up the stairs. "Yes, but that's all I'm doing. You need to heal."

He leaned in and nuzzled her neck. "Are you sure?"

She sucked in a breath and arched away from him, reaching out to push the bedroom door open. "You're a really bad patient."

"I just want my wife next to me."

She eased him onto the bed, then knelt to take his boots off. "I will be. At some point. I have to get Charlie settled first, and by then, you'll be sound asleep. You won't even know I'm there."

"Sure I will." He lay back and closed his eyes. She unbuttoned his jeans. He grinned. "I knew this was just a ploy to get me alone."

She laughed. "Drugged up and trying to get frisky. That's my husband."

"Yeah," he muttered. And drifted off to sleep.

IVY MANAGED to get Hank's jeans and shirt off him, but it was only because she had the strength of a shifter. Moving that much man would have been impossible otherwise. She covered him up, tucked the flash drive under his T-shirts in his dresser drawer, then jogged back down to the living room.

"Charlie, bedtime. Upstairs and teeth brushed."

"Aw, Mom, can't I play one more game?"

"Not tonight, honey. Tomorrow's going to be a busy day. You have your first day at sports camp."

He made a face. "I know."

Birdie clapped her hands. "Isn't that exciting, Charlie? Think of all the new friends you're going to make."

He shot her a look as he put the game controller away. Clearly he didn't share her enthusiasm.

Ivy laughed as Birdie stood. "I guess I should be going, too. Call me if you need anything."

"Thank you for everything. I'll see you tomorrow. I'm going to come to the station after I drop him off."

"Is Hank going to work tomorrow?"

Ivy rolled her eyes. "You think I can stop him?"

Birdie snorted softly. "Silly question. Oh, I almost forgot with all that business about the flash drive. Charlie and I did a little clothes shopping today and—"

"You got my son to go shopping? For clothes?" Ivy wondered if Birdie had a little witch in her, because dragging her son into a clothing store took a special kind of magic.

Birdie put her hand to her mouth and whispered, "I promised him ice cream."

"That would do it."

"Anyway, I got him some shorts and a few new T-shirts. For his sports camp. I hope that's okay."

"Okay? That's wonderful. I just realized I was going to have to do laundry tonight so I could send him to camp in something clean." Ivy hugged her. "Thank you so much. You can bribe my son with sweets anytime."

"I'll hold you to that." With a laugh and a happy grin, Birdie kissed Charlie on the cheek and headed out. "See you tomorrow! Have a good day at camp, Charlie boy!"

Ivy locked the house up after her, then herded Charlie to the bathroom for teeth brushing, finally getting him into bed ten minutes later. He was asleep in five, a sure sign that Birdie's gift of the Wii had been a gift for all of them.

With both her men out cold, Ivy slipped back downstairs and pulled out her cell phone. She wanted to call Sam and tell him about the info on the flash drive, but what if he was involved in it somehow? What if he hadn't been truthful with her about being done with the Kincaid business?

She stared at her phone, her heart aching with the possibilities. If Sam was involved, those decisions were on him. He might be her little brother, but he was also a grown man. She glanced upstairs. She had a new family now and her son to protect.

Plus, Hank had asked her to wait before she said anything.

Reluctantly, she plugged her phone in to charge and left it on the kitchen counter before turning the lights off and heading back up.

Tomorrow they'd all have answers.

Even if some of those answers weren't good ones.

26

Hank stared in amazement as Birdie set a cup of coffee on his desk. "You feeling all right?"

"Why?"

"You brought me coffee. Usually I have to get that myself."

She gave him the eye but answered, "You're convalescing. Actually, you shouldn't even be here, but since you're working on that...information we found last night, I'll give you a pass."

"Thank you, Dr. Birdie. And I'm fine now, just so you know. I took the stitches out this morning. I'm all healed up."

She looked at him, aghast. "You're not supposed to take your own stitches out."

"What are you going to do? Sue me for malpractice?"

"Hmph. All I do for you and that's the kind of sass I get." She lifted her chin as she strode back to her desk.

He smiled. It was good to be back at work. Good to have his routine back. He sipped his coffee as his gaze landed on the flash drive.

It would be even better when Ivy didn't have to worry about her family anymore. Well, he'd started the ball rolling this morning. Now it was just a matter of getting some questions answered.

The phone rang.

Birdie yelled, "Phone."

With a long-suffering sigh, Hank reached for the receiver. "Nocturne Falls Sheriff Department. Sheriff Merrow speaking."

"Morning, Sheriff. This is US Attorney Janet Fry. I understand you have some information that might interest me."

"Are you interested in putting Clemens Kincaid away?"

"Hell yes."

"Then I think we can do business. But that information comes with conditions."

"Such as?"

"I need total immunity for Sam, Ivy and Patsy Kincaid. That's the youngest son, the daughter and Clemens' wife." Not that he thought Ivy was guilty of anything, but he wanted her protected.

"Are they willing to testify?"

"They might be, but I don't think that will be necessary with the information I have."

"If that's true, I can guarantee them immunity. But whatever you have better lead to a conviction."

"It will. Send me the deal in writing and I'll pass

on what I have."

"I'll get it together. The Kincaid file is a thick one. I spoke to someone in the organized crime division and they're eager to close it. This could be a real feather in your cap, Sheriff."

Hank grunted. "I don't need a feather in my cap. What I need is my name kept out of it. Consider me an anonymous source."

Fry hesitated. "You're sure about that? A big arrest like this could lead to a commendation and who knows what?"

"I'm sure. Just get me that deal."

"Suit yourself. I'll have it to you before the end of the day." She hung up.

Half an hour later, Ivy popped in. "Hi, Birdie." She stuck her head around Hank's door. "You busy?"

"Not too busy for you." He got up. "How'd Charlie do at camp?"

"He wasn't happy at first, but by the time I left, he was already talking to some of the other kids."

"Good."

Worry bracketed her eyes. "You have any news?"

He slipped his arms around her waist. "I do. And it's all good."

She closed her eyes and exhaled, leaning her forehead against his cheek. "Thank you."

He kissed her temple. "Call Sam. It's time to fill him in."

Ivy stuck her hands under her legs to keep from fidgeting while Hank explained everything to Sam. Her brother sat stock still, listening like he was hearing the tale of their father's misdeeds for the first time.

"And that's about it," Hank finished.

Sam shook his head. "Are you sure about all this?"

Ivy put her hand on his arm. "We have proof, Sam."

He nodded, staring at his hands.

Her heart went out to him, but she had questions of her own. "You had to have known about this."

"I've had my suspicions for a long time, but Dad always shielded me from it." Sam let out a hard breath. "You know he's always pushed for me to go into law enforcement. Now I think that was probably so he'd have someone on the inside. Someone in the family, that is. He's already got a few local cops on the payroll."

Sam dropped his head, and the muscles in his jaw tightened. When he looked at Hank again, pain and determination shone in his eyes. "How much time am I going to have to do?"

"None. I've brokered a deal with the US Attorney

to give you, Ivy and your mother immunity with conditions."

Sam blinked hard. "No trial? No arrest?"

"No."

"I don't know how to thank you. That is...way more than I expected." Sam took a long, relieved breath. "If you need anything from me..."

"I need you to move here where your sister can keep an eye on you. And for you to make yourself a valuable part of your nephew's life." Hank's gaze tapered down. "You upset that boy once and I will make you very sorry."

"Wouldn't dream of it." Sam held his hands up. "As for moving here, consider it done. There's no life for me back home anyway." He smiled. "I'm going to be the best uncle that kid's ever had."

Hank's stern expression stayed put. "That's going to be hard to do considering his other uncle is my brother, Titus. Speaking of, Titus is willing to give you a job at the firehouse so long as you can pass the tests and training. I've already run a background check on you, and unlike your sister, you don't have an arrest record, so you qualify. You'll have to go to the Georgia Fire Academy. It won't be easy, but it's a fresh start if you're interested."

"I am. Thank you. So much." Sam grabbed Ivy's hand. "You, too. I'm sorry about everything."

"I know. I'm really happy you want to be part of

Charlie's life." She squeezed his hand, then gave him a hard, serious look. "But I'd like for you and Hank to be friends too."

"We can work on that." Sadness filled Sam's eyes again. "I owe Charlie big-time." He sighed. "I have a lot to make up for."

Hank nodded. "Why don't you come over for dinner tonight? We never did get to do our family run after the wedding. Full moon's gone, but better late than never."

Sam grinned. "That would be great. Any chance Bridget's going to be there?"

Hank frowned. "I just thought of another condition for you living here."

"Hank." Ivy gave him a look. She loved the idea of Bridget and Sam. So long as Bridget could see herself with a Kincaid. Maybe she'd get Birdie working on it. There wasn't anything that woman couldn't accomplish.

Hank managed a slim smile. "See you for dinner."

"See you," Sam said. "Bye, sis." He made his way out, leaving Ivy and Hank alone.

Hank leaned back in his chair. "That went well."

She tipped her head. "Did you really make his immunity conditional on him moving here?"

"No. But I figured you'd like it."

She smiled. "Very much. Thank you. I love you

more than I can adequately express right now."

He grinned. "In the words of Charlie: I know."

Having Sam over for dinner turned into having Birdie, Bridget, Titus and his girlfriend, too. Charlie was in heaven surrounded by his new fan club. After dinner, the whole lot of them went for a run, ending up at the waterfall.

Ivy stood proudly at Hank's side as Charlie splashed in the water. She nuzzled Hank's neck, almost undone by the happiness filling her. One thought repeated over and over in her head. *Life is good.*

It sure is.

She looked at Hank. *I heard your voice. In my head!*

He woofed a soft bark and gave her a wolfy grin. *That makes us bonded mates. There's no getting rid of me now.*

She returned his wolfy grin. *Good because you're stuck with me, too.*

Charlie came up to them and shook, spraying them both with water. Hank butted his head against Charlie's side and took off, inviting him to follow.

Charlie went after him, and the rest of the family joined the chase. By the time they reached the property line and shifted back to their human forms, they'd all worked off dinner.

Birdie patted her hair. "I don't know about you

all, but I'm ready for that peach cobbler and vanilla ice cream."

"Me, too," Charlie piped up. "Can I, Mom?"

"After that run? I'd say we've all earned it. Go with Aunt Birdie and see if she needs any help."

He grabbed Birdie's hand. "You need help, Aunt Birdie?"

Ivy laughed, and Hank shook his head.

"I'll help, too." Bridget looked at Sam. "You any good in the kitchen?"

Looking a little starry-eyed, Sam nodded. "Yeah, I can, uh, scoop the ice cream."

"C'mon, then," Bridget said.

Sam went after her with the same enthusiasm Charlie had shown for cobbler.

Hank and Ivy walked slowly, holding hands, letting Titus and his girlfriend, Zoe, get ahead of them. Hank released Ivy's hand to slip his arm around her waist. He hugged her close and his eyes flickered with something halfway between amusement and consternation. "I know what you're up to."

"I have no idea what you're talking about."

"Then you're not trying to fix my sister up with your brother?"

Ivy shrugged but didn't dare look at him for fear her eyes would give the truth away. "Don't blame me, blame nature. I can't help it if Merrows are naturally attracted to Kincaids."

He snorted. "Well, if that's the case, any chance you have a non-criminal uncle you could introduce Birdie to?"

She laughed and finally looked at him. "As a matter of fact..."

"Oh no, you don't." He picked her up, and she let out a surprised whoop, which only made him look more pleased with himself. "You're one of a kind, Ivy."

She put her arms around his neck. "And aren't you glad for that?"

He nodded. "I am. I'm also glad I'm the one who ended up with you." He kissed her, a brief but promise-filled seal of their love. "I hope there's whipped cream."

She made a face. "Whipped cream *and* ice cream on your cobbler? Really giving that shifter metabolism a workout, huh?"

"Oh, the whipped cream isn't for the cobbler, my love." Wicked intent gleamed golden in his eyes as he brought her closer for a kiss. "It's for later."

Want to be up to date on all books & release dates by Kristen Painter? Sign-up for my newsletter on my website, www.kristenpainter.com. No spam, just news (sales, freebies, and releases.)

If you loved the book and want to help the series grow, tell a friend about the book and take time to leave a review!

PARANORMAL WOMEN'S FICTION

First Fangs Club Series:

Sucks To Be Me

Suck It Up Buttercup

Sucker Punch

The Suck Stops Here

COZY MYSTERY:

Jayne Frost Series:

Miss Frost Solves A Cold Case: A Nocturne Falls Mystery

Miss Frost Ices The Imp: A Nocturne Falls Mystery

Miss Frost Saves The Sandman: A Nocturne Falls Mystery

Miss Frost Cracks A Caper: A Nocturne Falls Mystery

When Birdie Babysat Spider: A Jayne Frost Short

Miss Frost Braves The Blizzard: A Nocturne Falls Mystery

Miss Frost Says I Do: A Nocturne Falls Mystery

HappilyEverlasting Series:

Witchful Thinking

PARANORMAL ROMANCE

Nocturne Falls Series:

The Vampire's Mail Order Bride

The Werewolf Meets His Match

The Gargoyle Gets His Girl

The Professor Woos The Witch

The Witch's Halloween Hero – short story

The Werewolf's Christmas Wish – short story

The Vampire's Fake Fiancée

The Vampire's Valentine Surprise – short story

The Shifter Romances The Writer

The Vampire's True Love Trials – short story

The Vampire's Accidental Wife

The Reaper Rescues The Genie

The Detective Wins The Witch

The Vampire's Priceless Treasure

The Werewolf Dates The Deputy

The Siren Saves The Billionaire

Shadowvale Series:

The Trouble With Witches

The Vampire's Cursed Kiss

The Forgettable Miss French

Moody And The Beast

Sin City Collectors Series

Queen Of Hearts

Dead Man's Hand

Double or Nothing

Standalone Paranormal Romance:

Dark Kiss of the Reaper

Heart of Fire

Recipe for Magic

Miss Bramble and the Leviathan

All Fired Up

URBAN FANTASY

The House of Comarré series:

Forbidden Blood

Blood Rights

Flesh and Blood

Bad Blood

Out For Blood

Last Blood

The Crescent City series:

House of the Rising Sun

City of Eternal Night

Garden of Dreams and Desires

Nothing is completed without an amazing team.

Many thanks to:

Cover design: Janet Holmes
Interior Formating: Author E.M.S
Editor: Joyce Lamb
Copyedits/proofs: Dana Waganer
Beta Reader: Leslie Wolf Barnes

ABOUT THE AUTHOR

USA Today Best Selling Author Kristen Painter is a little obsessed with cats, books, chocolate, and shoes. It's a healthy mix. She loves to entertain her readers with interesting twists and unforgettable characters. She currently writes the best-selling paranormal romance series, Nocturne Falls, and award-winning urban fantasy. The former college English teacher can often be found all over social media where she loves to interact with readers.

For more information go to www.kristenpainter.com

Made in the USA
Middletown, DE
19 February 2024